Book 9 in the SEEIN

SERVING JESUS

A NOVEL

Jeffrey McClain Jones

SERVING JESUS

John 14:12 Publications

www.jeffreymcclainjones.com

Cover Design by Coverness.com

For my big sister, Terri—whom I still remember playing piano ...
long, long ago.

Chapter 1

Nightshift

Bethany Hight felt the gritty crunch as she twisted the top off the saltshaker. Instead of watching what she was doing with her hands, her attention was attached to that guy with the piercing eyes and the ponytail. He wasn't looking in her direction right now, so she ventured a longer study. Annabelle, the other waitress, had said he looked like an undercover cop. But Bethany couldn't see that. He was more like an artist or something creative—or more like a criminal than a cop if she had to go that direction. Though that could be the *undercover* part of Annabelle's speculation, come to think of it.

As if he had detected Bethany watching him, he looked straight at her, and she flipped her gaze away. And averting her eyes snapped her attention back to what she was doing with the salt and pepper. Her hand was covered with granules of salt that had escaped from the old glass shakers. She shook the tiny granules onto the pale blue tray on which she had collected the salt and pepper from the empty tables.

That undercover artist—or creative cop or whoever—was talking to a couple at the only table still occupied. The other guy also had long hair. Dark. He was pretty good looking, like a TV actor, though Bethany had only caught brief glimpses of his face from where she stood behind the counter. Annabelle had been the one waiting on the two men who were accompanied by a woman. Maybe about thirty, the woman had braids with gold and purple woven in and her skin was darker than that of the two men. She was pretty intriguing, herself. The woman and one of the men sat close in the booth in a way that caused Bethany to assume they were a couple. But she was probably seeing more than that.

Annabelle landed next to the counter, pausing to check the buttons on her blouse with one hand and then running that hand over her golden hair. She was taller and heavier than Bethany but still in good shape for a woman in her forties. Uninhibited male customers often highlighted her figure with comments, both complimentary and crude.

She was looking at that last table of customers. "I can't decide whether to tell them it's closing time." Annabelle rolled her eyes. She twisted her neck and checked the old analog clock on the wall. "Past closing time." She had teased Bethany about being too young to read that clock, with its pointy black hands and only twelve numbers on its white face.

At nineteen, Bethany relied on her phone and her smartwatch for mundane things like time and for the mostly ignored messages she'd received all evening from her dramatic roommate, Emily. It had been a busy night at the diner.

A big intake of air probably implied that Annabelle had decided to go talk to those last diners. But, as she rounded the end of the counter, the guy with the ponytail was standing up. The couple followed. The woman wiped at something on her cheek, then she and the other guy took turns hugging the ponytail guy. He definitely couldn't be a cop, as far as Bethany was concerned.

Maybe what Annabelle was seeing was strength. Authority. Confidence. But all that didn't have to come from a badge and a concealed weapon. There were other sources of strength and authority.

Bethany was thinking of her grandma as she carried the tray of shakers to the booth farthest from the departing customers.

Odd as it seemed, something about that guy with the ponytail called to mind her grandma.

The three customers smiled at Bethany as their eyes passed over her on their way to the front door. No, that ponytail guy was too friendly to be a criminal or undercover cop. More like a counselor, or maybe an AA sponsor—not that she'd ever met anyone who introduced themselves as an AA sponsor. Seeing them portrayed in movies probably distorted her ideas about what they would be like.

Her grandma didn't really make Bethany think of AA sponsors, so why was Bethany thinking of Grandma Hight now?

It was late. She was tired. The shift was almost over. Her mind was wandering.

But she couldn't escape the feeling that the ponytail guy, and maybe those other two as well, reminded her of Grandma. Or maybe she was just getting a subtle reminder that she should call her grandma.

In the supply room, next to the employee break room which Annabelle and Jose were occupying now, Bethany pulled out her phone. Through the thin walls she could pick out the tone of an intense discussion between the waitress and the cook who was managing the diner tonight. They were probably talking about hours or dollars.

"Hello, dear. You caught me just before I turned out the lights in the living room." Grandma's voice crackled just a little, as it revived with excitement, probably staving off the sleep for which she'd been preparing.

"Hi, Grandma. Sorry. I know it's late. I was just thinking of you and wondering if it was one of those prompts for me to call you. Are you okay?"

Grandma chuckled. "Well, I am okay. I hope I don't have to be sick or in trouble for you to get a prompt to call me."

"Oh. No. Of course, I don't."

"'Cause then I'd have to make something up just so you would talk to me."

"Ha. Well, don't let me lead you into temptation. Good point about me not needing a crisis or anything to get a reminder to call."

Bethany could hear the conversational tones lowering next door—maybe acceptance or a truce was on the way. Jose was not the manager of the diner—just in charge tonight. He was the senior cook and a levelheaded guy, but he wasn't the one to decide big things like raises or time off or whatever it was Annabelle wanted.

"Are you at the dorm?"

"No, at work. This is one of my regular nights." Bethany idly tapped on the bundles of plastic-wrapped paper napkins at eye level on the chrome rack next to her.

"Oh. And something at the diner prompted you to call?"

"Maybe I'm just missing you. But I saw some folks in here—the last ones to leave—that reminded me of you somehow."

"Huh. Were they old fogeys?"

"Ha. No, they were young, though older than me. There was just something about them. Or maybe it's just my imagination."

Grandma inhaled deeply. "Sure. Sometimes it's hard to tell the difference. But I'm very encouraged that you're listening just in case it's the Spirit leading you to do something." She chuckled again. "And I wouldn't put it past him to prompt you to call your old grandma out of simple kindness."

"Hmm. Kindness." Bethany gently punched the napkins with the side of her fist. "That's a good word to describe you, and maybe that's what I was seeing in those people. I could sorta tell they were kind to each other. They even left before Annabelle had to chase them out after closing." She stopped thumping the enticingly soft napkin packages. "I probably need to work on that. It's not my strongest thing."

"Kindness? Well, we can all work to get better at all sorts of things. Having more of the fruit of the Spirit is important." Grandma didn't sound like she had already concluded that her granddaughter needed to learn more about kindness, but maybe she was just treating Bethany's self-assessment with a little ... kindness.

"Okay. Well, I'll let you get to sleep."

"Are you heading home soon?"

"Soon. In half an hour or so. We just need to close things up."

"D'you have someone to walk you to the dorm?"

"It's only a few minutes' away. I usually go with Annabelle to the bus stop and wait there if her bus isn't close. Then it's just a few blocks to campus from there." It was more than ten blocks, but ten was fewer than twenty, she reasoned. She didn't want to worry her grandma.

"Not using the scooter anymore?"

"No. It got too messed up when I crashed."

"Well, I'm glad you didn't get *messed up* in that crash."

"Yeah. I was in better shape than the scooter afterward."

"Okay. I'll let you go, and I'll pray for safety and some good sleep tonight."

"Thanks, Grandma. I'll pray for you too."

When Bethany ended the call, she could hear Jose and Annabelle parting ways, apparently peacefully. Maybe Annabelle just needed to vent to someone. She has a kid to support and so does Jose. He would be sympathetic, and he was generally kind.

Nearly crashing into Jose as she dragged one of those packages of napkins out of the storage room, Bethany grunted an apology.

"Ha. That's okay. You can go ahead and crash into me as long as you're only carrying napkins. Knives would be a different thing." Jose did a dance step to get clear of Bethany and her load. He moved easily on his feet, considering he had been standing next to a grill all day. He was a big, round guy with sloping shoulders and a ready grin. A silver tooth showed in the front when he smiled broadly.

Bethany laughed wearily. After closing time, most of her reactions came automatically, if they came at all.

Jose paused before opening the cooler door. “You takin’ a sandwich home with you tonight?”

“No, thanks. I had a good sandwich at my supper break, remember? You have served me already, sir.”

“Ah, well, so many customers. Hard to keep track of ’em all.” He grinned and pulled on the cooler handle, disappearing into a faint vapor cloud.

Bethany knew what he meant. The crowd of customers on a busy night like this tended to blur together in her mind. Except, of course, that guy with the ponytail and the charming couple he was eating with. They remained sharp in her mind. Fascinating, in fact. Irrationally so.

Chapter 2

Crashing

The bus Annabelle hoped to catch was less than two blocks away, according to the tracking map on her phone, so Bethany waved goodbye and headed for campus. She didn't really miss riding her scooter. Grandma's mention of it on the phone tonight was the first time Bethany had given her former two-wheeler any thought this spring.

Back in the fall, she had dodged a little kid who barreled out of a restaurant. Bethany had to careen off the curb to avoid smashing into the little guy. Instead, she landed on the side of her scooter in the street. The gift from her dad took the brunt of it. It never worked right after that.

But walking was less tense, even if it was slower. Slower was good sometimes. She generally felt safe on these city streets. Tonight, she texted Emily as she walked, marking her progress toward the dorm with incoming and outgoing messages. Doing so felt less like walking alone. At least her roommate could call 911 if some threat leapt out at her.

No threats were in sight this night, not even threatening weather. It was in the fifties still this late in the day. Going into work had been a sacrifice that afternoon, with glorious sunshine and blossoming trees all around. Milwaukee could be beautiful when it wanted to be, when the weather cooperated in the late spring.

Engrossed in messages about the intricacies of the ever-shifting relationship between Emily and William, Bethany was on campus before she realized. She turned toward her dorm and checked her surroundings more carefully. It did feel a little scary to arrive somewhere without noticing her approach, especially this late at night.

As she strode to the glass doors of the tall dormitory, her mom's voice echoed in her head. "Your father apparently doesn't care if you get raped or murdered on the way home from work at night. If he's gonna support this whole fiasco, surely he could pay enough so you don't have to work at that diner."

The version of that tirade that replayed in Bethany's head was clear, whether she had assembled it from more than one such complaint. A bit of mental cut and paste, maybe.

Thanks, Mom. Thanks for that thought. She allowed a bit of sarcasm, even as she noted how much nicer it was to recall her mother's ominous warnings only *after* arriving in the lobby of the dorm.

The *fiasco* in question was Bethany's music education major, not the piano performance major her mother would have preferred. Mom had bailed out of paying for any of it when Bethany opted for a different career path than she had laid out for her daughter. As she trudged up the stairs to her third-floor suite, Bethany wondered if Emily's constant romantic trials were filling in as a substitute for her mother's former role as producer and director of life drama.

Bethany arrived at her door on the third floor to the sound of booming dance music just up the hall. The suite she shared included five beds, four of which were currently taken. Bethany and Emily shared a double bedroom, Jacqueline had a double to herself. Her roomie, Sandy, had left school due to an illness in her family. The single in the suite was occupied by Rosemary, a girl none of the others had known at the beginning of the year. Now, toward the end of the spring semester, Bethany still didn't feel like she knew Rosemary well.

Jacqueline and Sandy had been Emily's friends from freshman year, but Jacqueline was at least as close with Bethany now as with Emily. She seemed to have less tolerance than Bethany did for the constant romantic turmoil of Emily's life. Thus, the internal question about why Bethany was not so bothered by the drama. Maybe she needed someone to fill the role of the emotional volcano she lived next to. It was certainly better than *being* the source of emotional tremors and eruptions.

The electronic lock beeped when Bethany pressed her keycard against it. She wasn't supposed to have to touch the lock on her suite door with the card, but her security ID seemed to be at least as tired as Bethany was most days. Before she left school, Sandy had explained that these locks were using *near-field communication* and apparently *near* included actually touching. It made sense, in a dictionary sort of way.

Bethany could hear someone moving around in the bathroom, then heard the clunk of a case closing—maybe a makeup case.

Jacqueline poked her head out the bathroom door. She was wearing a mask of face cream. "Boo!"

With a start, Bethany blurted a laugh—a self-conscious laugh about how tired her reaction proved she surely was.

"Sorry. You gonna study, or do you wanna watch a movie?" Leaving the bathroom door open, Jacqueline turned her gangly frame back toward the mirror. Maybe she hadn't finished her application of that cream.

"I should study." Bethany slipped her phone into her front pants pocket and pulled her jacket off. "I *should* anyway. Not guaranteeing I'll be able to keep my eyes open."

"How was the diner?"

Bethany sometimes felt like Jacqueline was slumming it with the other girls. Her interest in Bethany's job rang a bit like anthropological research. Jacqueline was a history major—prelaw—but she seemed to have an almost scientific interest in the lives of the other girls.

"It was fine. There are always entertaining characters in there." Wasn't that what Jacqueline hoped to hear?

"Yeah? Any hot guys?" She turned her face, partially red from scrubbing, toward Bethany.

"Only older guys. I don't see many students in there."

"Who cares if they're older? That might be just what you need. Someone to guide you..." She kept talking, but the sound of her voice faded as Bethany walked away.

Bethany was pushing her bedroom door open, not sticking around to hear Jacqueline's relationship advice. Given the number of times Bethany had walked away from her suitemate when she talked like that, it didn't even feel rude anymore. She could hear Jacqueline still speaking, but she seemed to be facing the mirror or maybe headed to her own room. Just talking, not necessarily communicating.

Once she was dressed in sweats, fully intending to study, Bethany tucked her fried food scented work clothes into her laundry bag. Jacqueline tapped on her door, which was already open a few inches.

"Hey, sorry if I offended you back there." Her face was a fresh pink tone and her eyes shone with sincerity. She was taller than Bethany by a few inches. Her neck seemed perpetually bent forward, like a tall girl trying to hide her height. Or maybe just a girl who has read lots of books. Or one who was never taught to sit up straight while on a piano bench practicing for hours and hours.

"Thanks for saying that. Yeah. I have to resist lusting after guys I see at work. So ... right. I can't really think like that. It messes with my head."

"Understood. A working girl has to stay focused." Jacqueline would be working as an intern at a law firm this summer. She did that so she didn't have to work during the school year like Bethany did.

"Not just that. You know, it's also about ... you know, about my faith."

Jacqueline nodded slowly, her dark hair falling over one shoulder. "I know. That part I don't get, but I know it's important to you. So ... sorry."

"You are forgiven." Bethany made a gesture she had seen in a movie, the sign of the cross over her friend. Only about half joking.

Her suitemate bowed slightly and backed out of the room. Bethany watched her go, idly holding her electronic reader in her hand, signaling her sincerity about studying.

Bethany was hoping, not assuming, that actual work would get done before sleep. She forced herself to attempt reading a novel assigned for her literature class—Margaret Atwood's *A Handmaid's Tale*. Bethany was glad to see it on the class list because a lot of her fellow students had read it already in high school. Her reading list during high school was probably shorter than most of her friends'. Large swaths of her education were covered by her mother and by occasional tutors. Instead of attending a local high school, Bethany had more often traveled to play concerts and compete in piano performance. Her list of awards was longer than her reading list.

She sat on her bed with her legs pretzeled under her and made a sincere effort to read. She fought sleepy nods with persistent blinking and huffs of breath.

When Emily arrived in the room, Bethany's face was half buried in her pillow. She peered through the lashes of one eye at her roommate's attempts at stealth. Even as tired as she was, Bethany roused at the subtlest sounds—sounds that might inspire dreams about small burrowing animals moving into their suite. There was, after all, an empty bed these days.

Without saying anything to Emily, Bethany fell back asleep, only briefly wondering what she had done with her reader. Perhaps she dreamt about the location of that electronic device but that wasn't nearly as clear as the very unusual dream she had that night.

"Bethany. Bethany. It's me." That was the first part of the dream. Those words seemed to stand alone, except it happened three times. Just her name spoken by a man's friendly voice. Of course, it was someone who would know her well enough that he could simply identify himself as "me."

Next was an image that seemed to be connected to those few words, but the man didn't appear to speak. It was the image of the guy with the ponytail at the diner. His eyes were even kinder in her dream than what she had seen in real life.

He just gazed at her, smiling. It felt as if he were introducing himself, in a way. The words *Bethany, Bethany, it's me* didn't recur while she saw him, but they seemed to be part of the background of his image. It was an introduction by someone she already knew, apparently. Strangely.

As she looked at the loving kindness in that man's eyes, she grew uncomfortable. Some of what she had said to Jacqueline before bed came back. This guy was too old for her. She shouldn't be staring at that guy like that. But she told herself she wasn't doing it. He was the one looking at *her* like that. If anyone was being inappropriate, it was him. He looked at her like he was in love with her.

Then the dream ended—or moved on, with something like a black screen transition in a movie. The next image she saw looked like Jesus. The costume, the expression—everything about the man who appeared next in her dream said, *this is Jesus*. But it also might have been the same man as the one with the ponytail.

At least it might have been him.

Chapter 3

Overslept

Bethany overslept on Sunday morning in her windowless bedroom. Her watch informed her that she still had time to catch the church service online, but she would have to forego the trip to the cafeteria and settle for a granola bar breakfast.

"I'll consider it fasting." She said that aloud before recalling that Emily was sleeping on the other side of the room. Her roommate was buried under her lavender and white duvet. Only a glimpse of Emily's toes revealed her presence. She didn't stir in response to Bethany's unguarded comment.

Despite her roomie's comatose state, Bethany remained quiet on her way to the bathroom and while collecting her humble breakfast and sliding her laptop off her desk. She breathed a sigh when she settled onto her bed with her computer and her water bottle. With her legs stretched in front of her, she leaned on her pillow, wedged herself against the wall, and powered up the laptop.

All that was as automatic as a yawn, but when she had her earbuds in and the worship service appeared in a full-screen window, she paused over a nugget from her dreams during the night. It was like a shiny bit of gold amid the usual clods and gravel of her nocturnal landscape. It felt real and more substantial than her usual dreams. Certainly, it was more significant than the painfully common dream in which she tries to go to class, only to discover that she doesn't recall where the class meets and realizes she hadn't been attending that class all semester.

No, this was not an academic anxiety dream, and it wasn't one of the whirling confusing dreams that were also common. This new one was a *Jesus* dream, complete with a cameo appearance by that guy with the ponytail. The possible AA sponsor.

Could the two men be the same? In her dreams they could be, of course. She shook her head. Why would she make that connection, even in a dream? In Psychology 101, they had studied the part of the brain that streamed dreams. They learned to see dreams as an exercise of the subconscious mind. Nothing mysterious—just brain activity intended to deal with issues not resolved during waking hours.

Whatever it was, this dream was different from any before it, and she was a little worried about what it meant.

As she resettled one of her earbuds and focused on the second verse of the first song at church that morning, Bethany thought she heard a voice. An unexpected voice of someone invisible—like the sound of someone rising from the grave.

"Are you watching church?" It was Emily, speaking from beneath her duvet. She tried to fling her cover back but had to make two more attempts before her head was liberated.

Bethany pulled out one earbud. "Church. Yeah. You gonna get up and watch with me?"

"Can you come over here? I don't think I can move." For Emily, the line between *can* and *want to* was often faded.

But Bethany accommodated. Sliding off her bed, she gripped her slender laptop in one hand, dragged her water bottle with her other, and carried her pillow under one arm. She climbed over Emily and took up a position similar to the one she had just left behind. She draped her legs across her waif-like roommate so the two of them formed an uneven letter X.

Enabling the onboard speakers and removing her second earbud, Bethany settled her laptop where Emily could see it.

"Who's that on keyboards?"

"Her name is Jess or Jessica." Bethany recalled the jovial musician from when they first met. "She was part of that music camp last summer." That summer camp experience had confirmed Bethany's determination to do more than just perform music. She wanted to share music by empowering kids to make their own. Joyful Noise Music Camp had been an outreach idea from the youth pastor at the church, and he had recruited Bethany to provide keyboard lessons. It was a blast. She was hooked.

"You ever think of doing that? On stage with the band at church?" Emily's voice was starting to clear, becoming less perforated by sleepy obstructions. She had attended church with Bethany once. Emily's church back home was of a different brand. She wasn't attending any church most weeks, but she often joined Bethany when she watched her church online.

Bethany had played keyboards at some of the college group gatherings during this school year. Word got out about her skills after the music camp. "That still looks too much like *performing* up there on Sunday, even though I know it's really not. I guess I still don't trust myself to get past the way it looks, the way it feels to be up on a stage with people watching out there in the seats."

"Hmm. Lots of people at your church worship with their eyes closed."

Hissing a laugh through her teeth, Bethany nodded. "Good point. But this isn't about anybody but me. It's my problem."

"And it's about your mom."

Bethany laughed again but cut that short. "Hey, let me get into this service, will ya?"

"Mm-hmm." Emily was silent for a few seconds. "Got any more of those granola bars?"

Taking a deep breath, Bethany turned up the volume and began to hum the worship song, even as she set the laptop down and climbed off the bed. Breakfast in bed was not too great a kindness to provide her roommate, and if crumbs got under the duvet, Emily would have no one else to blame.

Hoisting herself into more of a sitting position, Emily bobbed her head gently to the music, then she stopped and watched Bethany climb back onto the bed. “I broke up with William last night, I think.”

“What?” Bethany wanted to shush her roomie again, to focus on the church service, but the deep line between Emily’s eyebrows appeared to have been carved by some serious pain.

“He was never gonna be right for me. He would never go to church with me, for example.”

“You broke up with William because he wouldn’t go to church with you?” Bethany turned the volume on the computer back down to where it had been before she got up to retrieve the granola bar. She handed Emily her breakfast. The fact that Emily rarely went to church didn’t seem to factor into the breakup.

“It was something we argued about last night. I really wasn’t asking him to go to church with me *today*, but it would have been nice to have it be an option, sort of.” She took a deep breath, pulling at the bright green granola bar wrapper with her delicate hands. “We were never right for each other.”

Never is a long time. It would even have to include last week when William was “definitely the one” for Emily. But Bethany would not point that out. Not this time. She would save it for when Emily tried to get back together with William next week. She said a silent prayer for deliverance from having to face that temptation in the future.

Instead of saying any of that aloud, Bethany offered sympathy. “Sorry, Em. Sorry it didn’t work out.”

“Thanks. At least I’ll have more time to hang out with you before summer vacation.” Her whole face formed a doll-like smile.

That was a happy prospect, even if it didn’t seem likely to come to pass. Finals loomed ahead of them. But Bethany repressed that counterpoint and smiled back with a nod. She wanted to at least catch the last of the worship songs.

And Emily did let her listen. Crunching away on the granola bar and dribbling water down her chin, breakfast kept her occupied for a couple minutes. She settled down after that, staying silent during the greeting and announcements and falling asleep during the sermon.

Bethany prayed for her roommate with a hand resting on one motionless leg. All the boy drama was about something else, of course, but Bethany could only guess what it was.

She checked in and out of the sermon, distracted by wondering about her own lack of boyfriends. Was Emily's love life enough drama for Bethany? No need for boys of her own? That was probably a lame explanation. Not a real answer.

When the sermon came to a close, Bethany was glad there wouldn't be a quiz over the contents of that talk. And, as the pastor was wrapping up, Bethany wondered if she had taken her dream from last night seriously enough. She could at least pass a quiz on what the man in her dream said.

She laughed. *The man of her dreams.*

Chapter 4

Caller

On the way out of the dining hall that afternoon, Bethany got a call from her dad. “Hey, girl. How are you doing?”

Her dad was living in Portage, in Central Wisconsin, these days. He was remarried. Portage was not too far away for Bethany to visit during breaks. She had driven there with friends over spring break. A bus had carried her home for Christmas.

Upon answering the call, she had detoured from crossing the lobby to exiting the building into the midday sunshine. “I’m good. A quiet day. Not working at the diner. Getting some studying done.” She waved at Penny, a friend from church who passed her on the sidewalk. Penny looked dressed up—she had probably made it to church. She was a good Christian.

As her dad filled her in on the contents and mood of his weekend, Bethany considered sharing her dream with him. But, as sympathetic as he generally was, he wasn’t the best person to review such things with, and she knew right away who she would call about it.

“Are you being safe? Your mom keeps messaging me about how you’re not being safe.” Dad sounded like he was fulfilling an obligation, not addressing a fear of his own.

“I didn’t know you two were talking.”

“Uh. Well, we didn’t used to, and I wouldn’t really call it talking.” He let his words coast for a few seconds. He was probably deleting a whole directory of things he was really thinking. He was pretty disciplined about not saying negative things about her mother.

Bethany responded to her mother's concern. "I am careful. I have friends at work and on campus who look out for me." Then she thought of something. "And God is looking out for me. Jesus is never far away, it seems. At least not far from my thoughts."

"Hmm, okay. Now you sound like your grandma."

"Thank you. I was planning to call her later." She raised her face toward the pristine blue sky. Something about the brightness of the day stirred more regret that she had missed going to church that morning.

"Oh, good. I usually call her on Sunday night, so I'll talk to her after you do." His voice faded as if he had turned away from his phone.

"When you call her, then, you can try to find out what secrets we keep together."

"Oh, yeah? You have secrets with your grandma? That's kinda reassuring. I'm glad you have her to talk to about things. Even secret things." His gladness sounded real but a bit muffled, like the difference between music coming through the walls and music being played in her room.

"Thanks, Dad. Thanks for trusting us."

"My daughter and my mom—I guess I trust you each on your own but together you are a force of nature."

"Ha. Well, we're probably the two women who pray for you the most."

"That seems likely. I wouldn't be surprised." This reply was polite and generic. Cruising in neutral. Dad had stayed clear of Grandma's and Bethany's faith, but he never criticized them about it.

"So, are you okay with me staying in Milwaukee this whole summer? I didn't hear a real clear response from you on that." She was looking at the blooming pink and white flowers in one of the planters near her dorm, thinking how nice it would be to see the campus in summer—also thinking she should remember what those flowers were called. Grandma might have told her their name. She used to grow these little round flowers at her house in Wisconsin.

"Have you considered spending part of the summer with your mom? I was thinking that might be good for you and for her."

"You want me to do that so she can stop bugging you?"

"Well, she bugs me because she cares about you and ... and she's worried."

"I don't think she's gonna worry less if we spend more time together. We spent so much time together before college. I think I still need a break from her."

"Okay. That was the only thing I was thinking about you staying in Milwaukee for the summer. I get it that the money is good at the diner. You can come here for a couple o' weekends, and you can see your grandma down in Illinois. That all makes sense, but I was just wondering if you had any thoughts about seeing your mom out in Oregon."

"No. Not yet. I will someday soon, I'm sure. Maybe next Christmas." It was a rough draft idea that popped out without any editing.

"Christmas? Well, I guess I can give up one Christmas with you."

When Bethany had lived with her mother, she usually spent Christmas with her dad, including visits to her grandma and her cousin Katie in the later years.

"Have you talked to Patty lately?" Bethany asked about her aunt, Katie's mom. As they spoke, she had looped back to the dorm, striding through the lobby now.

"I haven't. Not for a while." He ended the topic there.

Bethany decided not to intensify the questioning. Her dad's relationship with his sister was his business. She knew that relationship was complicated by Patty's similarities to Bethany's mother, at least when it came to bombarding her dad with her strident opinions. Bethany's dad was like one of those sandstone walls in a cave. He seemed to invite visitors to carve away at his surface, to make their mark.

Bethany tried not to yield to that temptation. She loved her dad. She didn't feel a need to make him into someone different.

They ended their call as she entered her dorm room. She found the suite entirely empty. She adjusted her plans—there would be no need to go to the library if the room was going to be so quiet.

She needed to do some reading in one of her hardbound textbooks. *Introduction to Biology*. Not the catchiest title. The book was basically what she expected for a core curriculum requirement. And, in contrast to the eBooks downloaded to her reader, this one weighed a few pounds. Somehow, that seemed appropriate for a book preoccupied with bodies, human and otherwise.

Bethany sat on her bed with legs folded under her, yellow highlighter in hand, and she read about avian biology—birds like the ones Grandma Hight loved to watch out the window of her apartment in the retirement home.

Wandering thoughts of her grandma recalled the strange dream of Jesus, which then reminded her what the pastor was saying in the streaming church service that morning. *Encountering Jesus* was the title of his talk. Grandma had some amazing stories of encountering Jesus, meeting him as if he was as physically present as the cinderblock of a biology textbook in Bethany's lap.

"An encounter like that would be so cool." She inhaled deeply. Over the last few years, since finally getting to know her Grandma Hight, Bethany had marveled at Grandma's stories like someone watching a drama streaming on her computer. They were great stories—believable as someone else's narrative.

But only as someone else's.

As she queued up regret over being distracted by these thoughts, someone knocked on the suite door.

"Maybe I *should* have gone to the library." Bethany slid off her bed, expecting to find one of her suite mates who had forgotten to take her keycard with her. Or maybe it was a neighbor checking on the assigned reading in one of her classes. She had no suitors these days—*suitor* was her grandma's word, one Grandma always used with a twinkle in her eye. A gentleman caller, perhaps?

Of all the people Bethany expected to see at her door, the man she found smiling at her in the hallway was not one of them.

Chapter 5

Knocking

As familiar as was the act of opening her suite door, what she found there was entirely disconnected from her real life. Bethany felt like she had suddenly slipped from normal physical reality into a dream. Or perhaps into her imagination.

It was like seeing a video version of one of her grandma's stories.

There he was.

Jesus, apparently, and he was wearing the classic costume of religious art and modern Gospel dramas.

Jesus was standing in the dorm hallway. Smiling at Bethany.

"Behold! I stand at the door and knock." He spoke clearly, confidently, then he laughed.

And he disappeared.

Bethany barked a surprised noise that she had probably never made before. She whipped her head left and then right. Her knees faltered. She gripped the doorpost. Where did he go? What just happened? Did he sprint down the hall? Would Jesus show up at her door, knock, and run? Of course not. But ...

She staggered two steps toward the stairs and the elevator. Uncertainty interrupted her progress, however, when she felt her bare feet on the hallway carpet and heard the suite door swinging closed behind her.

Lunging back toward her door, she slipped her fingers in just before it closed. She had neither her phone nor keycard in her pockets.

That was close.

Bethany stood in the hall, holding the door open a few inches, trying to decide what to do.

What did he say? It almost felt like a joke—like Jesus showed up at her door and told her a joke. "Behold, I stand at the door and knock." That was a quote from ... from someplace in the Bible. She wasn't sure who was supposed to have said it, exactly. But it was about Jesus, she was mostly sure. It was about him, but it surely didn't imply that he would come to her dorm room and literally knock on her door.

Pulling the door open wider, she considered slipping on shoes, grabbing her phone and keycard, and renewing her chase toward the disappearing man. If that's what she was doing out there in the hall.

There was a problem with that plan, however. The replay in her head confirmed that he had not run down the hall. He had vanished. When she looked squarely at her memory, she could see him standing there smiling at her and then he was gone. Vanished. Not striding down the hall toward the stairs or the elevator, just gone.

"What the ..." She stopped herself from finishing that sentence the way many of her friends surely would have. She had stopped herself from swearing. And, instead, she started to giggle. She could not stop herself from laughing as she wandered back through the suite, toward her bedroom.

"What was that?" She laughed harder. "That was wild!" Her upper back became electric. She continued to release an untamed and alien laugh in irregular bursts.

"Holy ... heck." She shook her head at herself now. "Did that really happen?"

Bethany stood in the middle of the floor in her bedroom looking at the collection of band posters Emily had stuck to the wall above her bed.

"That really happened!" She said it to the choir of pop stars staring back at her from those posters. "Jesus really knocked on my door!"

She released a huge sigh. "Wow. That was crazy!"

"I have to call Grandma."

As she searched for her phone, which had slipped beneath a pillow on her bed, she considered whether this would be a good time to call Grandma. "I know I can't tell anyone else. That's for sure." She briefly considered whether the pastor who preached about encountering Jesus that morning would believe her.

And she started to laugh again. A harder, deeper laugh.

In her head, the laughter sounded a bit insane. But in her chest, it felt really good. It felt like she was exhaling something that had been lodged inside her. That thing pulled free and shot right out, like a reversal of Cupid's arrow—an arrow extracted, a wound set free.

Her laughter shifted to a lower gear. "Huh. That's a weird thought." Her own diagnostic pause prompted her to laugh a little longer. The notion about her heart, an arrow, and a wound wasn't objectively funny, but she laughed anyway.

She really wanted to call Grandma, so she pulled herself together and tapped her grandma's number in her recent calls list. She had already planned to call her that afternoon, to talk about the dream. Now she had to tell someone about that visitor.

"Hello, dear." Grandma cleared her throat.

"Did I wake you up?" A Sunday afternoon nap didn't sound unreasonable. Actually, it sounded pretty attractive to Bethany at that moment.

"Uh. Well, not exactly. I just woke up half a minute ago, and I was thinking about you. Just thinking, not worrying, I promise." Grandma chuckled. Then she made a dull grunting noise, like the sound of a woman in her eighties sitting up. "So, what happened?"

"Ha! How do you know something happened? I could just be calling to talk, like we were saying last night."

"Oh, sure. That's true." Grandma paused a second. "But what happened?"

Bethany was chuckling again. She could sense the approach of more of that crazy laughter. She strained to stifle it, out of mercy for her grandma, not wanting to worry her favorite person.

"Something did happen." She released a vocalized breath. "Huuuuhhhh." It was a sound she had heard Grandma make when telling fun stories, including stories about Jesus showing up in her house.

"Well, it sounds like it's a *good* thing." Grandma's voice was full of hope and invitation.

"I can only tell *you* about this. No one else will believe me."

"Oh, Bethany." This time Grandma's reply was more hushed.

The awe evident in her voice gave her granddaughter a shiver. "Whoa, it's like you already know. You know that Jesus came to my dorm room. He knocked on my door."

"Is he still there now?" Only Grandma would ask *that* question. Of course, she would ask that because she would be remembering Jesus staying with her, first in her house and then wherever she went for at least a week. He even disappeared once and then came back to speak with her and follow her around again.

A slice of Bethany's heart slipped from the lofty overlook she had been teetering on when she decided to call Grandma. That Jesus had disappeared from her so quickly, however, didn't banish the wonder of what had happened.

"No. He just came to my door and knocked."

"Like in the Bible. *The Book of Revelations*." Grandma's hushed tone was mixed now with recognition.

"Oh, yeah. That's where it is." Bethany hummed for a second, not sure what difference it made to know the exact chapter and verse. "He smiled like he was enjoying himself. He was at my door, and he said, 'I stand at your door and knock.'" She laughed. "Uh, he even started with 'Behold!' I think." And her chortling became uncontrollable again.

When she started to get a grip on herself, she could hear Grandma laughing too. Her chuckles were both deep in her chest and chirpy, then Grandma started coughing. Perhaps she pulled the phone away from her face or covered the microphone, but she came back with high pitched exhalations that were like icing on top of the sweet laughter.

Grandma cleared her throat again. "Oh, I can picture it. That is so much like something he would do. Hmm, I even think maybe he told me that once. He was standing at my bedroom door. That's definitely his personality at its finest." She was starting to sound more like a woman recently awakened from a nap or maybe a grandma who needed to get back to sleep.

But Bethany had questions. "Why do you think he did it? Oh, and he was in my dream too. There was this man at the diner late last night, and he was ..." She flipped through the snapshots in her head. "It seems like it might have been him. It might have been Jesus, only dressed like a modern guy." She had gotten off track. "Anyway, back to the dream. I had a dream where Jesus ..." She did another one of those video replays. "I really think it was the same Jesus as at my door. I mean, he looked just like the Jesus at my door."

"Wait. What happened? You had a dream last night?"

"Yes. It happened after I saw this guy at the diner. He was pretty memorable. I ... I was really ... impressed by his smile, in a way." She took another deep breath. "He's the one that made me want to call you last night." She sighed. "I guess I would say now that it was him. And not just because he came to my door and knocked." She repressed a new set of giggles. "No, he came to me in my dream and said, 'Bethany, it's me.' Yeah. It was him." She sniffed a wistful laugh.

"Ooohhh, that gives me even more chills." Grandma released another hushed breath into the phone.

Bethany relaxed her shoulders and tried to sort her thoughts. "So, why do you think he did all that?"

"Why? Oh, well, I expect only he can tell you for sure why he did any of it. But you can be sure that it's all for *your* good and to please God. That's what Jesus always does. He does what pleases God and he does what benefits us." Grandma's voice scratched a little, perhaps still recovering from the cold that had recently slowed her down.

"That sounds right. I can believe that. And ... I guess I can wait for him to explain to me why he did it." Bethany paused at the sound of Grandma coughing again. "Okay. I don't wanna keep you from your nap."

"Oh, no problem. I am tired but never too tired to hear from you. Let me know what he does next. I'm sure he'll keep reaching out to you, in his time. And he'll explain it all to you."

"Thanks, Grandma. I don't know what I would've done if I didn't have you to tell about this. Maybe I would have freaked out one of my friends just because I was desperate to tell someone."

"Well, of course, I'm here to listen."

"You're pretty sure there's more?"

"Well, dear, with Jesus there's always more."

Chapter 6

Waiting

After classes on Monday, Bethany worked a shift at the diner. Savannah was the other waitress for the night. It was Annabelle's day off. Savannah was a few years older than Bethany. She was an athletic woman, who managed to appear unfazed no matter how intense the customer demands.

"Well, girl, what you been up to? You look like a chick that's got a secret."

Bethany stood in the break room, staring at Savannah's wide dark eyes, noting a hint of smile on her generous lips. "Me? A secret?" Of course, she knew that she *did* have a secret, which was an unusual situation for her. She had a story she wouldn't tell anyone except her grandma. But how could Savannah know she had a secret?

"Sometimes I get a sense of these sorta things." Savannah pushed at the side of her afro as if she had just picked it and needed to settle it down a little tighter. Or maybe it was just a nervous habit. She seemed to do that when male customers got aggressively friendly.

"Uh, okay, but ... if it's a secret, how come you know about it?" Bethany felt like she was imitating her other grandma—Grandma Marconi, a clever and argumentative woman, back when she had been more alert.

Savannah had no answer for this challenge. With a bob of her head, she abandoned her expedition into Bethany's life, or maybe just put it on hold, and ambled away from the doorway.

Jose and Diego, the assistant cook, were speaking Spanish loudly in the kitchen. As far as Bethany knew, Jose was supposed to be leaving. The beginning of the week was usually pretty quiet and Diego sometimes closed the diner on a Monday. Today Diego didn't sound happy.

Bethany knew enough Spanish to translate the key points.

"I got obligations too. This is *your* night." The conclusive tone of Jose's reply seemed to settle the matter.

Diego must have been trying to get Jose to take over for him. Apparently, that didn't work with Jose's schedule. His obligations included his son, Guillermo. Jose called him Memo—which seemed like a better name for a three-year-old, as far as Bethany was concerned.

Tying on her apron, Bethany stepped aside so Diego could push past her and grab his hat from his locker. He was shorter and thinner than Jose, though not really short or thin. He was kind of a junior version of Jose, probably ten years younger. Maybe he would someday grow up to be like Jose—as big as Jose, if not as gracious. Diego must have been optimistic about his prospects for getting off tonight because he'd left his chef's hat in the break room. The abrasive rush in and out of the room and the muttering under his breath twisted Bethany's insides even tighter than the string she was tying on her apron. Working with Diego might be miserable if he was in a bad mood.

After Diego barged back out of the room, Savannah poked her head in the door. She raised her neat eyebrows at Bethany. "You ready for this?"

"Maybe it won't be that busy." She shrugged. "You've closed with Diego before?"

Savannah nodded slowly. "And I worked with him when he was in a bad mood before too. The food is fine, but his manners are awful."

Bethany breathed a sigh and headed for the dining counter. "Well, I got your back."

Savannah chuckle. "And I got yours."

Jose didn't leave until well past seven, probably later than he intended, but there was a bigger supper rush than was usual for most Mondays. Some event on campus or somewhere downtown probably brought people to the area. Bethany didn't know what it was this time, but she recalled a few Monday night, off-peak concerts she had played in various cities when she was fifteen and sixteen. Her mom had believed in exposure and was glad to take a dead night of the week as an opportunity for her girl to get more experience in front of a live—though small—audience.

This recollection didn't do anything to elevate Bethany's mood, but Diego's mood was even worse. He muttered and swore loudly enough that she could hear him whenever she picked up an order. But his profanity—both English and Spanish—couldn't be heard from the tables. That was good for business but not good for Bethany's enjoyment of her work.

She wished she could close the diner for Diego. He probably had to do something with his family, judging from the way Jose had spoken to him earlier. Maybe there was a birthday celebration he forgot until too late or a cousin that needed help—something that would put him in a bad light for not being there.

Annabelle had closed the diner a couple times. She knew the combination to the safe, or at least she knew where it was hidden. Bethany doubted Annabelle had memorized it for use twice a year. But Bethany and Savannah were both junior to Annabelle and worked part-time, compared to Annabelle's full-time.

Around eight-thirty that night, Bethany was pondering these things when she noticed the old woman at the back table had finished her soup. She approached to check if the woman was interested in dessert, and the disheveled woman cast a glance at Bethany before hastily turning to look ahead of her, as if she could see out one of the windows from there.

"How was the soup?" Bethany really was curious. Ham and beans wasn't a soup she had tried. It was too heavy for her, but some people liked it. This woman looked as if she could use a few hot and hearty meals. Her sunken cheeks were lined in swirls almost like old wood, stained and etched and stained again.

The woman only glanced at Bethany. "It was fine. Uh, very good actually." She spoke as if addressing someone under the table or talking into a microphone on her collar. Then she peeked at Bethany under her eyebrows.

"Can I get you anything else?" Bethany paused, then decided to follow an impulse. "What about a refill of the soup?" This was not something they offered. There was no bottomless soup bowl on the menu or on the daily specials card. A second bowl would have to be paid for, if anyone ever asked for a refill.

The woman looked up now. She focused on Bethany's eyes before her head ticked to the right, as if breaking that link between them. "Uh, no. That's ... I can't ... I couldn't pay for that."

"It's on the house. Free refills Monday." Was it okay to just make that up? Essentially, it was a lie intended to benefit someone who seemed to be in need.

"Huh? Really?" The old woman could probably tell Bethany was just inventing that option. "If you're serious, I could eat another of those." She checked Bethany's face again, evidently searching for seriousness.

"Sure. And more bread?"

"Uh, yes, please. If you don't mind." The wounded humility of this woman nearly drove Bethany to tears.

She turned away hastily, the empty soup bowl in her hand. As she closed in on the kitchen, she could hear Diego. He must have been talking on his phone. Maybe he would be too distracted to notice her filling another soup bowl and collecting another basket of rolls.

But he was scowling at her as she located a clean soup bowl and filled another breadbasket. She almost got out of the kitchen without any questions.

But he called to her when he hung up his phone. "Hey. Who's that for? Not the same woman, is it?"

For half a second, Bethany considered lying to him. She could say the woman found something in the soup. Something that merited a fresh bowl. Bethany had slipped the dirty bowl into the pile next to the sink. Diego wouldn't know whether the woman had finished her first bowl of soup. The guy washing dishes—she couldn't remember his name—wouldn't say anything. These calculations about whether that lie might work, and the inherent hesitation that came with contemplating such deception, kept Bethany from answering at all.

"Hey. Where are you going with that? She has to pay for a second bowl, you know."

Bethany glanced over her shoulder, her gaze passing over Savannah, whose eyebrows were locked in question mode. Bethany only acknowledged Diego's words with a nod.

Following one step behind her, Savannah stopped at the end of the counter. There was a man sipping coffee with his elbows on the linoleum. He was looking at something on his phone. Savannah didn't say anything to him. She must have been following Bethany with her eyes, if not with her feet.

"Here you go. Your free refill." Bethany lowered her voice to half volume in case Savannah was tuned in, though she didn't think her coworker would tattle on her.

The old woman looked at the steaming bowl of bean soup, her rumpled hands resting by their heels on the edge of the melamine table. She looked at Bethany more pointedly than before. She started to say something but stopped.

"Don't worry." That was all Bethany could think to say.

"But ... I can't ..." The woman glanced toward the kitchen.

Bethany resisted looking over her shoulder. She didn't want to find Diego there watching her, so she refused to check. "Can't ...?"

Leaning forward, looking at Bethany's waistline instead of her face, the woman said, "I can't pay."

Bethany whispered back. "But it's a free ..." She stopped herself when she realized what the woman was saying. Now she did look over her shoulder. And Diego *was* there in the kitchen doorway with a towel in his hands, staring at her.

A couple at one of Savannah's tables called her over, and the dishwasher said something to Diego, drawing him back to the kitchen.

Bethany leaned forward. She spoke just above a whisper. "Don't worry about it. I got you covered." She tried to wink like her grandma would in a situation like this, but it probably looked more like a wince. Winking was not something Bethany practiced much.

A young guy came in the front door, and Bethany took the opportunity to leave the woman to eat in peace. Relative peace, given the angst she seemed to wear like a shroud.

Bethany asked the lone guy if he wanted to sit at the counter or in a booth. They didn't use the front tables this late at night.

"I have two friends coming, so a booth, please."

"Will you want the full menu?" It was late. Late for Bethany to eat supper on any day, whether she was working or not, but she couldn't assume anything about this guy and his friends. She gestured to a nearby table.

"Uh. Yeah, full menu. They'll be hungry." The guy looked to be in his mid-twenties. Slender, sculpted cheekbones, deep blue eyes. His hair was a patch of brown sprouted from the top of his head, with the sides buzzed short. He lowered his eyebrows when Bethany stared at him too long. He reminded her of someone. She was trying to figure out who.

"Okay, I'll bring you the menus. Do you want anything to drink while you wait?"

He ordered coffee after settling into his seat. Maybe he was a graduate student at one of the universities—a late-night coffee drinker.

When Bethany came back with the menus, she glanced toward the old woman. She was spooning soup, puckering her lips, and blowing to cool it. She had half a dinner roll in her other hand.

Turning her attention to the new arrival, Bethany slowed. A woman and a small girl were cautiously entering the front door. They accelerated, however, when they laid their eyes on the man in the booth, where he faced the door. Two generations of smiles lit their faces, and they slid into the booth across the table from him.

Bethany was holding four menus. She had forgotten how many friends the guy said were coming, so she set three of menus on the table and asked if the woman and the girl wanted something to drink.

"Do you have sodas?" The woman looked at the man and back at Bethany. She must have been at least ten years older than the guy or maybe was someone with a harder life than the clean-cheeked man. She seemed to be seeking permission from him before ordering drinks.

"Sure. We have Coke products."

"So, like, Sprite?" The woman glanced at the little girl who seemed a bit overwhelmed by something ... or by everything about the evening.

Bethany returned to the counter with another order for coffee—which she noted she had not delivered yet to the young man—and an order for one small Sprite for the girl.

Savannah said goodbye to her last customer and cruised to a stop next to the coffee pots. "Should I take this new crew, or do you want me to start cleaning up?"

Looking at Savannah to measure what she would prefer, Bethany shrugged. "You take whoever else comes in. I'll finish these two tables." That was diner protocol, but it was more than that for Bethany tonight. She didn't always feel it, but tonight she wanted to serve these particular people. The old woman who couldn't pay for her soup, the young man who seemed to be playing host to the humble woman and her daughter—Bethany was invested in serving all of them.

While the new trio reviewed the menu, Bethany visited the old woman. She was done with her soup and had just slipped the last of the bread into a backpack in the seat next to her. Without thinking about it, Bethany grabbed a few single-serving margarine tubs left on the next table and placed them in front of the woman without a word about it.

"How was the soup?" Never mind that she had already asked this.

The woman nodded, raising her eyes from the little margarine offering to assess Bethany. She scooped the margarine packets into the backpack after a glance toward the kitchen. "It was good. All good." Then she seemed to switch roles suddenly. She looked up at Bethany, sighed gently, and said, "Thank you. Thank you so much."

That was all. And that was plenty.

"You're welcome. I know that God loves you very much." She smiled. "Take care of yourself." She nodded and turned back to the counter, before getting a signal from the young man near the front of the diner. She was calculating how much she had received in tips compared to how much to charge herself for two bowls of soup. The latter wouldn't wipe out her tips entirely, but it would inflict a large dent. It had been busy for a Monday but not very rich in tips.

She stuffed those thoughts down as she arrived next to the other table. The old woman shuffled past her, slowing Bethany's response for a few seconds.

Savannah was at the near end of the counter. "You have a good night, dear." She called to her as the old woman pulled the front door open.

The woman glanced at Savannah, waved, and nodded.

When Bethany dedicated her attention to the three in the booth before her, she found three questioning gazes. What was the question? Maybe it was about her distraction with the old woman, which was surely obvious.

"What can I get you?"

The three each ordered entrees, which worried Bethany. How would Diego react to a full order just fifteen minutes before closing? He had already sent the dishwasher home for the night.

The young man stopped Bethany as she turned toward the kitchen. “Uh, do you have any kind of cake?”

“We have Boston cream pie, which, of course, is really cake with a vanilla pudding layer in the middle.”

The man grinned. “Do you suppose folks in Boston don’t know that it’s really cake?”

His Wisconsin accent excused his poke at folks not present. Bethany had never lived anywhere on the east coast, but she hadn’t yet adopted a midwestern antagonism toward either coast.

She laughed. “It’s good cake, even if they call it pie.” She assured them, with a particular pause to look at the little girl.

“We’ll take one piece to share among us.”

“Wise choice. The pieces are huge.”

All three customers glowed at this news.

Bethany helped Savannah clean behind the counter, until the other waitress collected the supplies to start on the tables. Then Bethany delivered the dinners, with the little girl getting hers first—a small burger with fries. Bethany had dumped the fries Diego originally gave her and waited a couple minutes to scoop fresh ones when the fryer finished. Diego didn’t seem to care. He was intent on cleaning the grill. If his grumpiness turned inward, that would be fine with her. Though maybe she would repent of that thought later.

When the three remaining customers finished their entrees, Bethany brought out the big slice of cake, with three forks and two extra plates. She had cut the piece a bit larger than usual. It was the end of the day, after all, and the rest of the cake would probably go home with one of the staff if it wasn’t dropped in the dumpster.

The eyes of the little girl expanded beyond what Bethany would have thought possible. Her mouth fell open, revealing a sporadic row of teeth. As the girl exclaimed over the cake and her mother fended off her venturing fingers, the man dug something from his shirt pocket. Two small candles. Then he pulled out a lighter.

"I hope there's not a law against bringing our own candles." He glanced at Bethany, a little apologetic.

"Or your own fire." Bethany raised her eyebrows. She could sense Savannah looking their way.

It was past nine. Savannah had turned the sign in the window to *Closed*. Now she was just two tables away with her cleaning project.

Bethany took a step toward the kitchen, once the candles were planted and the lighter lit. She checked for signs that Diego was watching. Maybe there *was* some rule against bringing your own candles and lighter to the diner. She even suspected Diego might invent such a rule, if his mood was bad enough.

When she started to round the counter, Bethany stopped suddenly. The young man was *trying* to sing "Happy Birthday" but he was way off key. The mother seemed shy, or maybe just unsure how to sing in that awkward key.

Bethany turned back and she picked up the song where the young man seemed to be flaying the tune and pounding it with a rusty hammer.

She had been an accomplished concert pianist by the age of thirteen. Bethany had perfect pitch, though not the greatest voice. She knew how to apply her voice to keeping a tune. Tonight, she used it to revive the birthday song. Her singing evidently invited the mother to join more heartily and elevated the game of the young man. By the time they finished the final line, Savannah had joined in from where she stood next to the adjacent table.

The gratitude in the eyes of the mother was only overshadowed by the wondrous smile of the little girl as she blew out her candles. The grateful grin of the young man was satisfying as well. Bethany just nodded in acknowledgment and turned her toes toward the kitchen, a warm grace accompanying her on her way.

Chapter 7

Company

With those three customers gone and only a smear of chocolate frosting left on the dessert plate, Bethany locked the front door. Through the glass she returned one last wave to the little girl, whose name—according to the birthday song—was Lapita. The girl's birthday celebration had provided a merry ending to what started as a tense night.

Wedged between her cleaning and waiting on that last table, Bethany had deposited exact change into the till to cover two bowls of soup and the accompanying salad and bread. The generous tip from the guy with the birthday candles covered nearly half the cost of the old lady's meal, and Bethany didn't feel badly about any of it.

When she returned to the cake keeper, checking the date on the Boston cream pie again, she called into the kitchen. "Hey, Diego, the Boston cream pie has to go tonight. You wanna take it with you?"

He snorted through his nose then appeared to relax. He looked up from the metal pan he was washing. "You know, that would be nice. There's still half a cake, right?"

"Or half a pie, depending on how you look at it." Savannah was dropping damp towels into the laundry bin near Diego.

Diego chuckled. He was usually a pretty mellow guy, but here was the first sign of humanity from him that evening. Bethany greeted it with a grin that was really aimed at Savannah. The other waitress was scrutinizing Bethany the way she had at the beginning of her shift, when she made that comment about her having a secret. What secret was Bethany giving away now?

She was able to exit the front door by 9:40. The slow last hour had allowed them to get a head start on the cleaning. Diego was also highly motivated to get out as soon as possible. Bethany prayed for him and his family obligation, as well as about the chance he had cut some corners to close early. She prayed for grace and mercy—he needed those. Everyone did.

Pulling her phone out, checking what messages she had missed since her short dinner break, Bethany tugged the zipper on her gray hoodie a bit higher. The night was clear and crisp. The wide arterial street was quiet. Only distant cars could be heard accelerating or bumping over seams in the pavement.

Raising her hood against the cool air might obscure the fact that a young woman was walking alone at night. Too bad she didn't really know how to *walk* like a guy. She might get it wrong if she tried and be mistaken for a drunk or something, so she just walked like herself—quick and focused on her phone.

That focus was broken when she noted a man standing near the corner convenience store just ahead of her. She kept her eyes on her phone but diverted some attention to that man as she hurried past. Her impression of his clothes was familiar. She hadn't gotten a look at his face.

"That was beautiful, Bethany. The soup for that woman and singing 'Happy Birthday' for Lapita. Oh, the old woman's name is Jan, by the way."

Bethany stopped in the middle of the sidewalk. Her heart was racing. She could barely breathe.

It was the man with the ponytail.

"It's me, Bethany." He said it with a mischievous grin. He sounded just like the man in her dream.

Her mind seemed to be scattered around her like the pieces of a vase dropped on the pavement.

This guy seemed to know all about what she had done at work that night. That was creepy.

He also knew her name ... and he sounded like that guy in her dream. Actually, it ... it *was* the guy in her dream.

Since she had not taken off running toward campus or dashed toward the fire station three blocks away, she had clearly decided to endure the creepiness. Realizing this, she felt like she was caught in the sort of delay that comes just before she gets a joke.

A joke.

That grin.

She looked the man squarely in the eyes. And, in those eyes, she saw the person who had knocked at her door in the dorm. Only the costume had changed.

For some reason she wondered what he was using to hold his hair in that ponytail. His ponytail was like the one she wore at work.

"You ..." She lost what she was going to say, but she consoled herself by focusing on how great it was to just look at him. She had never been in love before, but this must be what *love at first sight* felt like.

"I'm a bit old for you, dear." He faked a scowl then guffawed. "At least two thousand years too old, depending on when you start counting." He continued laughing at his own joke or maybe laughing at the expression on her face. She was probably looking pretty dumb.

He responded to her thoughts. "No, dear. You could never look unintelligent. Surprised is not the same as dumb."

First, he had responded to what she did at work, where he was nowhere in sight. Now he was responding to her thoughts.

But that made sense ... if he was ... HIM.

"I'm so glad to see you." Her eyes began to water as she stood planted in the middle of the sidewalk.

He stepped closer, pecked her on the cheek, and put his arm around her. "Let's get you back to your dorm, so your mother isn't justified in her worrying."

His arm was firm around her shoulders. He was solid. And he was Jesus.

"This is like what you did with my grandma." Her voice gurgled in her throat. She swallowed hard.

"Yes. Like, but not the same. My relationship with everyone is unique. There is no one like your grandma. No one in my life is identical to Gladys."

"Huh." Her head seemed to be levitating and maybe her body would soon follow. Something about what Jesus said about her grandma's role in his life changed the atmosphere. Altered gravity.

"Don't worry. I got you." He squeezed her a little tighter, anchoring her to the ground.

How could this be? Then she started to shuffle through some of her grandma's stories.

When she was fifteen, Bethany's dad had arranged to drop her at her grandmother's house for a visit. He had gone to court to get the right to take her out of Oregon, where her mother's home address was, though Bethany and her mother were rarely at that address.

At the start, Grandma Hight had treated Bethany like one of the birds that gathered by the feeder in her back yard—careful not to chase her away. But on the last night of her visit, Grandma risked scaring Bethany away by telling her about Jesus coming to visit. It was a wild and unbelievable story, except that, somehow, Bethany did believe it. Maybe she just *wanted* to believe it. She wanted a grandma. She wanted *this* grandma. And if this gracious and kind old lady—who seemed to demand nothing of Bethany—thought she had seen and talked to Jesus, then so be it. From this old woman who offered such unconditional love, Bethany could accept even the craziest of tales.

Now she was assessing her own crazy story. "Are you only visible to me?" She looked around to see if anyone was close enough to see her with her friend.

Jesus pointed his nose at a woman slipping into a car next to the curb, twenty yards ahead of them. "Hello! Miss!" He waved at the woman as they drew closer.

That was when Bethany noticed the woman's long spring coat dangling outside the car door, just about to be pinned there.

The woman leaned out the door and looked right at Bethany ... and at Jesus.

"Your coat." He pointed to where a corner of pale fabric hung halfway to the pavement.

"Oh, thanks." She pulled the hem into the car and hesitated as she looked at Jesus again. She was definitely looking at Jesus.

Bethany glanced at him, as he grinned at the woman and nodded acknowledgment of her thanks. Bethany started to giggle again, bowing her head and covering her mouth.

Bowing her head like that reminded Bethany that her hood was still pulled up. She had been so enamored with Jesus's appearance that she had missed that awkward fact. Flipping the hood away from her face, it landed against Jesus's arm. He released his wrap around her and settled the hood beneath her ponytail. Then he took her hand.

Holding hands with Jesus. That warm reality brought back the first time Bethany held hands with a boy—Danny Anderson, a secret sweetheart of her early teen years. Having a boyfriend was between difficult and impossible around her stringent practice and concert schedules, especially under her mother's surveillance.

Tipping his head toward her, he held eye contact. "She was never trying to harm you, even if it did do some harm."

"My mother?" She knew he was talking about her mother. Bethany just wondered what he was telling her about her own history, bypassing the oddity of talking to someone who was responding to her thoughts. "She *did* harm me?"

"Of course. It's difficult to be deeply involved in anyone's life without doing some harm. The real question for you is whether it was more harm than you can forgive."

"Oh." Like a shade pulled down to block the morning sun, this challenge from Jesus darkened the environment around them. Bethany glanced at him. "I've known I should forgive my mother for all kinds of things. I guess I'm just waiting to be ready. Does that make sense?"

Jesus stopped at the corner, next to a crossing light. From there, Bethany could see the campus and her path to the dorm.

"Can we stay out a little longer?" She had to force that request through a thickening in her throat, as if a big swallow of honey was inhibiting her voice.

"Of course, dear. I won't tell your mother, but you're free to tell her if you like." He beamed at her then stepped off the curb when the *Walk* signal appeared.

She laughed again, but this time tears seemed to be on the verge. She throttled her emotions and took a deep breath. "I guess I should ask you for help forgiving my mother." She snorted. "That just seems so typical, like a cliché or something."

Jesus let go of her hand after they stepped up onto the curb. He turned right, away from her dorm. Three young people, probably students, approached from that direction. Bethany wondered if Jesus broke their physical contact to protect her reputation. Or something like that.

"You would, of course, get questions about that strange man you were seen walking with, even holding hands with, but it wouldn't be like when your mother caught you holding hands with Danny." His mention of Danny and the embarrassing incident induced a huddled feeling, as if Jesus, Bethany, and Danny Andersen had all been close friends.

But in those days, Bethany had no relationship with Jesus that she could see from this distance. It wasn't until she met her grandma that she started to explore faith in God and in Jesus. This trail of thoughts led right into a lingering question in the dark corners of her mind. Did she turn so readily toward pursuing God just to spite her mother?

She looked at Jesus. His eyes seemed to contain a question of his own, but which question was that?

"The question is, what difference does it make now?" He shrugged slightly. "People have often turned to me out of less than perfect motives. Think of disaster and disease. Lots of people treat my father and I like insurance they wish they had purchased *before* tragedy struck, but that doesn't mean we reject them when they approach that way."

Another big breath prepped her response. "Okay. So, say I listened to Grandma when she talked about you, mostly because I knew it would piss ... I mean, it would upset my mom. That's in the past. Are you saying I'm beyond that now?"

"Yes, you are. Our relationship is real. It stands on its own. Your grandma is a wonderful support, as are your friends from church. But facing the less lofty motivations that influenced your start on this path is part of that bigger question. How much is too much to forgive?"

"Huh. I guess it's sort of twisted. If my first reason for following you was to rebel against my mom, then ... maybe her trying to control my life had kind of ... a long-term benefit to it."

He nodded slowly. "Her tight control had many long-term benefits. She protected you from getting into a whole list of troubles. Substance abuse. Harmful relationships. And she instilled some good habits with her vigilant supervision."

"So, I'm supposed to be grateful for all that?"

"Life is full of mixtures, Bethany. Consider my story about the wheat and the weeds. In this world, under the regime of my enemy, the best you can hope for is a mixture of the good with the troublesome. But don't worry, I will win in the end."

She laughed. "You will win? Pretty sure of yourself, are you?"

He laughed loud. "Yes, dear. You will find that I am very sure of myself, and I hope to have my own long-term effects on your life in that direction."

"Giving me confidence that you will win?"

"Confidence that you and I win?"

For the next hour, they walked along quiet residential streets that surrounded the campus. Bethany could not have retraced the route the next morning. Jesus was leading the way, and he was gently leading the discussion as well. The discussion wove in and out of issues of resentment and unnoticed benefits related to her mother's parenting style, but it didn't crescendo in one cathartic moment of forgiveness.

Maybe that would come later. Bethany hoped there would be a later.

"Can I see you like this again?" They were at an intersection where a broad sidewalk led into the heart of campus.

Jesus appeared to be ending their walk there. He smiled gently at her. "There is always more for you and me, Bethany. More to say, more to do—and we will see each other again." His eyes remained fastened on her. "One way you will see me is in the people you serve—at school and at the diner. When you serve them, you serve me."

She forced her brow to relax when she realized she was scowling at him. "Okay. I guess I'm tired. I'll have to think about that." She searched his dark eyes. "I do feel like I will see you again, so that's a relief."

"Peace, little sister. Sleep well. I love you." He hugged her then turned to walk away.

For several seconds, Bethany stood alone in the shadows fighting the urge to chase after him. How could she just let him walk away like that?

I never leave you. It was a voice inside her head. A voice like her own but also very much like the voice she had been listening to for the past hour.

The voice of Jesus was inside her head.

Chapter 8

Distracted

Tuesdays were busy classroom days for Bethany. She spent more than four hours in lecture halls. It was a day she didn't work at the diner. Not being on her feet for six hours in a row was welcomed, even a bit luxurious.

Keeping focused on school was particularly difficult this Tuesday. Most of her classes were general education requirements. Sometimes interesting, but not always, and never as interesting as walking around talking with Jesus. Or even as interesting as reexamining that extraterrestrial experience.

"Where were you today? You didn't ask any questions at all." Mark was walking with her, away from the Intro to Education lecture hall. He hoisted his backpack higher on his skinny shoulder.

"I know. It's amazing there was any discussion at all." Bethany knew she was deflecting, but Mark was only an acquaintance, not even what she would call a friend. He was the second most likely student to make comments and ask questions in that class.

"Well, I hope you appreciate me carrying the load for you today." He flashed a quick grin. He was probably flirting. He flipped his long brown bangs to one side, using the fingers of one hand like a comb.

Bethany liked him but wasn't interested in anything beyond a good education-related discussion with him. He took good notes and was an amazingly rapid keyboard artist—in the laptop sense. "I'll help you out next time." Half-hearted was the best she could do just then. It was lunch time, and she was being dragged down by low blood sugar.

Geri, another student in that class, slid in next to Mark. “You guys going to lunch? I'm starved.”

“Yeah. Bethany's buying lunch to make up for letting us down in class discussion today.”

“Yes, I'm buying, as long as you both have your student IDs with you.”

“And fully paid meal plans.” Geri offered her usual cherubic grin. Her eyes were large halfmoons, her round cheeks exaggerating the orange slice shape of those dark eyes when she grinned like that. She had dyed one side of her hair magenta recently, the side opposite the ear that had a half dozen piercings.

“Very generous, I know.” Bethany returned the grin and nodded sideways toward the dining hall nearest the education building.

Mark bumped shoulders with Bethany and Geri, trying to wedge himself between them, and he continued his interrogation. “So, you never answered my question. What's up? You seemed really distracted.”

Bethany checked herself on that characterization of his questions as an interrogation. She had often accused her mother of interrogating her. Any unusual behavior on Bethany's part was subject to scrutiny and questioning. That was about her mother, not about Mark.

“I had a busy day yesterday. Worked at the diner and had a long talk with a friend late last night.”

“A guy friend?” Geri's voice lilted. As far as Bethany knew, Geri was not into guys, but apparently she knew Bethany was.

If only Geri knew how *into* this particular guy Bethany was.

It occurred to her that this post-class conversation might really be an opportunity for her to talk about Jesus. “It was a person who identifies as male. Yes, it was.” That was her attempt to be both relevant and coy. Maybe not so smooth. She really was hungry.

"A late-night talk, huh?" Mark had fallen half a step behind as they passed from the shade of the education building into the sunshine. That sunshine faded almost as soon as they stepped into it. A herd of clouds was grazing across the spring blue sky.

"Yes. A talk. I was working on some issues about my mom." Bethany bumped hips with Geri, apologizing only with her eyes.

"Oh, a *serious* talk." Geri's mood seemed to deflate a bit.

"Yes. And a familiar topic." Mark nodded a greeting to two students walking the opposite direction. "Did you figure anything out?"

For the first time, Bethany paused to savor a growing realization about that conversation with Jesus. "Yes. In fact, I think I did." She checked for signs that her classmates were really interested in this topic. She saw no evidence of boredom yet. "I realized that some of her hardline tactics probably actually benefited me in the end. As much as I didn't like being under lockdown, I can see now how some of my mom's restrictions eventually worked out okay for me."

"Like how?" Geri looked back at her, having moved a half a step ahead.

Bethany's pedestrian pace was probably being slowed by her constant calculations regarding how much to say. "Well, one big thing is that I got into going to ... church because I knew it would cheese her off."

"Ah, good use of culturally relevant colloquialism." Mark was a word nerd.

"Okay, cheesehead." Geri led the way through the glass door into the resident hall dining facility.

Mark animated a singsong reply as they entered the dining hall. "Sticks and stones may break my bones, but cheese will never hurt me."

"Is that, like, the state motto?" Geri was from Illinois or Indiana, as far as Bethany recalled. Geri was quick to make fun of Wisconsinites.

Bethany wasn't offended. She was just a Wisconsinite because her dad was. His residency was one reason she chose to go to school in the state, getting some benefits from using his address. Come to think of it, that choice too had originally been enhanced by the extent to which it upset her mother.

"So you went to church, as in signed up for religion, to get back at your mom?" Geri had not missed that part of Bethany's confession.

Running her keycard over the scanner, Bethany waited for Mark to catch up. "Yeah. I did it for that reason to start, but I stuck around after that because church really meant a lot to me. Unintended consequences."

Mark signaled his interest in a different buffet line and parted from Bethany and Geri as they settled into the salad bar queue. Prime lunch time, the place was buzzing.

"So, what kind of church is it, if you don't mind me asking?" Geri lifted a tray and handed it to Bethany then took one for herself.

"No. I'm glad to talk about it." She named the church she was attending and set her tray next to the large bowl of salad greens. "It was my grandma that helped me figure out which one to choose, though it's not exactly like the church she goes to."

Geri started dishing greens onto a dinner plate. "Your grandma is a little old church lady?"

Bethany laughed at those words applied to her Grandma Hight. "She is that, and I think she would fully identify herself that way."

"Sounds like you get along well with your grandma."

"I do. What about you? Do you have a favorite grandparent?" Bethany was happy to tell her story, but the conversation was becoming too one-sided.

"Not really. I have a grandpa that lives in New Jersey and a grandma that lives near Tallahassee. I don't see 'em much. Just a phone call now and again. Birthday cards."

"Do they, like, send you five dollars for your birthday?" Bethany always found that phenomenon charming and a little sad when her friends told her about it.

"Ha. No. My grandpa is pretty rich. I get, like, a check for a hundred dollars in a fancy card from him. But my other grandma—my mom's mom—is not so like that. Just sends a card. I don't mind. I don't know how rich she is. She's retired and living on her own. She has enough to worry about."

When they finally spilled out of the salad bar to the main thoroughfare of the dining hall, Mark was there holding his tray loaded with a burger and fries and three pieces of fruit—banana, pear, and orange. No judgments were spoken among them, and Bethany led the way to a table near the windows.

Mark pulled out his chair. "You were saying you went to church to tick off your parents. I had to go to church to keep mine happy." He raised his eyebrows in an inquiring way. Maybe he was wondering if this was still the topic at hand.

"Yeah, I get that. My mom just wasn't into God at all. She still isn't, as far as I know."

"You don't talk to her now?" Geri picked up her fork and seemed to be searching for the best way to attack the mound of salad she had amassed.

"We talk some, but she hasn't forgiven me for coming to school here."

"Oh. There's more to this story." Mark chewed a french fry and made bug eyes.

"I was a piano prodigy as a kid, but I decided to go into music education instead of performance. My mom was all into the performance. Classic stage mom, I guess."

Both Mark and Geri were already chewing vigorously when Bethany finally began to dig into her lunch, starting with a small scoop of cottage cheese.

Around bites of food, Bethany recounted the history of her piano competitions and concerts and her eventual escape from her mom's dreams for her life. She was tired of talking and done delaying fully digging into her food, so she turned a question back on Mark.

"So, that's me. But what was it you were saying about only going to church to please your parents?"

Mark wiped one hand on a paper napkin. "It's pretty typical where I grew up in Wauwatosa, I think. Kids go to church because parents make them. It wasn't worth it to fight to get out of it. And, with so many of us *forced* to go, it just became the main place to get in trouble. I saw more crime and sex and drugs in Sunday school and youth group than anywhere else."

"That can't be true." Geri scowled at Mark and took a sip from her water glass.

"It is, though. Take a bunch of sulky kids and make 'em sit through boring lessons, and you get teens just itching to sneak out back and make out or get high."

Bethany cringed. "Dang. That is *not* the way youth group is advertised at my church."

Mark laughed. "No one advertises that stuff, but it might be worth thinking about before forcing *your* kids to go to church." He looked at Bethany as if she had children she was planning to drag with her to Sunday school and youth group this week.

"Not happening any time soon."

"You can put a reminder in your phone for when it comes up," Mark joked as he watched Geri tapping something into her phone.

Chapter 9

Missed

After her last class of the day, Bethany returned to her suite. Emily was there talking on the phone with someone, her voice mousy and expressive. It was decently warm outside, so Bethany dropped off her books and laptop and took her eReader out of her backpack. She switched from sneakers to flipflops and grabbed a light hoodie. She would find a shady spot to sit and read until supper.

Waving to Emily on her way out, Bethany started to wonder if she had missed an opportunity at lunch with Mark and Geri. It was rare that she got to talk about church at school, at least with people who didn't attend church with her. What Mark said about the delinquents in his church youth group might have been overstated. But having not been a church kid, Bethany couldn't decide. And, of course, just because that was how it was at *his* church wouldn't mean it was typical.

She was still thinking about this when she reached the sunny patio across the path from her dorm. Straight ahead, one concrete bench was available in a patch of shade. But as she drew closer to the seat, she could sense someone else approaching at an angle. A big guy to her right.

Bethany restrained the urge to run and beat him to that spot. She checked whether he was really headed to the same seat. He looked at her and smiled. It was Colson, a guy from her church.

"Hey, Bethany. Good to see you. I never see you on campus."

"Yeah. Our schedules must be out of sync or something. How are you?" She gave him a one-armed side hug.

"I'm great. Just getting some reading done before I head to work."

"Where do you work?" By now they had arrived at that empty bench. A pair of girls approached from behind but veered off when Bethany sat down. Clearly this shade was in high demand today.

He sat on the other end of the bench. He was wearing a pale blue t-shirt with the name of some business that she couldn't see from that angle. "I work at a copy place just off campus. I do tech support for the computers they have in there." He pulled at the t-shirt as a visual aid.

Bethany still didn't catch the exact name. "Wow. That's cool. But do people still use a copy place and computers and all?"

"Yeah, for some things like specialty printing. We have 3D printers, for instance."

"Oh, sure. That makes sense. I was just picturing old people who still haven't bought a home computer yet."

He laughed briefly then sobered. "Actually, there are some people without computers who come in there, but it's more often poor people. Like, someone who has a computer at home, but it crashed and they can't afford to get it fixed. They could try using a computer at the library maybe, but those are all taken sometimes, so they have to pay up at the copy shop."

"Oh. That doesn't sound good. Not really an economical solution, right? How much does it cost?"

"Like, fifty cents a minute."

"A minute? You charge by the minute?"

"Hey, it's not my shop. I just work there." He held up two hands as if to slow her recriminations.

"Oh. Yeah, but still, that's thirty dollars an hour."

"I know. I sometimes give kids a break if they need to use it that long. My manager hasn't stopped me from doing that yet. I mean, I can't imagine charging some child thirty bucks to use the computer to do his homework."

"Ouch. Yeah, I get it." She dragged her lavender hoodie off her shoulders and slipped her arms into the sleeves. There was a breeze, and the concrete bench was even cooler than the air.

"Well, I got reading to do. And you too, huh?"

"Yeah. *History of Education in America*."

"Ah, just fun reading then."

"Ha! Exactly." She booted up her reader and watched Colson pull a small hardbound book from his bag.

He showed her. *The Great Gatsby*. "I know most people read this in high school, but my school wasn't so good." That book looked small in his big hand.

She grinned sympathetically. "I was mostly homeschooled, so I have the same problem."

"Oh, I didn't know that. Yeah, a lot of church people do that, I guess."

"I didn't grow up in church. My mom did homeschooling so I could focus on piano."

"Oh, yeah. I've heard you play at the college group a few times. Yeah, you're good." He snickered. "But I guess that's pretty obvious."

"I try to stay out of the spotlight these days. Had enough of that as a kid."

"Oh, sure. Yeah, that makes sense. Well, look at it this way, you really bless us with your gift. So, praise God for that."

"That's the best way to look at it. Thanks."

They did both get to their reading, but Bethany repeatedly drifted toward wondering again about the impact her mother had on her life. Now she was considering whether she was allowing her mother to still have too much influence. Staying away from pianos on stages was a reaction to Bethany's overexposure as a girl. Couldn't she let go of that and start using her music as a gift that blesses other people? It didn't have to be a performance thing.

Gemma, one of the young adult pastors at church, had said something to her about that. Bethany wasn't ready to hear it and pretty much discounted all such appeals at the time. But maybe now she was ready to rethink it. People at church hadn't kept hounding her to play when she explained her history, and that was helpful—a stark contrast to her mother.

Colson stood from the bench after about twenty minutes, tucked his novel into his backpack, and waved to her. "Take care, Bethany. Blessings on your studies."

"Thanks, Colson. Blessings on your work."

He grinned and strode away at a healthy pace.

As she watched him walking from shade to sunlight to shade and away, Bethany blinked at something in her eye. Or ... maybe something was in the air. A sort of blur between her and Colson. The brief impression might have even been a human figure, like on a single frame of a film.

I am still here. That was the clear thought in her head. Not really a voice but a thought that seemed to come from the mind of someone else.

"You're *always* here. I just miss that fact most of the time." She said that aloud, talking to the flash of light that had caught her attention and the voiceless thoughts in her head.

Chapter 10

Group

Not working in the diner on Tuesday evening meant Bethany could go to a house group meeting with people from church. She was the youngest person in the group, but she treasured the advice and support she got from the folks who gathered there every week. The Tuesday contact was important too because she often worked weekend evenings, which was the most likely time for church college group activities.

Waiting in front of the dorm for Mildred Kim to pick her up, Bethany began debating with herself about whether to say anything to the group about meeting Jesus. Then she included him in the conversation. *Should I tell them?* She waited. No answer—no words, at least. She did sense a rising feeling, an affirmative feeling.

Should I just tell them when they ask how the week has been? During the sharing time? That was the most obvious approach, but that seemed awkward. Most people shared briefly about a tough day at work, a doctor's appointment, or an argument with a roommate or family member. Wouldn't she blow up the meeting with her news?

She wondered how much it would shock people to know she met with Jesus this week. But what if she just kept it to herself?

Mildred pulled up in her compact car, a late model hybrid. She worked in a bank as some kind of midlevel manager in the investments department. That was as much as Bethany understood. What she saw firsthand was a woman who insisted on giving her a ride, but who often seemed to be rushing from one thing to the next.

"Hello. How are you doing, Bethany?" Mildred's black hair was cut in a pageboy, she wore what Bethany assumed was her business suit from work.

"Great, how are you, Mildred?" She settled into the passenger seat and found the seatbelt.

"Good. Good. Hang on." She maneuvered away from the curb and slowed to avoid a guy on a skateboard.

In her head, Bethany tested an idea. *What if I just ask Mildred what I should say?*

The next thought that entered her head was, *Feel free*. Though it was probably an answer to the present question, she paused at the feeling that those two words might cover more than just what to say to Mildred. Feeling free seemed to describe everything she had seen of Jesus.

"So, what's up with you these days?" Mildred laid out a bright new invitation. It seemed to call for full disclosure. At least today it did.

"I had a really crazy weekend. Like, mind-blowing." That was not one of Bethany's most articulate preambles, but she was hastily shoving herself out there where she would be forced to follow through with some genuinely crazy and mind-blowing news. She wouldn't be able to back out and make something up. She didn't have that good an imagination.

"Really? What's that about?"

"About Jesus. I had a very real encounter with Jesus." That phrase from the Sunday sermon popped out. Maybe that was just a matter of adopting familiar language to describe a very unfamiliar experience.

"Really? That sounds awesome! Are you gonna share it with the whole group?" Mildred was a nervous driver, which meant she normally glanced only briefly at Bethany. But Bethany's introduction to her revelation seemed to be inspiring an adventurously longer gape.

"Well, I was hoping you could help me decide what to do about that. I'm afraid of blowing up the meeting with my story."

"Oh, I get it." Mildred hit her blinker and checked all directions before taking a left. "But, I mean, if it's that great a thing, then I think everyone would want to hear about it. It would be inspiring, right?"

Here was an echo of what Bethany had been contemplating about playing piano on stage. She really wanted to keep a low profile, but what about inspiring others with a gift she has to share?

"Yeah. I don't wanna hog the meeting or take away from Sam's agenda or whatever. But maybe it would inspire others." She felt her own words trying to click her thoughts together into a solid shape. "But what if people don't believe me?"

"Oh, it's that good, is it?" Mildred stared at her for two full seconds, with thin eyebrows raised. She had to apply the brakes a bit abruptly when the next traffic light changed.

Mildred was being generous, giving Bethany the benefit of the doubt. She was also allowing Bethany to hang on to her news instead of pressing for details. Even so, the driver had adopted a permanent grin. A bigger grin than usual.

Their small group met in a spacious apartment in the Third Ward, a short distance from campus. It was too far to walk comfortably, but an easy drive. If she still had her scooter, Bethany would consider attempting the trip on two wheels in good weather. After parking on the street, she and Mildred passed through the lobby of the old building which must have been used for some commercial purpose in centuries past. The floor tiles looked like a chessboard—large, shiny black and white squares.

Like in the dorm, Bethany walked up the stairs to the third floor, having convinced Mildred earlier in the year that bypassing the elevator was good for them. Now it was their habit. Her driver was a bit heavier than Bethany, with shorter legs, puffing when they reached the third floor. But Mildred didn't complain.

Sam Culver met them at the door to his apartment. The group was all singles. Sam had the biggest apartment of the members, a two-plus bedroom place that doubled as his office.

"Hello, Mildred. Hello, Bethany. Welcome, welcome. Come on in." Sam was tall and slender, almost ghostly pale. He might have said those exact words every week. It was part of a greeting ritual among church members who tended to downplay rituals.

Part of the attraction of the group was their comfortable familiarity. The all-singles gathering also helped Bethany not feel like an infant among the adults. In broadest strokes, they were all in the same life stage, even though Mildred was almost twice as old as Bethany. And Sam was also well past thirty. Still, it was billed as a young singles house group. Or *apartment group*, as Sam liked to point out, with a sly squint of his big gray eyes.

Cheri Miller and Donna Andrews were already sitting on the couch in the living room. The place was brightly lit even at seven p.m., with tall windows that faced the lake front, though without a clear view of the water. Bethany was looking at the building next door when Steve Engel and Matt Weiland arrived. The members present probably constituted a quorum. It was time to start.

Her palms sweating, Bethany anticipated her chance to share her story. She sat in one of the armchairs facing away from the windows, giving her a good view of the others around the rough circle. Cheri, a stout woman in her early thirties, with straight brown hair, was tuning her guitar, final touches that made it obvious she had tuned it before Bethany arrived. Cheri tuned by ear. She had a good ear.

From her seat, Bethany was distracted by the red rims around Donna's eyes, eyes bent toward the coffee table in the center of the circle. A tray of cups sat on that table, as usual, next to a thermal pot of coffee and another pot of hot water for tea. As Cheri began strumming with more intention, Wendy Penner came bustling through the front door, pulling off her coat, probably too warm from overestimating the need for winter outerwear. Her blonde curls were flying in all directions.

Wendy looked like she wanted to apologize for being late but clamped her lips as Cheri started a song Bethany recognized. She suspected it was an old classic in churches like theirs, but she couldn't know for sure, given her short experience in this congregation. Or any congregation, for that matter.

Catching a knowing smile from Mildred, who added a flash of wide eyes, Bethany took solace in her friend's expectancy around her news. But that didn't help with the sweaty palms.

As they sang a third song, Sara Shultz arrived, raising the woman-to-man ratio toward the usual proportion. Bethany had noted Sam's relief in avoiding the awkwardness of being the only guy in the group whenever other men arrived.

When Cheri relaxed and set her guitar against the end of the couch, Sam led in prayer before opening the nonmusical portion of the meeting.

"Okay, does anyone have anything they want to share from the week? Any big news? Things we should be praying about?"

Bethany inhaled a preliminary breath, pausing to see if there were any other takers. Donna seemed to do that same air intake, but her exhale came with a cataract of sobbing tears. She had brought a personal crisis to group before. The group had seen Donna cry like this at least one other time, but no one showed any hint of impatience with the pale and round young woman. Even Mildred seemed to forget about Bethany's promised news as she focused on Donna, who told of medical tests she had undergone that week to explain a problem with her pituitary gland. There was a chance she had a tumor.

They all listened to the medical details and Donna's worst fears. And they gathered around her to lay hands on her sloping shoulders to pray, but it didn't end there. During the prayer time Donna continued to weep, and when they all settled back into their seats, she recalled her mother's painful, and ultimately terminal, battle with a brain tumor.

The meeting was usually divided into sections—music, sharing, discussion of a topic that Sam presented from a Gospel story, then closing prayer. Socializing was optional afterward. Mildred had to work early in the morning, so Bethany usually missed most of the socializing. That was probably easier, anyway, being so much younger than the others in the group. Donna was probably the next youngest, and she was in her late twenties, as far as Bethany could tell.

Donna's crisis, her medical concern, and the intense feelings it stirred about her mother, used up all the sharing time. She apologized repeatedly about that. After a pause Sam jumped into the scripture reading and his study questions for the group.

Breathing shallowly during the tension over whether she would get a chance to tell her story, and then over whether she should just give a brief summary, Bethany finally relaxed when it was clear she wouldn't be able to say anything. She avoided looking at Mildred, who sat with Wendy in the loveseat to her left. Bethany didn't want to see a question or a regret on Mildred's face. Her own feelings dodged and dashed in patterns too complicated to describe through mute eye contact.

During the reading and discussion of the passage where a man born blind is healed by Jesus, Bethany tried to sneak a mental peek toward the Jesus she had met. The one who had also been speaking to her in her head lately. She was sure the guy with the ponytail would not be attending this meeting, though he qualified as a young single, according to this group's membership. But wasn't he still present? Listening, maybe even speaking somehow.

In the Gospel of John, the story of the man born blind was one of the cautionary tales about religious opposition to God's miraculous interventions—interventions that often shattered expectations. That was how Sam was presenting it. Others engaged in an open discussion, some sharing personal experiences brought to mind by the opposition Jesus faced from the religious leaders of his day.

It was a story from Cheri to which Sam responded when he said, "Yeah. It's amazing how preoccupation with pleasing people and fulfilling religious obligations can get in the way of receiving Jesus himself. Right?"

That statement sounded mostly theoretical to Bethany. She had faced little opposition in her life from religious people. Her greatest conflict was with her mother, a woman without religion. But a more present question was raising her blood pressure and shallowing her respiration again. Had this group missed an important encounter with Jesus in favor of politely listening to one person's medical concerns? That thought was clearly never going to see the light of day, especially because Bethany was not fully certain how others in the group would even receive her fantastic story.

The prayer time at the end of the meeting included more petitions for Donna's health and consolation for her ongoing emotional pain. They also prayed about concerns from others, including the approaching end of Bethany's semester. It was probably a mischievous child inside her that contemplated asking prayer for her to have another walk and talk with Jesus after work one day this week. She would never actually say such a thing. She was surprised she'd even thought of it.

On the way home, Mildred did recall Bethany's news. "I'm sorry you didn't get to share with the group. Do you need to talk about it?"

Their ride was usually less than ten minutes on the way home, with traffic reduced after the fall of darkness. Did Bethany need to talk about it? She was feeling disappointed at not getting to share with the group, but what about just telling Mildred?

Go ahead. It'll do her some good. That was the input from an invisible person who might have been wedged into the back seat or maybe just riding inside Bethany's head.

Either way, Bethany proceeded to tell Mildred the story of seeing Jesus at the diner and at her dorm room door. And finally on the long walk after work.

By the time she finished, they were parked in front of the dorms. "Oh, Bethany! Oh, my gosh!" Her eyes had been gaping for most of the story, her lower lip quivering part of the time. Now Mildred exploded. "Oh, dear. We should go back. Some of them are probably still at Sam's. You should tell them. You should have told them even if it seemed like ..." Maybe she stopped there because she saw the look of doubt and concern on Bethany's face.

Finally laughing awkwardly, Bethany answered her hasty proposal. "I don't think we have to go back. I just felt like I was supposed to tell you."

"Supposed to?"

"I felt like Jesus told me it would do you some good."

Her eyes welling with tears immediately, Mildred grabbed Bethany's near arm. "Really? Jesus told you that? About me?" She covered her mouth and continued to stare, her watery eyes still gaping.

Bethany patted Mildred's hand. "Well, I guess he was right. Seems like it did do you some good."

Mildred laughed at that, a little hysterically, perhaps.

Chapter 11

Paradoxes

Emily was in the room when Bethany arrived back from small group just past nine o'clock. This was early for Emily to be in. "Hey. How was your meeting?" She asked it even though she had earbuds in and wasn't looking at Bethany.

Getting a glimpse of a scientific diagram of some kind, Bethany was glad to see Emily was doing schoolwork on her tablet computer.

"The meeting was fine. The usual suspects." Bethany didn't imagine Emily was particularly interested in the church meeting. Something about the way she tended to ask about the small group meetings brought to mind a preoccupied parent greeting a kid coming home from an activity. Emily probably couldn't even hear all of Bethany's response with her buds in.

With her nose just inches from the glowing tablet screen, Emily didn't seem to be inviting questions about *her* evening either. But maybe there *are* times to invite oneself into a conversation. Standing by her closet, idly stowing her fleece jacket, Bethany thought again about whether she should have been more assertive at the small group meeting. It felt like Donna had preempted all other sharing with her anxiety about the prospect of a problem. It wasn't a real problem yet, but that might be unfair. How to measure someone else's pain, their anxiety, and its justification was well beyond her.

As Bethany pulled out her biology textbook, she thought about Donna's intense worries and recalled something Grandma Hight had said to her. "If you spend a lot of energy worrying about something before it happens, then when it does happen you just have to suffer it a second time." Or something like that. Probably Grandma didn't invent that saying, but it had seemed like good advice when Bethany was considering quitting the competition and concert circuits and going to college instead. She had been stockpiling anxiety over what it would mean for her to quit, what her mother would do, and what the future would hold.

Tonight, she should probably repent of assuming Donna was being unnecessarily anxious. How could Bethany know? Given that, she was glad she hadn't tried to force her news into the meeting. *Hello, I just wanted to tell you that I'm seeing Jesus in Milwaukee these days.* She snorted a quiet laugh.

Getting to work, she sat on her bed and cracked open the textbook. She snickered at the novelty of that sound, realizing it was rare to open a hardbound book in a quiet room where she wasn't wearing earbuds. She checked with Emily to see if she noticed the snicker.

Nope. She was gone to the world and still scowling at some chart.

Trying to focus on the chapter she needed to finish tonight, Bethany kept wandering toward what would happen if she told Emily, or someone else, about her Jesus encounter. What would they think? Bethany had never told Emily about Grandma's adventures with Jesus. That seemed like wise discretion, but maybe this was different. It was about Bethany's personal experience. Her own truth.

Gripping her forehead with one hand, she tried to drive concentration into her *cranium*. That was a word in the biology book. Maybe that cranium pressure worked. She got through the chapter. But typing up the summary due in class Thursday seemed to involve lead weights and a lack of oxygen. Her head nodding, she sighed voluminously several times.

When she woke up, the lights were out but Emily wasn't in the room. Bethany reached over the side of her bed and settled the heavy textbook and her laptop onto the floor, taking care not to put them where she would stub her toe in the morning.

But, lying there on her side, she couldn't get back to sleep. It was nearly eleven o'clock. Time for bed on most days. It was clearly past time today, given how she had nodded off in the middle of homework.

She queued the usual debate about sitting up and starting to read again. Reading the biology textbook seemed likely to solve any problem with sleeplessness. But she lost track of that idea when she paused to recall what she had told Mildred about Jesus. Her friend's intense wonder was a very persuasive argument that Bethany should have said something at group tonight. She laughed lightly at Mildred's attempt to get her to return to the meeting and tell the group her story over chips and sodas.

I told you it would do her some good. And maybe you too.

She thought that was a voice in her head. A pretty clear voice, given that it had to penetrate all that gray matter ... inside her cranium. But then she heard another noise. Fabric brushing against fabric. She twisted her head toward Emily's bed. Maybe she was wrong about her roommate being gone.

No sign of her.

Then came a tapping on her door.

"Wha ... who ... uh, come in?" Pieces of embarrassment fluttered into the air above her bed. She was clutching the comforter to her chin, with most of her back exposed to the room. She was still dressed, however.

"Wanna come out for a walk?" A male voice.

His voice.

He peeked in her door. "Bundle up. It's getting colder outside."

Focused on what it meant to bundle up, as she climbed out of bed, she did notice that the wind had increased, buffeting the tall building. There was no sound of rain that she could hear. Or snow. How much colder was it?

"Oh, not so cold by Wisconsin standards, but you *will* need that puffy coat." He was watching her reach for her purple winter coat in the closet. A hat fell out of one sleeve when she pulled it off the hanger. She caught her white knitted scarf before it dropped out of the other sleeve. That was a Christmas gift from Katie during her freshman year. She dropped the scarf on the bed.

The man was wearing the same classic brown suede jacket she had seen him in before. There was no hat on his head, but that didn't seem strange or problematic, somehow. Was that because Bethany really thought of him as ... less real than her? Less physically present?

He was smiling and nodding as if he was listening to her thoughts. Backing away from the door so she could squeeze past him, he responded to those ponderings. "This is part of the paradox of my life. I'm here but not *only* here. Physical but *also* spiritual." He held the suite door for her. "But these, my dear, are also part of *your* experience."

It sounded like the beginning of a lesson. A lesson in philosophy? Theology?

"The people in seminary call it Christology, which is entwined with anthropology right now." He grinned at her.

Bethany sensed a tease in that grin. It felt as if he knew these polysyllabic words were making her dizzy—not because she didn't recognize them but because it was late at night, and *he* was the one saying them.

He paused in the hallway as she checked again for her phone and keycard, then the man in the ponytail led the way to the stairwell, pulling the door open for her. This floor was mixed, male and female students, though the suites were each segregated. A man on the floor would not be noteworthy, but this guy appeared older than most of the students.

"There's that guy in your sociology course last semester. The military veteran. He's older."

"Yeah, and he lives upstairs. That's right." The sound of her own voice alerted her to the fact that these were her first spoken words since she woke up. Silent as a sleepwalker, she had simply followed him, limiting her end of their conversation to unspoken thoughts.

"If you wanted to conceal my identity from your friends and neighbors, that might work."

"Conceal your identity?" She was plodding down the stairs just ahead of him, her hands in her pockets. She hadn't even looked for her mittens. There wasn't much call for mittens in May. And she wasn't entirely awake yet. Her head was gliding down the stairs like she was skiing down a bunny slope on a modest Wisconsin mountain.

"Because of what people will think about you when you tell them about this encounter, you are tempted to conceal it. And I'm not insisting that you have to tell. Not everyone will benefit as much as Mildred did."

"Hmm. She really did seem to ... get it. I guess it was good for her. Though I can't say I know how."

"You can just trust me on that. You don't need to know all about it."

"Need to know, huh?"

Her roommate, Emily, was an avid fan of spy movies, old or new, silly or intense. Bethany had endured quite a few of those films while sitting shoulder to shoulder with her.

Jesus led Bethany through the lobby to the front doors, pushing through as vigorously as a college guy. Or maybe as an older guy with no obligations to normal physics. He turned and smiled at Bethany as he held the outer door open for her.

Then he sobered. "Of course, everyone needs to know about me, but not everyone needs to know every detail about our private relationship with each other."

"Private? Huh, I would have thought you would say *personal.*"

"You were thinking of spy movies and the *need to know.*" He shrugged then revamped his smile. "I'm just saying that it's okay to keep some things to yourself. I know you have a struggle with that. Your mother is dedicated to her own privacy, but she didn't always protect yours."

"And my friends at school and at church are suspicious of too much privacy." She cast a thought toward whether this conversation was about the meeting tonight. "So I worry about which one is right."

"Yes. Sharing what's going on in your life is sort of a contract you have with your church house group, or apartment group, as the case may be." He seemed to be always grinning.

"But you're making a serious point here, I assume."

Jesus slipped an arm around her shoulders. "Yes. The point is for you not to worry that you might have missed an opportunity at small group tonight. You have no way of knowing how they would have responded or how much it would have hurt Donna to feel her news swept aside."

"Oh. Yeah, that was what I was worrying about." She hesitated. "But *you* know how they would have responded, even though I don't."

"Well, that takes us back to those paradoxes of which I spoke a few minutes ago." He released his grip on her shoulder and slipped both hands into his pockets.

Bethany did the same and then recognized a guy from her education class approaching with a few other guys she didn't know. Her classmate looked at her but didn't say anything, which left Bethany wondering about Jesus breaking contact with her just before that guy could see them clearly.

"Uh, paradoxes?"

"I have been to every part of the future, and I can run any number of hypotheticals based on my detailed knowledge of all the people involved in any scenario. I can see and know all that *might* have happened, but I don't focus on those hypothetical timelines."

"What?" Bethany laughed. "You sound like that theoretical physics grad student guy in church."

"Lucas. And it's kind of you to characterize him by his field of study and not primarily by his nerdiness."

"Ha. You think Lucas is nerdy?"

"Just saying ..." He chuckled. "Remember I can even hear what people say in their heads."

"Really, and that's not an invasion of their privacy?"

"Is it an invasion of your privacy for your best friend to know how you feel about something?"

"Uh. No, but ... is that the same?"

"The same? Well, we get back to our word of the evening. Paradox. I am the same as you. You are the same as me, in potential. Your friends know you and can guess some of the things that go through your head, even how you might react. I'm just a better friend who guesses much more accurately ... all the time."

"Just that?" Her head had not stopped spinning. But, perhaps, she was getting to like the sensation more.

They transitioned to talking about some of her friends, especially the ones at church. He sympathized with her regrets that she couldn't spend more time with them. She hadn't had many Christian friends before, especially ones her age.

Jesus seemed well informed, fully invested, and completely free of anxiety as he and Bethany wound in and out of all those relationships.

Bethany was still anxious about what to tell her small group. "Will I get a chance to tell them about these talks?"

"Of course you will. Whether you take advantage of those chances is entirely up to you, just as it is up to you whether you tell Emily, or Jacqueline, or any of the others."

They had arrived in front of the dorm tower in which she lived. The wind had been building during their walk around the neighboring streets. Now dots of moisture were landing on her face from three sides, as the wind whipped and waned.

"Okay, dear. You need to sleep. I will help you rest if you let me."

"Let you? How?"

"Welcome me into your thoughts. No invasion required. Just invite me in to calm and settle the storm that threatens your rest." He raised his head toward a wind-whipped tree. "I'm good at calming storms." As he said that, the wind died suddenly, and the rain ceased for several seconds before it all started up again.

Bethany let her mouth drop open.

"I didn't want to go all the way with that. I don't want any meteorologists to lose their jobs for getting the forecast completely wrong." He chuckled, hugged her, and he turned to walk away.

As she puzzled over the weather trick, if it really was a trick, she watched him walking into the windy darkness. He was walking away but not really leaving, she reminded herself. Despite appearances.

Then he vanished.

Hmm. Despite disappearances?

Chapter 12

Sharing

With finals approaching like troops goosestepping through the streets in one of Emily's beloved WWII spy movies, Bethany's roomie was bunkered in the room more often. But they didn't talk more. Earbuds prevented some of that as well as a palpable tension in Emily's physical posture and facial expression. The most approachable expression on that small, elven face was chagrin and suffering. She was certainly suffering the consequences of the weeks of neglect that had cornered her into the prospect of not passing some of her courses.

Bethany could never live like that. She had been trained to practice and prepare. The discipline acquired through playing piano served her well when it came to balancing her classes with her work schedule and getting it all done on time.

On Friday of that week, Bethany worked at the diner. It was raw and far too cold for a day in May. Which was just fine for keeping her focused on studying. But it was not pleasant for the long walk to work. With the wind too strong to keep her umbrella safely above her head, she had to surrender to a cold soaking late that afternoon.

Her slacks were damp, and she was grouchy about that and about the mounting pressure around the end of the term. That all probably accounted for her elevated annoyance at an older man who seemed to be staring at her as she waited on other tables later that evening.

The man, with steel gray hair—swept back and held in place by some sort of gel—had ruddy skin and a pocked complexion. His eyes were gray or dull blue. She hadn't made eye contact with him, really. She just checked occasionally to confirm that he was still watching her from his table by the front windows.

Annabelle was serving him. "You want me to spit in his food?" She was watching him past the door frame between the kitchen and the counter area. The guy was visible in profile when they looked down the counter.

"No, of course not." Bethany frowned at Annabelle and tugged at her black pants where they seemed to be creeping up from behind.

"I haven't seen him checking out your backside, for what it's worth."

Bethany had, of course, noticed men doing that before. Generally forcing herself to ignore that rude behavior. Now she got tangled up in wondering how often Annabelle had noticed it on her behalf. She got even more tangled around Annabelle's use of the word *backside*. Was that unusually polite vocabulary influenced by Bethany?

What difference did it make that the man who was definitely staring at her was not just checking out her ... backside?

Jose interrupted this inquiry by calling out an order for her to deliver, and someone else seemed to catch her attention internally.

You could go talk to that man and find out what he's looking at.

She grimaced at the thought. It was so unexpected and, of course, so unwise. That old guy could be dangerous. Who knew what he could be capable of?

I know.

Those words came through so clearly that Bethany looked around, checking for the man in the ponytail. But she had to pay attention to her hands and feet to keep from dumping the tray laden with burgers, fries, meatloaf, and mashed potatoes. A fork had been driven down through the meatloaf, holding in place a tomato slice and connecting the meat and potatoes concoction to two slices of bread on the bottom. It was the meatloaf special. The fork quivered as Bethany steadied her load.

After delivering the food to a young couple and their toddler—fish sticks had already been delivered to the little blondie—she glanced toward the old man. He was glowering into his coffee, stroking his chin like a man who was used to having whiskers. Though she would hate to defend her actions in court, or in the manager's office, something in the old man's gestures assured her that it would be okay.

Yes. It will be okay. That voice came again, assuring and still vague.

As she turned toward the front table, not one she normally served, Bethany caught a warning glare from Annabelle, who was on her way back to the kitchen. Annabelle nearly stumbled under the strain she put into twisting her neck to watch Bethany's bizarre behavior.

Bethany cleared her throat when she arrived at the side of the man's small table.

He raised his eyes and immediately recoiled when he saw her face. "Oh. Uh ... you ..." He tried to smile but appeared to be interrupted by a small spasm from his lips, one that expanded to include the rest of his face.

"Hi. I hope you don't mind me asking but I noticed you were looking at me." Her voice lodged in her throat, blocked perhaps by her own incredulity at how truly foolish this felt.

He frowned and shook his head, but he truncated that to look into her eyes. He settled on a pleading gaze. "I am so sorry. I didn't mean to bother you. It's just that you look ... you remind me ... so much ... of someone ... I lost." He glanced away and then checked back as if looking for her forgiveness. Then he heaved a ragged sigh.

"Who ... who was it?" Her voice came out as a mumble carried on a whisper.

He moaned. Was he going to cry? When he focused on Bethany again, his gray blue eyes were still full of pleading. "My daughter. It was a long time ago. She was killed. Hitchhiking, we think. She got in a car with a ... a man."

Bethany's hand rose to her mouth. "Oh, my. I am so sorry. Oh, dear Jesus." As that name still hung in the air over that table, the front door opened and in came that man. *The* man. The man with the ponytail.

He nodded to Bethany then looked at the old gentleman. "Earl. Good to see you."

Earl's bushy eyebrows hunkered toward the deep crease above his nose. "Do I ...? Oh." He breathed silently for a second. "Sure." Then he nodded, only briefly checking with Bethany. Maybe he was checking if it was okay for him to talk to the new arrival instead of her.

"Well ... I'll leave you two to talk." Her voice shook. She stepped back, nearly crashing into Annabelle just behind her. Bethany's knees were shaking like they had often done on the way to a piano at center stage.

Annabelle was holding a water pitcher but seemed to have forgotten where she was headed with it. Standing like a cardboard cutout of a woman Bethany once worked with at in a diner, she stared right through Bethany.

Locking her eyes on the man in the ponytail, Annabelle finally spoke. "Can I get you anything ... sir?" A waitress for most of her adult life, longer than Bethany had been alive, that question was reflexive—a useful reflex in the midst of mental paralysis.

"Coffee will be fine, Annabelle. Thanks. Cream and sugar." He smiled. The man. He smiled at Annabelle.

Bethany was pretty sure she saw love in that smile, and she was pretty sure she had just shared Jesus with one or two other people without even meaning to do it.

Chapter 13

Heartache

Bethany was still laughing, her sides a bit sore as she walked on the mostly dry sidewalk. She was on her way home at the end of her shift, her jacket zipped high against the jostling wind.

Annabelle was the primary source of her laughter.

"Do you know him?" Bethany had asked her coworker when they were both behind the counter, next to the coffee machines.

"Sure. He comes in here once in a while." Annabelle was still staring at the guy.

"Do you know his name?" Bethany's voice quaked a little, anticipating the answer.

"Well, I think he said his name was ... Jesús." She pronounced it like it was Spanish—*Hey-zoos*. "You think he looks Hispanic?"

Bethany had to go into the cooler to release the laughter that threatened to explode out of her. Maybe her sides hurt so much now because she had forced that laugh to wait until she found a place to release it.

She was chuckling again when her phone rang in her pocket. Her aunt Patty was calling.

"Patty?"

"Bethany. I guessed that it would be okay to call you this late."

"Yeah. I'm walking home from work."

"Oh. Okay." Patty was almost panting. "Well, I called your dad already. I just wanted to tell you as soon as possible."

"What? What is it?"

"Your grandma. My mom. She's in the hospital. She had some chest pains today. They took her in an ambulance before we could get over there. I guess one of her neighbors called 9-1-1." Grandma lived in a retirement home, in an independent apartment. She didn't have any kind of medical staff in her building, so that explained her neighbor having to call it in.

"Uh. Okay." Bethany's thoughts flew all over the place, but they seemed to be doing it in slow motion. "Chest pains? How serious is it?"

"Well, we don't know yet. She was treating it like indigestion, just taking antacids. But she was having trouble breathing at dinner when one of her friends convinced her to take it seriously." Patty inhaled deeply. "I guess Mom called me while she was waiting for the ambulance. I kind of panicked and tried to get to her place before the EMTs. I don't know. Anyway. Me and Katie are here in the hospital, waiting for news. Derek is out of town. Oh, I guess that's too much information." She harumphed at herself.

"No. That's fine, Patty. I'll start praying for Grandma. Please let me know as soon as you find out anything."

"I will. Of course, I will. Even if it's late. You can just set your phone to ... well, you know what to do."

"Sure. No problem."

"Okay. Bye, Bethany."

"Bye, Patty." She ended the call and briefly considered changing her phone settings. She could set it so an incoming call would buzz overnight. She could keep her phone in bed with her. This assumed Grandma's condition was critical, and Bethany would need to get down there right away.

But she didn't know if that's what was likely to come next.

"Her life is not in danger right now. She will make it through the night." Jesus was walking beside her again.

She shuddered at the shock of his sudden appearing. "Huh. You ... you know that for sure? What about ... paradoxes?" She noted that he was wearing his Sunday school Jesus costume.

"Some things are not obscured from your eyes by the potential choices of the individuals involved. No one is deciding whether to let your grandma make it through the night. No one that my father and I haven't already defeated, that is."

"Oh. Okay." She was a bit distracted by what it meant that he appeared to glow and that he was wearing the ancient costume. There were layers of complexity in his explanation about Grandma that also slowed her response.

Apparently, he sensed Bethany's discomfort. He morphed in a single second to being the ponytail guy, who was reportedly named Jesús.

"You liked that, didn't you?" He smiled at her and laughed lightly.

She assumed he was responding to her thoughts again. "The Jesús trick with Annabelle? Yeah. I nearly injured myself laughing."

"But it felt good, didn't it?"

She took a deep breath. Her ribs weren't hurting anymore. She hadn't done any serious damage. "I guess it did feel good. I think I was feeling kinda relieved that all this is really happening. I mean, like, glad for more evidence that others can see you too."

"I didn't actually tell her what my name is, but Annabelle invented something out of what she was sensing."

"What? How's that?"

"People need to make sense of things, to compose a story that explains what's happening. Annabelle could sense something about me that's different, but she couldn't figure out what it was. What came to mind for her was my real name. Then she corrected herself, because she was sure it could not possibly be the name the way you pronounce it in English, the way she heard it pronounced in church when she was a kid."

"She went to church when she was a kid?" Bethany was truly curious about Annabelle's past, but she knew there were more important questions to ask right now. "So, Grandma's gonna be okay?"

He nodded, allowing the conversation to shift with her concerns. "She has water around her heart. That's the cause of the pain and discomfort. Chest pain and shortness of breath started the sirens blaring."

"But they should, shouldn't they?"

"Sure. No one acted improperly in calling that ambulance but no one besides your grandma asked *me* to intervene."

"It was okay to call an ambulance, but they should have been praying to you at the same time?"

"Something like that." He strode casually next to her, no anxiety evident in his pace or his demeanor, evidently waiting for her next question.

"So, I shouldn't worry. I'll find out how bad it is tomorrow."

"Yes. That's right. Generally, you shouldn't worry, but I don't spend much time telling people that. It's more effective for me to simply show you."

"Show me ... not to worry?"

"Show you that you ultimately have no reason to worry. You worry because you are afraid that either no one is in charge or the ones in charge of your life are not very good at it. Or you even fear that they might be evil."

She batted her eyes for a while, blinking against the wind that buffeted her face. "I know I'm not supposed to worry. But I guess I never really ... sort of documented why I do it anyway." Then she captured one of the bits of wisdom Jesus had let loose into the cool and windy air. "So how do you show me not to worry?"

"By showing you that I am in charge of your life, and I am very good at it. And ... I am good."

Of course, from anyone else this would be a laugh line. But this man walking next to her was not anyone else. And he was not kidding. Not trying to provoke a laugh ... this time. He was serious and he was seriously good.

"So, you showed me, like, by coming into the diner when I was talking to Earl, right where I said your name?"

"Very sharp." His smile spread wide. "You didn't miss that and you haven't forgotten. It helps to remind yourself of times I've intervened, times I have faithfully met your needs."

"Hmm. I think of my grandma as the best intervention you ever did for me."

He nodded, taking a deep breath. "She has been important, and she will continue to be important to you long after she has left this earth."

"Uh. I don't wanna think about her doing that."

"Right. It feels like too much right now, but I will give you grace to survive it when the time comes."

She twisted her neck more fully toward him. "Does that mean I'll feel more ready when it really is her time?"

"It's possible. But not guaranteed."

She nodded slowly, sidestepping a deep puddle. As they got closer to campus, the pavement was still damp in spots. Where the squares of concrete sidewalk were tilted, little triangular reservoirs of water remained.

"You offer me these promises, but they always seem like they have a catch to them. Or, like, a limit."

"The limit is always in you, never with me."

Here was another of those statements she wouldn't tolerate from anyone other than the Son of God.

"You're God. And I'm not, right?" One of the pastors at her church liked to say that line.

"Yes. That's right. Which brings us back to our paradoxes."

"Will this be on the final?"

He laughed so loud Bethany worried the neighbors would be disturbed by the rowdy students walking down their street. She never wanted to be one of those disrespectful college students that the rest of the city dreaded or feared.

"You're not likely to scare the neighbors, dear." Jesus laughed more softly now.

Chapter 14

Questioning

Saturday was the day for updates. The first, and most important for Bethany, was an update on her grandma's health.

"She's feeling okay. Not good but okay. The doctors say it's not a heart attack, but water around her heart." Patty sounded tired. She must have been up most of the night.

Bethany was stunned into silence at hearing an echo of Jesus's explanation of Grandma's health issue, his supernatural diagnosis. Then she nearly laughed aloud at the notion. Of course, his diagnosis had been accurate.

She breathed easier. "So, it's something they can treat?" Bethany was sitting at her desk in her dorm room, waiting for a turn in the shower.

"Yes. They want to monitor it for a while to make sure it's not increasing. It might even go away on its own. It could just be fluid leftover from a virus she had last month."

"Oh. That doesn't sound so bad. Then no surgery or anything?" Bethany looked up at Emily, returning from the shower, two towels constituting her wardrobe. The one on her head was a pink turban, the one wrapped around her tiny torso a maroon bath sheet. She loved her towels.

Mouthing something about Rosemary taking the shower next, Emily headed to her closet. Bethany checked the time on her phone. Still early. There was plenty of time to study before the walk to the diner for a long Saturday shift.

"Not surgery. They have ways of reducing the fluid, but not like open heart surgery or anything like that." Patty's reply seemed to circle around the details of the medical procedure.

"Okay. Thanks for calling me again. I'll check my phone all day for news. I need to think about whether I should come down there and see her."

"Oh, of course, she would love to see you. But you know she would want you to stick with school and work, as long as it looks like she's gonna be okay."

"So, you think she is gonna be okay?" Part of the point of those questions was testing what Patty felt, past the medical data. Her more general perception of her mother's aging health.

"I hope so. She's pretty feisty still. You might get a call from her later this morning. She has to go through another scan then she'll probably wanna talk. She'll wanna let you know she's okay. You know."

"Right. I know."

After finally getting her turn at the shower, not usually so difficult on a Saturday, Bethany joined the prefinals flow to the dining hall then to the library. She had to check out a reading folder to access a few items that were not online for her health class. Copyright issues, apparently. The reading was simple and quick. She took a few notes on her laptop before heading back to her room to do some reading. The Margaret Atwood novel was calling her, and the library was too crowded for concentrated reading.

On her way back to her room, Bethany received a call from Mildred.

"Hey. How are you doing?" Bethany worried when she saw it was her Tuesday night friend calling on a Saturday. Mildred rarely called about anything other than small group meetings and transportation.

"Hi. I hope I'm not disturbing you."

"No. I'm just on my way from the library to my dorm room. What's up?"

"Well ... I was wondering how things are going with you ... and with seeing Jesus and talking to him."

Bethany laughed for a couple seconds. Here was a very strange inquiry that made perfect sense. "You probably said that with a straight face, but I laugh because it happened again. It was new and different—sort of a double appearance. One for a guy at the diner then Jesus walking me home from work."

Mildred was quiet for a few seconds. She almost whispered her response. "I love that he walks you home."

Pausing to absorb the coziness of Mildred's reply, Bethany couldn't repress her smile. "I suppose it could all just be my imagination." She only said that to leave room for Mildred. Offering an opportunity for her to be okay with the same sort of encounter not happening to her.

"Hmm. I guess it could be, but I wish I had such a wonderful imagination as that." She paused. "You don't think it is, really? Do you? You don't think it really is just your imagination?"

"No. Huh. It helped that Jesus showed up at work and sat down to talk to this guy that I met there. This older man had lost his daughter. He was staring at me because I reminded him of his daughter, and I felt like Jesus told me to go talk to him, even though I was creeped out by the guy."

"Whoa. That's crazy. Wow." She squawked. "And *he* saw Jesus? This man saw Jesus?"

"Yep. And one of the other waitresses did too. Or, I guess, everyone at the diner could see him. Though Jesus just looked like this cool guy in his thirties with long hair in a ponytail."

"Ha. Well, I guess he could have a ponytail these days. It's modern times and all." Mildred's voice danced childishly.

They talked a little longer, wandering to more mundane topics. Bethany couldn't easily hold her focus on Mildred's call when the topic drifted away from seeing Jesus. Leftovers from the talk with Patty were still cluttering her mind.

When the call with Mildred ended, Bethany could sense something unfinished. Something unsatisfied, unanswered. An issue? A problem? A wrong that had not been set right?

She had to get to reading. But reading a book that was all about wrongs that had not been set right only intensified the struggle that seemed to be threatening to break into all-out war.

What's that about? She didn't say it aloud. Maybe she didn't expect an answer.

Who are you listening to? That was another of those thoughts that landed like a voice but this time the voice seemed more distant.

She paused to look around her room. What was she looking for? Fatigue that flowed from her head down to her feet warned her not to waste energy trying to find whatever it was. Whoever was calling for her attention would just have to wait.

At work that afternoon, Bethany bobbled plates, forgot parts of orders, and seemed to be causing some kind of abrasion with Savannah. When a particularly demanding customer said, "I asked you twice if this dressing was vegan," Bethany answered the question and faked a smile. She cut a short path to the kitchen, where she found a clean towel and covered her face to release an exasperated growl.

Raising her head from her sheltering towel, she found the boss watching her.

Ralph Augustino was the son of the original owner and a former cook in the diner. A squat man with a dark brown combover, he managed the diner as well as a coffee shop and two laundromats. He was at least partial owner of all those, as far as Bethany knew.

"Hey, kid. Take a break. Go grab a smoke out back or something." His tone was gruff, even when he was trying to console.

She chuckled weakly. "But I don't smoke."

"You might think about starting." He waved dismissively and headed toward the front of the restaurant. Ralph would probably do a circuit around the tables, checking on customer satisfaction. The late lunchers were paying and trooping out the door by then. Dinner would start ramping up in a couple hours.

Bethany did go out the back door. She stood with her back to the building and took a deep breath, glad to find the wind was not coming across the dumpster. A flash of yellow caught her eye. A goldfinch flitted from branch to branch in the yard across the alley.

"Huh." She watched the bright yellow and black bird until it dashed off toward some other destination. She knew the name of the species because of Grandma Hight. On one of her visits to Grandma's house in southeast Wisconsin, before Grandma moved to the retirement home, a highlighter-colored bird excited her old grandma.

"Oh, dear. Come here quick. A goldfinch is on the back fence. Oh, what a beauty."

Bethany was fifteen at the time, allowed to visit her grandma's house for the second time. Spying the bird, Bethany had smiled mostly at her grandma's enthusiasm, still getting used to the old woman's cheerful lack of inhibitions.

Now, standing against the cool brick wall of the diner, next to a stack of pallets and plastic crates, the bird stirred some concoction of emotions. Fear. That was part of it. Dread somehow related to the distractions she had been battling all day, even since she got the call about Grandma being in the hospital.

It almost felt like she was mad at Grandma. Just as she paused to ponder that possibility, the back door opened, and Savannah poked her head out.

"Table six is ready for their check."

Bethany didn't hesitate. She dared not. A deep and dangerous bog surrounded the dark thoughts she had just stumbled upon. She would go right back to work and retreat quickly from whatever monsters awaited in that dank wilderness.

She patted Savannah on the shoulder on her way past, in an effort to make peace. A silent apology for her fractured attention, which had surely made her difficult to work with that afternoon.

The impatient customer left no tip, but Bethany didn't pause long to resent that. She would do better and provide no excuses for other customers to stiff her. Moments of pause and distraction brought back the image of the goldfinch in the tree next door. Not the goldfinch at Grandma's house. She couldn't recall that one so clearly.

It was half an hour till closing when Earl, the old man from the previous night, came into the diner. He looked around as if hoping to find someone. The last person Bethany had seen him with was Jesus—or Jesús. It was a joke. Sort of a joke. But she didn't find it so funny tonight.

Annabelle interrupted these thoughts by patting Bethany on the shoulder. "See ya later, kid."

"G'bye, Annabelle. Have a safe trip home." Why did she say that? It wasn't her usual parting, but tonight she wouldn't be walking Annabelle to the bus stop.

Annabelle just waved and disappeared into the kitchen.

As she watched Savannah seating Earl, Bethany breathed deeply. The old man looked at her with eyes that almost smiled. He blinked placidly. His face was much more tranquil tonight. How was that? Wasn't his daughter still gone? His conversation with Jesus last night had surely not brought her back. She snorted at herself and thanked the fates that Earl was seated at one of Savannah's tables.

Earl was there until closing, eating apple pie and drinking decaf. No one joined him, but he still seemed more content than when Bethany first noticed him the previous night, before Jesus sat down with him.

Something urged Bethany to talk to Earl again, but she resisted. She was tired. She had work to do. Savannah was responsible for that table. And Earl did nothing to invite Bethany to talk. She smiled at him in passing, after turning the *Open* sign to *Closed*. But she felt no curiosity about his situation or the details of his talk with Jesus.

She mostly felt nothing. She was numbed by weariness or maybe preoccupied with worries of her own.

Chapter 15

Imposter

On the way back to campus, Bethany wondered if she should start renting a bike or a scooter for her work commutes. How much did the electric conveyances cost? There was a rack full of them right outside her dorm. The walk to and from the diner took her almost fifteen minutes. With finals approaching, that time seemed wasted.

Except when Jesus walked with her, of course. Tonight that *of course* was tainted with irony. Where was he?

A thought faded into focus again. *Who are you listening to?*

Wasn't that the same thing she had heard during work, as she worried about Grandma?

"Who?" She replied aloud. A partial reply to a thought. Or was she responding to another person? Where was that person?

Who are you listening to? This time it felt like an accusation. The questioner seemed to know the answer and just wanted her to admit it. Right?

Who are you listening to?

"What? What are you saying?" Speaking aloud again, as she crossed a residential street, she did feel as if someone was there, but it didn't feel the same as when Jesus went invisible and still talked to her.

This realization rode with her onto campus and into her dorm, up the stairs and onto her floor. She was hauling a back-pack cluttered with some kind of revelation. But, like something in her backpack, that revelation remained behind her, out of reach and out of sight.

She went to bed early. There was no sign of any of the other girls. They were probably out studying or partying. Or both.

Emily coming in during the small hours of the morning only raised Bethany's consciousness slightly. She knew it was happening but did nothing about it. Then she had a dream.

She was at work. All the tables were full of students. So many students. What were they doing there? Bethany was the only waitress. She knew the reason no one else was working, but she spent no time thinking about what it was. She had no time to think.

This crowd of students was definitely from the university, an unusual congregation at the diner. Though she knew in the dream that they were fellow students, she didn't recognize any of them. Their identities were blurry even if their faces were not. Not only did she not know them, she also didn't know what they wanted. They were talking among themselves and expecting her to serve them without bothering to give her their orders.

She tried collecting whatever plates came up in the kitchen and searching for someone who wanted the sandwich, the salad, or the soup on those plates. But it was too loud for her to be heard as she called out dishes and searched for recognition from someone among the crowd. Finally, she dropped the tray she was holding onto the nearest table and tugged her apron off. She was out of there. She couldn't take it anymore.

Dashing out the back door, she found it still light outside and there were birds flying all around the parking lot. Red birds and yellow ones, blue birds and green ones. Unusual colors. Nameless birds. She kept her head down, not wanting to see them. Not wanting to have to explain what species they were or where they came from.

She couldn't stop thinking about those strange birds even as she was looking for a scooter she could ride back to campus. Surely one of the students had left an electric scooter parked outside the diner. But she didn't recognize the parking lot or the street. Where was she? She was worried now that it wasn't safe for her to be walking alone.

Then *he* was there. The man with the ponytail was with her, though walking two paces behind. And when she turned to check why he stayed behind her, his face changed. She saw it change, as if catching him at some trick. He was not Jesus. He was someone else. When he realized she recognized his deception, he started to chase her.

She ran back toward campus, tripping over the ridges and cracks in the sidewalk, losing her shoes and then running harder, as if her thick-soled work shoes had been holding her back.

Still, the man was right behind her. He was always two steps away from capturing her, and he followed her into the lobby and into the stairwell of the dorm. There he finally caught her, grabbing her, spinning her around and insisting..

"Who are you listening to?"

It was him. He was the one asking that question.

He turned into Jesus again, but only briefly.

When he switched back to that nameless, faceless imposter, Bethany took advantage of that gap and wrenched free from him, dashing up the stairs as fast as she could. He was only a step behind her, grabbing at her feet.

She woke up kicking at the sheets on her bed.

Chapter 16

Church

On Sunday morning, Bethany rolled toward her night table to collect her phone and nearly cursed when she saw the time. How had she slept so late? She got to bed early. She sighed. It had been a strenuous sleep.

Bouncing off the bed, her sheets trailing onto the floor, she slowed when she noticed Emily looking at her through narrowed eyes, her face mushed against the mattress, her pillow on the floor.

"Hey."

"Hey." Bethany scuttled to the bathroom.

When she came back to collect clean clothes before getting into the shower, she found Emily hugging her pillow.

Emily opened her eyes almost halfway this time. "Who were you fighting with in your sleep last night?"

Bethany stopped, puffed her lips, and took a stab at the answer. "I think it was something about my grandma being in the hospital. I think I'm mad at somebody about that."

"Whoa. I hope you weren't kicking your grandma."

"Ha. Yeah. Me too." It was a throwaway comment, grumbled as she turned toward the shower. But something about it started a cascade, like pulling an orange out of a pyramid in the grocery store, the whole pile coming loose and tumbling around her feet.

Grandma couldn't die. That would be so unfair. After all these years, Bethany finally got to know her grandma. That sweet old lady introduced her to Jesus and a whole new world. Grandma showed her true freedom and gave her the courage to defy her mother and to pursue her true calling. At eighteen, Bethany even took her dad's last name so she could have the same name as Grandma Hight.

Grandma can't die. She just can't.

Her shower was a streaming blur, like the identity of those people in her dream. Should she be going to church? Was it worth this rush to skip breakfast and give up study time?

But she needed something and maybe she would find it at church. Maybe she would find Jesus at church. She sputtered water when she laughed, turning off the shower. She was questioning going to church when she had a chance to actually make it this week. The rise of internal resistance somehow reinforced the feeling that she needed something she would find there.

Is this spiritual warfare? She didn't say it aloud. She aimed that question at the voice that had been directing her. Maybe at the voice that had been accusing her.

As she toweled off, she checked her phone. Time. Temperature. What jacket would she need? Any chance for a bite to eat?

Clutching a granola bar, she arrived in front of the dorm as the last student was climbing into the van. The last one before her, of course.

"Hey, Bethany." Colson scooted over to free a seat for her.

"Hey. I just made it."

Rhonda patted her on the shoulder from behind. "Good job."

Ashwani, whom they all called *Ash,* was the one who had slipped into the last seat before Bethany. "What did she do this time?"

Bethany answered. "I got out of bed."

"Nice. You gotta start somewhere, right?" He grinned and slid his black, plastic-rimmed glasses up his nose.

From there the conversation swirled around and past her. Bethany only laughed occasionally, laughter muted by her granola bar and her numbness. She was beginning to welcome the numbness as they neared the church. The alternative seemed to be busting out of the van and running away. Kind of like in her dream.

Considering that urge to flee, and rerunning parts of that frantic dream, filled the remaining minutes before the van stopped next to the front doors of the church building.

"All out, recruits." Rhonda bopped the seat behind Bethany as if she knew she had to break her out of the vortex that was threatening to drag her away from the real world.

The students filed out of the van and into the sanctuary, an older man named James holding the door open for them. He had done that almost every Sunday Bethany attended, but she still didn't know his last name. In her mind, instead of The Apostle James, he was The Doorman James. Something like that.

Odd thoughts seemed to suspend her away from everyone else. It was like she was walking through transparent gelatin. She felt encased even as she flowed with the herd of people taking seats in the auditorium. The building used to be some kind of industrial site, maybe manufacturing. These days it had a shiny concrete floor with rows and rows of padded chairs facing a low stage. Low, but still a stage. It was just tall enough to keep her away from it.

Without thinking about it—she seemed unable to link together two cogent thoughts—Bethany joined a half dozen other students in available seats near the back.

"Table for six. We have a spot for you back here." Ash said that. She couldn't see him but knew his voice amidst the murmuring crowd.

Forcing herself to slow her breathing, Bethany responded to a question from Kendra Miller. Maybe that was Kendra's second try at a question about finals.

"Uh. Not too bad for me. Only, like, two really intense exams. A couple papers. Some smallish stuff." Bethany forced herself to focus on Kendra.

Kendra had short blondish hair. She tended to wear baggy clothes, as if she used to be much larger. Not just heavier. Bigger. Bethany only wondered from a polite distance about this wardrobe tendency.

"Uh, what about you? Monster finals?"

Kendra shrugged. "Chemistry. Chemistry will be a beast. Calculus is open book. And I got my philosophy paper drafted. Just have to edit. No, not too bad overall." She squinched her eyes half shut, a habit Bethany had noticed before. Maybe Kendra wore uncomfortable contact lenses.

The worship band started to play, and Bethany stood for an opening song with the rest of the congregation. She could see one of the pastors with a microphone, but the slender woman in her forties was clearly waiting for the song to run first. This was the order of the service about half the time, Bethany noticed. A song and then an exhortation of some kind.

Right now, Bethany was noticing that she noticed things like that. She suspected she was hiding behind these observations, as opposed to actually worshipping.

What was she hiding from?

"Who are you listening to?" That sounded like a literal voice, but she restrained herself from looking around this time.

In that moment, she knew the answer to the question. The answer right then was that she wasn't listening to anyone, and that was intentional. At least on some level, she had decided not to listen. Shutting down felt safer. Like taking shelter from hostile fire that was coming from not so far away.

Odd. Why was she thinking about war and shooting? That was not her usual way of looking at the world. She wasn't a war movie fan and didn't even like the spy movies Emily adored.

When that first song ended, after only a couple minutes, Bethany could feel herself postponing listening. She was hiding from understanding what all the chatter was about.

The pastor was praying, calling on Jesus to make his presence known to all gathered there.

Jesus. Where are you?

A response. *Did you come here to find me? Why?*

She couldn't tell if the question was about *why* she was looking for him or *why* she would look at church.

Throughout the music set at the beginning of the service, she restrained that urge to look around for Jesus. She thought of that old man, Earl, as she had seen him last night at the diner. He was looking for someone. Now she was too.

Bethany managed to remain in that gelatin suspension throughout the singing, during the greetings, and through the sermon. The service was usually an hour and a half. This one seemed both longer and shorter. By the end she felt exhausted.

She wore half a grin as she listened to Kendra talking to Rhonda about her little brother's knee being healed so he could play baseball this year. It was a cool story. Rhonda's golden-brown face glowed with joy. Bethany knew it was remarkable, but she didn't feel anything about it.

Then Rhonda turned to Bethany. "Hey. Would you mind if I pray for you? I feel like there's this intense conflict going on around you. Like you could use a boost."

Kendra seemed to take that as an opening for her to slide down the row and out into the aisle. But Colson and Lucas slid closer, standing in the row just ahead of Rhonda and Bethany.

Wondering what the right answer would be to Rhonda's offer, Bethany tried to speak but something was wrong with her jaw. Or maybe it was a problem with all her joints. She was locked in place. Encased. Not in that giant Jell-O mold but inside an iron cage so small it constricted her on all sides.

Colson didn't wait for Bethany to answer Rhonda's offer. "I bless you in the name of Jesus to be free. Freedom! I declare freedom over you, Bethany, right now."

That declaration worked like a key unlocking that iron cage. Instantly, she knew she could talk, but the words she said made no sense. There were broken bits of words, syllables unrelated to each other. She gave up after uttering a gaggle of those nonsense syllables. She kept her eyes closed so she didn't have to witness the confusion on the faces of the people around her.

Lucas, a tall pale guy who was a few years older than her, leaned in close and spoke in a low, confidential tone. "I break off the attack of the enemy, right now. Bethany belongs to Jesus. She is victorious, in his name."

Those words, though gently spoken, had a jarring effect. Bethany's hands flew up to her chest and she let out another meaningless syllable. "Ja." She opened her eyes and blinked hard. Suddenly her nonsense words seemed extremely funny, and she let loose a barrage of laughter.

When she wobbled, as if the room were rocking in white-water rapids, all three of the young people praying for her grabbed her shoulders. Rhonda slid her strong hand around Bethany's upper back and steadied her.

Bethany leaned to her left until her head rested on Rhonda's substantial shoulder. She kept laughing, but this laughter felt less crazy, less out of control. And it felt good. She felt good.

Raising her head to look at her friends and to thank them, Bethany froze. That guy was standing behind Rhonda. That guy? What was she thinking? It was Jesus.

Not exactly sure why it was happening, Bethany felt herself tilting backward. She heard chairs sliding, metal over concrete, and exclamations all around her. And she felt a half a dozen hands lowering her gently onto the chairs next to where she had been sitting during the service. That slow ride toward horizontalness seemed to call for more laughter, so she met the call. She laughed until she cried, and she cried until she was tired of crying.

When her friends finally helped her to her feet, she had to blindly follow Rhonda and Colson up the aisle. Someone had reminded them that the van back to campus was waiting. Bethany was grateful for support behind and in front. She faltered a few times between pitching forward and falling over backward. Lucas was behind, propping her gently, following them to the van. Bethany and her supporters were the last to arrive.

Colson climbed in first. Rhonda followed, squeezing into the same seat she occupied before. Lucas held Bethany's arm as she lifted one foot into the van. When she noticed his hand on her arm, she turned around and set both feet on the ground again. She flung her arms around his neck and gave him a hug that included banging her chin into his collar bone.

Laughing in surprise, Lucas patted her on the back. “Are you gonna be okay?”

“Oh yeah. Much better now. Much better.” She was on the brink of starting to cry again but releasing her hold on Lucas seemed to keep her back from that edge. And, as she took the last seat on the van next to Colson and Ash, she waved girlishly at Lucas.

He laughed again, shook his head, and waved back.

Bethany really liked Lucas. Now she was wondering why she hadn’t noticed that before.

“Okay, so what happened to you?” Ash leaned forward to see Bethany past Colson.

She smiled at him, as other faces turned toward her, and she let loose her story. The whole story. She started with Jesus knocking on her dorm suite door.

About two minutes into her narrative, she noticed how easily the words flowed. Her mouth was free. Maybe too free. But she was willing to take the chance of needing to apologize later. When they arrived at campus, Bruce, the driver, sat with everyone else listening to Bethany’s perception of what had happened that morning. Colson and Rhonda each piped in to help her with that part.

When she was finished, Bethany could hear sniffles all around. That amid dead silence.

“Dang, girl! You’ve had an awesome week.” Ash got a few laughs with that.

Probably due to the impact of her story, most of the students from the van stayed together for lunch in the dining hall in Bethany’s dorm. They filled one big, round table. And Bethany got to hear other people’s stories about receiving direction from Jesus and of finding freedom from spiritual attacks.

Several times their laughter and their exclamations attracted curious eyes from nearby tables, and Bethany was pleased to find that she didn't much care who heard them or noticed how crazy they all sounded. She was even glad to embrace the possibility that she might be the craziest one of all.

Chapter 17

Listening

In her dorm room after lunch, Bethany breathed relief. The prayer time at the end of church had released her from some kind of personal captivity. Telling the story of Jesus walking and talking with her seemed to further scrape away inhibition about what people would think. But getting back to her home at school, the dorm room, brought another sort of relief. She had gone through a lot for one morning. Her room was a welcome refuge.

But she didn't linger in that quiet place for long. She called Grandma again. The call on Saturday had caught her grandma napping, according to Patty's text, so Bethany hadn't followed the voicemail she left.

Today, Grandma answered. "Hello, dear. How are you doing?"

"I'm doing great, Grandma. I've had all kinds of adventures with Jesus." The giggles came back for a second, but she got a handle on that. "And I had a really powerful prayer time at church this morning." She fully expected Grandma would have an idea what she meant, even if she couldn't guess the details.

"Well, I hope you're gonna tell me all about it. I'm getting bored here in the hospital."

"You really wanna hear all the embarrassing bits?" Bethany knew the answer to that.

"Only as much as you feel comfortable telling me."

"I can tell you all of it. I was just teasing. And some of it is about you."

"Oh. How's that?"

"Well ... I was worried about you ... going away." She held her breath for a second. But Grandma didn't interrupt. "And that seemed to get something stirred up about Mom. About her keeping me away from you all those years. Like I was mad at her for you being in the hospital because I was mad at her for keeping us apart."

"Oh, dear. That's a lot. And what did Jesus say about all that?"

"Huh. Well, I think he kept saying, 'who are you listening to?' Although I didn't actually see him saying it. It seemed sorta like he was reminding me to listen to him not to ... like ... listen to my fears or my anger at Mom."

"Or even listening to the devil."

"Uh. Yeah, I guess that's part of it. Which explains this morning." She reported what happened at church. The story made Grandma laugh for some reason. But then, Bethany hadn't really explained—even to herself—what *she* had been laughing about at the end of the prayer time.

Grandma's chuckling tapered to a low hum. "So, I think the part about listening to the devil was listening to accusations against your mother." Grandma seemed to pause for a reply. Hearing none, she carried on. "You see, he's the accuser. That's his way. He accuses people, and he even accuses us about real things. You could even say he's right sometimes, but it's not our business to listen to what he says. Even if he's right *by law*, we don't live by the law anymore."

It was a load of truth for Bethany to absorb, but she knew the next time she saw him she could ask that guy named Jesús what he thought about what Grandma was saying. For now, she was concerned about Grandma's breathing.

"You sound winded."

"Yes, I can't take as deep a breath as I'd like. They tell me that tomorrow they're gonna pull some of that fluid out."

"Pull it out? How do they do that?"

She laughed very softly. "Are you sure you want to know that? It involves a very big needle." She breathed what might have been one more laugh.

"Oh. Wow. Well, let me pray for you now, that everything will go as well as possible."

"Sure, I'd appreciate that. Though you might also bring Jesus down here to just take care of the whole thing for me." Another soft breathy laugh followed.

Assuming Grandma wasn't serious about her coming down to Illinois with Jesus, Bethany just prayed over the phone for Grandma's recovery by whatever means necessary—even a very big needle. Or a visit from Jesus.

Bethany said goodbye, sensing she was taxing Grandma too much. And, of course, there was studying to do.

She had to finish the draft of her final Intro to Education paper, so she could upload it for approval by Tuesday, before finishing it. She renewed her search on standardized testing, sitting with her laptop on her desk. Sometimes she had to sit at the desk to keep herself on task. But it wasn't so hard today, as if one of the most distracting voices had been banished from her head.

But, of course, I'm still here. It was *his* voice. Maybe only in her head.

She filled out the remaining subpoints of her findings and reread the conclusion, then she checked her phone for weather. Fifty-eight degrees now. Not much wind. Sunny. Time to go outside and find a place to read in the sunlight. She powered down her laptop and picked up her electronic reader and a baseball cap, in lieu of sunblock.

Her light blue jacket flapped as she walked briskly toward the forest preserve just outside campus. But, as she detoured around some new construction, she noticed a rumpled woman walking in the middle of the street. It was Sunday and no cars were around. But the woman seemed unsteady. She wore clothes in faded shades of gray and pink and brown. Her hair was like a yellowish gray helmet. As Bethany drew closer, she could see the raw, red complexion of a person who lives outside most of the year.

"Where's the mental health clinic? I need the emergency mental health clinic, and I know it's around here somewhere." She stopped and stared at Bethany from fifteen feet away.

Bethany approached slowly, uncertain whether she should reduce that distance. She slipped her reader into the side pocket of her softshell jacket, trying not to linger on the contrast between her spotless coat and the ragged clothes of the woman who was eyeing her suspiciously.

"You know that this is the university campus? I don't think the clinic you're looking for is here, but I can look it up." She had pulled her phone from her other jacket pocket and unlocked it.

An approaching car caused Bethany' to look up. A city police SUV slowed at the intersection half a block behind the woman. Bethany had no idea what the police would think about this woman wandering onto campus. She wasn't sure what the jurisdiction arrangement was between Milwaukee police and campus security, but it was clear the officer had spotted the woman and the vehicle was rolling toward them.

"Emergency mental health clinic. That's what I would look up if I still had a phone, and if Richard didn't take it from me. So that's what you could be looking up now if you were so inclined." The woman spoke to Bethany in a gravelly voice, but she was turning gradually toward the police officer who was exiting his vehicle and speaking into a radio attached to his body armor.

"Hello, officer. Do I know you?" The woman addressed the new arrival before Bethany could.

That was just as well. Bethany didn't know what to say to him.

"Do you need some help, ma'am?"

"I ain't done nothin' wrong."

The officer nodded. "Are you looking for something?" He was close enough that Bethany could sense when he looked at her instead of the woman.

But she kept her eyes on her phone for a couple more taps. "Okay. I see it. An emergency mental health clinic. But it's not very close. Like, over a mile away from here." She raised her head, aware of the officer but still focused on the woman.

"She was asking you for directions?" The officer stayed six feet away from Bethany and about the same distance from the woman. They formed an uncertain equilateral triangle.

Bethany faced him. "Yes. Not a problem." Her voice wavered a bit. She rarely had contact with the police. On a few occasions, an officer had eaten at the diner during one of her shifts, and once a pair of officers came to usher an unruly guy out the front door.

"It looks like it might be kinda far to walk." Bethany held up her phone and looked a question at the officer.

"Would you like a ride to the clinic, ma'am?" He rested a hand idly on the grip of his automatic pistol, which was still securely strapped into its holster.

"A ride? In a police car? What will people think?" The woman's voice was deadpan serious.

Bethany might have laughed at that reply during an earlier stage of her life, but she was feeling genuinely concerned for the woman and hoping the cop was there to help. Everything about the situation was uncertain to her. She glanced from the woman to the officer. He seemed at a loss for words as well. Maybe he was working silently at repressing his own laughter.

"I, personally, would think the kind officer is doing you a service. Serving and protecting, right?" Bethany only peered at the cop when she finished this serious, and seriously awkward, response.

"Yes, ma'am. I would be glad to give you a ride. You're not in any kind of trouble. No handcuffs." He held out his hands and smiled. He was a large man with a gray goatee and pink skin, pretty convincing in the part of the friendly policeman.

"Do you want me to ride with you?" Bethany offered that without knowing whether it was an option.

The woman formed an impressed pucker with her lips. "That's very nice of you, dear, but I don't think that will be necessary. You have your own reputation to protect, of course."

Bethany smiled. "I appreciate you thinking of me. I was just trying to help."

"Good try. I'll do it. I'll take a ride from the officer. I don't mind if I do."

The officer bowed slightly as he and the woman turned toward the police car. "Thanks, miss." And he left Bethany holding her phone and wondering if she had done everything she was supposed to.

Just fine, dear. You did just fine. That was the voice in her head, which had returned this afternoon. His voice was encouraging in all kinds of situations.

Chapter 18

Checking

Before going to work at the diner on Monday afternoon, Bethany called her grandma but the call went to voicemail. She left a message and, as if Patty was monitoring Grandma's phone, Bethany got a call from her almost immediately.

"Hello, Bethany. Your grandma is resting now. They had to give her some pain meds for the extraction, or whatever they call it."

"You mean pulling out the fluid?"

"Yes. That." She paused. "I think she's gonna be fine. They're giving her some antibiotics to prevent an infection from the procedures. That might mess up her eating for a while, they think, so they're gonna keep her here to monitor how she's doing. And, really, I'm glad they are. She's not as young as she used to be."

"You sound tired. Do you want me to come down there and be with Grandma for a while?"

Patty laughed. "No, dear. You finish your semester. Come see her when you're done with school."

"Hmm. Okay." She thought of Katie. They had been texting that morning. Her cousin had a couple weeks left of her junior year of high school. Her youngest still in school, Patty sounded like a school mom, with her calendar divided into semesters and breaks.

After getting off the phone with Patty and changing into her work clothes, Bethany noticed a text from Colson. **"Lucas was wanting your number. Okay for me to give him?"**

Lucas? The graduate student science guy with the friendly smile?

"Sure. No problem." She wasn't sure if Colson would buy her cool response. Why was that older guy wanting her number? Maybe just to follow up on the prayer time Sunday. It had been intense, and he seemed like a very responsible person. His eyes always seemed interested and compassionate. He had brown eyes, she was pretty sure.

Lucas was one of the oldest members of their young adults group, which mostly consisted of college students. He was at least three years older than Bethany. Maybe his interest was purely spiritual.

Or maybe not.

During her dinner break that evening, just after the modest Monday rush at the diner, Bethany got a text from a new number.

"Hello, Bethany. This is Lucas."

She wiped a remnant of balsamic dressing off her hand and added his number to her contacts before responding.

"Hey. How are you?"

"I'm good. Was wondering how you're doing after that prayer time yesterday."

If anyone was paying attention, they would have noticed her long sigh and her descending shoulders. A ministry follow-up was not as exciting as other possibilities she had been considering.

I'm *paying attention*. Jesus, her internal companion answered her thoughts again. Her invisible friend was apparently monitoring her communications and her imaginations. She sniffed a laugh at that notion.

"Thanks for asking. I feel great. A load off." If anyone had been monitoring her thoughts over the past twenty-four hours, they would have noted only sparse attention to the significance of that prayer time. The results seemed clearly good, but exactly what happened was not perfectly clear.

"Cool. One reason I wanted to contact you was an idea that came to mind as we were praying."

"Yeah? What's that?"

"It was something about your mother. About a debt she owes and your part in holding her in debt. Does that seem relevant?"

Bethany was exhaling another laugh when the cook stepped into the break room. Jose grabbed a large blue towel out of a locker and pulled off his hat to wipe at the sweat. He grunted at her and left the break room without saying a word.

Taking a deep breath, she answered Lucas. **"That is very relevant. Thanks for sharing it. Very much on point."**

"Okay. Good. Blessings!"

"Thanks. Thanks for reaching out."

She waited for a response. Maybe he would take the next step. An invite or something. But nothing arrived during the few minutes before the end of her break. Oh well, he's probably not interested in a kid Bethany's age.

To me you are a beloved child, but to many people you are no longer a kid. That was the unsolicited reply from the voice that needed no invitation, apparently. Like a mother, pretty much.

As she set her dishes next to the sink and washed her hands, she thought about her mother. Was Bethany supposed to do something for her now? Something about that debt?

It's worth considering. That thought might have been her own or that of her spiritual passenger. Or a mixture of the two, perhaps—a blend of two minds.

When her shift ended, Bethany threw a bag of garbage into the dumpster before turning toward campus, and she felt a warmth next to her. Or something like warmth. Maybe it was just her imagination. How much of an imagination did she really have? Her mom had discouraged too much imagination.

As a concert pianist, Bethany was taught to exude emotion from her shoulders through her fingers and into the tightly tuned air of an auditorium stage. They were planned and imagined emotions. Not the kind of imagination that inspired Chopin and Debussy to compose. She was not a composer. She was a performer.

Or she *had been* a performer. When was the last time she touched a real piano? The keyboard she used in her dorm room was not real. Her teachers from years past would be appalled to find her running her fingers up and down an electronic keyboard—even the high-tech compact keyboard her dad had bought her.

Running her mind up and down her regrets about all those years of practice and performance and neglecting her skills recently was like the exercises she should be doing more of, even on her fake keyboard. What about playing keys in church? Yeah, what about that?

"It is entirely up to you, of course."

She jumped half a step forward when Jesus appeared next to her. Her second response was to look around for anyone who might have witnessed this sudden arrival. And then there was the issue of his wardrobe—the flowing robes of a first century rabbi. It was not the usual garb for people in Milwaukee these days.

"Don't worry, no one sees." The night was dim between the streetlights. They were turning away from the main thoroughfare and into one of the neighborhoods bordering the campus.

"Hmm." She was stalling while she tried to recapture what she had been thinking about before this epiphany.

"Playing piano or keyboards at church." He reminded her of the topic and articulated it more precisely than she would have expected.

What did he care about the difference between piano and keyboard?

"I care about what you care about."

She turned her head fully toward him to search for the joke in his eyes.

"No joke." He smiled. "I am invested in you, and that means I am invested in the same things you are. I care about what you care about."

"But not always in the same way, right?"

"Well, worrying is not something I can do, but I am moved by what moves your heart."

"You *can't* worry?"

He shook his head. "It's a handicap. I know. But I just can't do it." Then he grinned and winked.

"A handicap? You're teasing me."

"A little." He slipped an arm around her shoulders. "Worry is about powerlessness. You worry when you feel you have no other useful response. Things in the future, for example, are hard to control. You feel powerless about the future, so you worry."

"But you ... are incapable of feeling powerless."

"Right. Which is complicated by the fact that I don't always get my way. Not everything works out the way I would like. You could see that as a sort of powerlessness. But it's not something that rules my thoughts or feelings. I devote my efforts in your life to what I *can* affect. Not what is in the hands of others."

She walked in silence for a couple steps, then a few more while looking at him. He grabbed her tighter when she stumbled.

"Is there something I should be doing for Grandma?"

"Pray. Tell me what you want for her. Invite the very best I have for her by inviting me into her situation."

"But she already invited you in ... into her life, right?"

"She has done that, of course, but she's tired now. You could help her out."

"By praying?"

"Patty's right. You don't need to go see Grandma before you finish finals, but you should go see her soon after that."

"Is she gonna be ... in trouble?"

He hummed. "I could just be urging you to go see her for your benefit."

"You could ..." She drew out that last word, offering him a chance to fill in the rest of that thought.

He just grinned at her again then he stopped walking. "This is where I go invisible."

She glanced up the sidewalk. She couldn't see anyone, but she could hear the laughter of someone approaching.

"Okay. Thanks for ... showing up."

"I am always with you." And he went invisible.

She could no longer see him. She could no longer feel his arm around her, but Bethany would take his word for it that he was still with her.

"Still there?" She spoke without moving her lips as three students came into view.

Yes, dear. Thanks for checking.

Chapter 19

Working

For Bethany, hard work was natural. It was a habit carved into her and coated with lacquer to make it last. That lacquer was the reward her work usually earned. At the diner, she earned a decent wage. Tips were good and her employer paid her more per hour than the law required.

Regarding schoolwork, the reward of her discipline included less stress at the end of the semester. Some of her friends and dormmates seemed to need emergency triage tents set up on campus to deal with their overwhelming stress. Absent such emergency facilities, Bethany prayed for them. She prayed for Emily a lot.

"I can't get an extension on my history paper. I'm screwed." Emily moaned when she came back to the room on Wednesday.

Bethany was packing up her laptop and heading to the library. "Oh, dear. I'm sorry about that." The sympathy took a little effort, but she did worry about Emily—worry that Jesus apparently wouldn't share. But maybe he couldn't affect Emily's behavior any more than Bethany could. At least not much more.

"You still praying for me?" Emily asked that even as she was falling facedown into the piled blankets on her bed.

"Yes, I am. All the time."

"Good. I need it."

Bethany paused over what to say next. She had friends who would dive into a spiritual lesson of some kind. Bethany could imagine some changes that would be good for her roommate, but her need to protect her relationship with Emily seemed to complicate things.

Instead of diving into God's plan for a more disciplined life, Bethany offered a pat on the back and a spontaneous prayer. "Bless Emily, Lord. Give her energy and creativity and confidence. Thank you, Jesus."

Muffled by her duvet, Emily mirrored those last three words. "Thank you, Bethany."

With a big sigh, Bethany departed, hiking her backpack up her shoulders and checking for her phone and keycard. On her way down the hall, she received a phone call from her mother.

"Hello, Mom. How are you doing?"

"I'm fine. Just wanted to check on you. I guess it's a ... time of ... for students." Either her mom glitched or the call connection did.

"It's not too bad for me. All those years of piano practice pay off with schoolwork."

"Are you still practicing?"

"Not as much as I'd like. I put in at least twenty hours a week at the diner and there's schoolwork. And church." She was trying to respond without complaining, and while banishing all tones of irony over the way her busyness was directly impacted by her mother's refusal to help pay for school.

A big breath from her mom. "Okay. I heard about your grandma. I hope she's gonna recover."

"I think she is. Patty says she's doing okay."

"Mm-hmm."

It was one of those moments when Bethany wondered why her mother even bothered. But she wanted to do her part, to do the work she could to stay connected to her mother. "So how are you doing? Any new clients?"

Her mother was selling real estate these days. "Things have slowed down. There's lots of uncertainty in the market, but I'm doing okay."

"How about Grandma Marconi? How is she?" Her other grandmother was in a facility that specialized in Alzheimer's care.

"Still the same. Her memory is gone, but she's as healthy as I am. Only older." Her voice fell at that last comment.

Grandma Marconi was in Oregon. Bethany would visit her if she went back there for a week or two, but her mother had not invited her and Bethany didn't want to give up hours at the diner. Her grandmother's inability to recognize her was another inhibiting factor.

"Okay. I'll let you get back to work. I'm glad your schoolwork is under control."

"Thanks, Mom. Thanks for calling." Bethany paused at a menu of things she could say next.

But her mom said goodbye and that ended the call.

Staying in touch with her mom was a drag on her mood any given day, but Bethany was thinking about what Lucas had said, and about Jesus's words regarding forgiveness. And then there was Grandma Hight and what she said about accusations against Bethany's mother. That added up to quite a total. Maybe a debt Bethany owed her mother.

Bethany snuffled a laugh as she added up all that input and tugged on the tall glass door to the library. *I get the message. I guess it's gonna take some work. But it's important work.* Thoughts unspoken.

But not unacknowledged. *Good girl. And good work.*

She could tolerate her Jesus calling her a girl the same way she could tolerate it from Grandma Hight. Jesus was even older than Grandma, after all.

She was pretty sure that thought elicited a laugh. At least a quiet one contained in her head.

Some of the research for her final paper in education class was on reserve in the library. She had exhausted the online publications she knew of. Today she would peruse actual copies of standardized tests that hadn't been scanned into the system—old tests. Bethany probably already had all the research she needed for the paper, but she was curious about what had changed in standardized tests over time. She was concentrating on the middle grades for the paper. Part of that was strategic—it was easier for her to comprehend tests on that level in a short amount of time. She also assumed she would teach in a middle school someday.

The summer camp experience that solidified her decision to teach music had been with kids ages four to sixteen. But she liked the eleven-, twelve-, and thirteen-year-olds the best. In her mind, they were potentially difficult to work with but worth the effort.

She set aside worries about both her grandmothers, about her mom and about her future career, and she waited in line at the reference reserve desk. Even there she didn't really feel like she could set aside one distraction—the presence of her invisible friend.

Me? A distraction?

Just checking to see if you were listening.

Chapter 20

Finally

Despite her discipline and preparation, the stress of finals erased almost a week of Bethany's life. The combination of tests and papers, pressed against her work hours at the diner, was draining. But the corporate exhaustion of her fellow students created a camaraderie she was starting to appreciate at the completion of her fourth semester.

With her sophomore year officially finished, even if grades weren't yet released, she planned to go to church on Sunday. She didn't expect the van would be available during the months ahead. Few students stayed in the dorms over the summer and none of the regular van riders were staying, as far as she knew. Those electric scooters and bikes were more attractive this time of year anyway.

The van was only half full that final Sunday. Rhonda and most of the others had evacuated the city on Friday or Saturday but Colson and Ash were along for the ride.

"Do I look like I lost weight?" Ash was a stickman and it was a facetious question, judging by his glowing eyes and broad grin.

"You might've shaved off a couple ounces." Colson was willing to play along, one eyebrow cocked.

"Because I feel so much lighter with finals done." Ash chortled. "And I got good news about next year. I get to be a graduate assistant even before I graduate."

"When are you graduating?"

"December. But in the fall, I get to work for the same chemistry professor I've had for most of my upper-level classes. I already know him really well and it should be a breeze."

From the smattering of congratulations his fellow students offered Ash, the conversation turned to summer employment options.

Colson leaned against the side of the van, glancing out the window. "My dad is a building contractor. I always get a laborer position with his construction crew in the summer. At least since I was big enough to do the work."

"Dude. You must have been big enough for that kind of work by the time you were, like, seven." Skinny Ash prodded hefty Colson, a guy who looked like he could break up the stickman for kindling.

But Colson only laughed. "No child labor violations were involved. I was fully occupied with soccer and baseball and basketball camps during the summer, until I was about fifteen."

"Really? Did you give up sports after that?" Bethany was wondering at that early cutoff date. It was similar to when she started looking for a way out of piano competitions.

He smirked. "I hurt my knee sophomore year. I messed it up too bad for varsity soccer but not too bad for pickin' up wood scraps and carrying tools."

"That's not what you're gonna do after school, is it?" Ash couldn't possibly conceive of a construction career for himself, obviously, but not for Colson either.

"No. I'm a criminal justice major. I'm thinking about law school."

"Oh, man that would be cool. So, you'd be, like, a public defender or something?"

Colson nodded. "Maybe something like that."

"Did you ever get healing prayer for your knee and for the trauma of losing your sports dreams?" Bethany was thinking about some of what Jesus had been offering her regarding her mother, and she was recalling how Colson had prayed for her last week.

He raised his parentheses-like eyebrows. “No. I haven’t. But, now that you mention it, I could get some prayer for that after the service.”

Bethany shrugged. “What about praying for you here?” She guessed they were still at least five minutes from the church building.

Colson rested his gaze on her, took a slow breath, and agreed to give it a try. Bethany wondered why he just looked at her and not the others. She wasn’t planning to be the only one praying.

When she glanced around at the other passengers, she felt like she was missing someone. Ash was next to her. Carrie had turned around in the seat ahead, looking willing. Behind them were Harim and Daisy. Harim gave a willing shrug in reply to Bethany’s unspoken invitation. But there was someone else.

A warm sensation of someone resting his weight on her back and leaning over her shoulder gave Bethany a start.

Nodding his head steadily now, Colson looked like a guy getting warmed up. Maybe even wound up. And before any of the others said a word, a silent tear rolled down his cheek.

Ash jumped into the pause this provoked and started to pray for healing to Colson’s heart, for recovery from the loss of his dreams. He shifted easily out of joking into praying, as Bethany had witnessed a few times before.

When she saw a semitransparent hand reaching around her, just barely touching Colson’s near knee, Bethany stretched her hand to match it. “Is ... is this the knee ... that got injured?” She was trying to focus on Colson and not get sucked into the shock of seeing that otherworldly hand. She seemed to be the only one seeing the mysterious participant.

“Yeah. That’s the one,” he whispered roughly.

“Okay, then. Jesus heals the injury. Any leftover pain or limitations, be healed in Jesus’s name.” She had heard her grandma and a few people at church pray like that, but Bethany had never said anything like it before.

"Huh." Colson puckered. "Feels good, warm. Yeah, that feels good." Then he sniffled and smiled at Bethany. "Did Jesus show you that?"

She wasn't sure what part Colson was asking about, but the answer was the same for all of it. "Yes, he did. I believe he did."

"Hmm. Feels better. Thanks."

As Ash asked more diagnostic questions, Bethany turned her attention back to that warm presence, warm and welcoming. For a second, she thought she could feel Jesus's pleasure, if it were possible to feel an invisible smile.

That odd thought led her on a mental meander that kept her tongue tied for the rest of the ride.

Chapter 21

Lifesaving

With increased tourism in the city during the summer months, the diner became even busier. It was one of the few diners near downtown and had a reputation that had spread around Wisconsin and over the internet. But Bethany still didn't work full-time. She would be taking a single class at the university for a few weeks after Memorial Day, which allowed her to continue living in the dorm at the same cost.

Even with work and that one class, it felt like she was on a break. For one thing, there were fewer people around. Sandy had come back to school to finish some classes and to take the first summer term, but that was just two of them in a suite meant for five. Sandy's room had a window. Bethany didn't move in there for that occasional sunlight, however. This time of year, she could just go outside to find the sun. And she savored having her room to herself. It's how she had grown up, as an only child. Apparently, she missed that, at least a little.

Late May and early June were the best days to be in Milwaukee. Just ask all the music festival attendees crowding the lake front. The walk to work was sometimes a bit sweaty, but Bethany carried her work clothes on days like that and wore shorts and a t-shirt for the afternoon stroll.

About a week after spring term ended, Bethany was walking toward campus from the diner. At 9:45 p.m. there was still twilight in the west, as the longest days approached. She was thinking about the train to Chicago and the one out to Naperville, where she would see Grandma Hight on Sunday. Bethany figured that missing church to see Grandma was fitting.

"Yes, if it wasn't for her, you wouldn't go to church at all." The man she had seen walking toward her on the wide commercial sidewalk was suddenly familiar. Had he shape-shifted? Or did she just not recognize him from a distance?

"You." She breathed a laugh. "I haven't seen you for a while."

"You saw my hand on the van last Sunday."

"Ha. Yeah. That's true, I did." She chuckled some more. "So where have you been? What have you been up to? Are you on summer break?"

He laughed loudly then pivoted to walk beside her toward campus. "A nice night for a walk."

It was beautiful. The temperature was in the mid-seventies, with a modest breeze. Just enough wind to keep the mosquitos away. The restaurant had been warm in the dining room and hot in the kitchen. The fresh air revived Bethany.

"A nice night to walk with *you*." She grinned up at him. He was wearing his modern costume, so she expected he would stay visible to her all the way back to campus. Or maybe they could prolong the walk as they had the first night he accompanied her home from work.

His reflected smile was warm and generous, not in a hurry to break eye contact as she would expect from most people. No curious squint in eyes wondering what she meant by her words of affection. She savored how comfortable they were together.

"Yes. But I'm going to ask you to do something tonight that's uncomfortable."

"Oh yeah? What's that?" She tried to anticipate the joke but when she checked his face, she found no humor posted there.

"Someone needs your help. They need an act of kindness, an act of faith."

"Whoa. That sounds important." She still reserved a teaspoon of hope that he was kidding or maybe speaking metaphorically. Perhaps he was telling her a parable.

"There is an older gentleman who is home alone and has started having chest pains. These chest pains are not like your grandma's. He is having a heart attack. He needs someone to help him."

"Where? Where is ... this ... man?" Walking home with Jesus had abruptly turned into a scene from a nightmare. A man having a heart attack? What could Bethany do about a heart attack? She hadn't even taken real CPR training. There was only the brief video she was required to watch last year when they hired her at the diner.

"You have your phone?" Jesus looked at her backpack.

She had put her phone in there because she was damp with sweat from work and preferred not to have the warm phone in her pocket. It always seemed to heat up as she walked between work and campus. A computer science major friend had explained that phenomenon to her in the dining hall once. Something about her phone searching for cell towers. During her winter walks she thought of it as the handwarmer app.

Her mind was drifting, maybe trying to escape from what Jesus was asking of her.

"Fear not. I have your back."

"So, you're gonna go with me to this ... this man's house?"

"Of course, I never leave you." He angled his head to the right and led the way onto a side street she usually bypassed. "Though I won't be visible to you or him, I can still lead you even if you can't see me."

"Uh-huh." She was distracted by the unfamiliar street. She might have walked on it in daylight a few times. Her route from campus to work was variable, but she only used a variation on the usual route when she was feeling bored or adventuresome. And she rarely did the same on the way back to campus at night.

"This will be a lifesaving adventure." He raised his hand towards a bungalow with golden light easing out of several windows. "He's in here. Mr. Pienkowski."

Bethany turned up the concrete sidewalk toward a tall front porch. "He ..." She was going to ask if the man knew she was coming but that made no sense. What did she really want to ask? What did she need to know?

"You're going to have to knock and then open the front door yourself. He can't come to the door. That's why he needs your help." Jesus didn't sound anxious or even very urgent.

That revived Bethany's hope that this wasn't real, just a joke or maybe a test to see what she would be willing to do for him.

"He needs you now, Bethany." Jesus stopped next to the door. The porch squeaked under his weight, just like it did under Bethany's thick work shoes.

She looked at Jesus, standing on the porch of a stranger. She could see him. She knew it was him. How could she doubt what he was saying?

"Knock." He nodded to the door.

She knocked three times but it was too weak. She pounded with the side of her fist then she noticed the doorbell button. She pressed it but heard nothing.

"It doesn't work."

Of course not. Otherwise, Jesus would have told her to hit the doorbell instead of knocking. She shook her head at herself.

No one was answering the door.

"Go ahead. It's unlocked. Open it and call out."

She gripped the handle and looked at Jesus.

"Do it, Bethany. He needs you, and he will be glad you let yourself into his house." Now he sounded more urgent.

Briefly, she considered how nonthreatening she looked. Jesus was more intimidating than she was, but she set that diversion aside to push the door open.

"Hello. Hello, Mr. Pien ... kowski?" Did she get the name right?

She looked at Jesus. He nodded.

"Mr. Pienkowski, my name is Bethany. Do you need some help?" She had her head inside the door. Her voice was thin and apologetic.

She heard a groan and a dull thump. That propelled her to step through the narrow entryway. "Do you need help? Where are you?"

Then came another noise, like someone rubbing a rough surface. She followed that sound to where she found an elderly man in gray slacks and a white t-shirt lying face down on the floor in the living room. Bethany dashed into the room.

"Are you okay? Do you need help?" She dropped her backpack onto a cluttered coffee table.

The man slowly rolled to his side, clutching at his chest with one hand. He pressed his eyes shut.

"I'll call for an ambulance." She fumbled for her phone, finally getting it clear of her backpack and unlocking it with facial recognition. Apparently, her phone still recognized her face when she was in a total panic.

Only as she dialed 9-1-1 did she notice that Jesus wasn't with her. Except he said he would be.

Her call connected. "9-1-1. What is your emergency?"

"An older gentleman is having a heart attack, I think. He's on the floor grabbing his chest."

"What is the address where you are calling from?"

Her mind went as blank as a page awaiting her answer on a final exam. Bethany looked around, her eyes falling on two envelopes amidst the piles on the coffee table. She saw that they were both addressed to Paul Pienkowski. She recited the address to the operator.

As the operator repeated the address back, Bethany wondered why Jesus hadn't provided her with that information. Then she rebuked herself with the fact that she had turned the corner under a street sign and walked onto a porch that probably had an address posted on it. If she hadn't been panicking and doubting Jesus's directions, she might have collected that valuable data before she got inside. Then another thought arrived, as if as a correction. Jesus didn't need to tell her the address because she found it easily on those envelopes.

"All right. Who am I speaking with?"

"This is Bethany Hight."

"We are dispatching a paramedic team. Please stay with this gentleman. Are you a relative?"

"No. I was ... I was just passing by. I don't even know him."

"All right. Is he outside on the sidewalk?"

"No, he's in his house on the floor of the living room."

There was a long pause. A pause as wide as the gap in the middle of Bethany's story. She thought of an excuse. Actually, she thought of a lie. She could say he had called out for help. In reality, the small moans he had made since she entered his house could never be characterized as a proper call for anything.

But the woman on the phone didn't ask for more details about that. Instead, she said, "Is he conscious? Can he speak?"

Bethany scooted closer to Mr. Pienkowski. "He's not moving." She leaned down to see if she could hear him breathing. With her ear inches from his mouth, she heard a long, low moan, barely louder than a breath. "He's groaning."

"Okay. Just stay with him. See if you can get him to speak. Try and keep him awake."

"Help me, Jesus." She said it as a reflex, probably. But she got an answer.

Put your hand on his cheek. Your hands are cool. It will revive him a little. That was a voice in her head. A very valuable voice.

She placed the palm of one hand on his cheek. His face was warmer than her hand. That was true. "Mr. Pienkowski. Stay awake if you can. There's a paramedic ... some ... paramedics are on the way."

"They're just over two minutes away now." The operator was still audible, even though Bethany had let the phone drift away from her ear.

"Just two minutes. Can you hear me?"

The old man nodded slightly. Then he said, "Uh-huh."

"Okay. Good. Good. You're doing good. Doing well."

Still lying on his side, he pried his near eye open and rotated it slowly toward her.

"Hi there. I'm Bethany. Jesus told me you needed help, and I found you in here on the floor like this. He said you were having a heart attack."

Mr. Pienkowski closed that eye and nodded minutely.

Bethany could hear a siren. As she listened, she could tell it was getting closer. "I can hear them. They're on their way."

The operator answered. "Yes. About a minute. They're almost there."

"Do you hear them, Mr. Pienkowski? Here they come. They'll take good care of you."

He nodded even more subtly this time, and his mouth tightened into a weak smile or maybe a grimace.

A siren roared to a halt. After a moment, the door burst open. Three husky men and one athletic woman in uniforms. They spoke in confident voices. Brightly-colored equipment filled the room. The next two minutes were a churn of sight and sound.

Bethany danced away and tried to find a place to stand where she wouldn't hinder the rescuers. She resorted to leaning against the doorway to the dining room.

She checked with Jesus. *Should I stick around? They don't need me anymore.*

Just another minute.

Not having received the syllabus for this class in Jesus-inspired search and rescue, she didn't really know what he expected of her. But that question slid aside as the paramedics lifted Mr. Pienkowski onto the gurney. When they raised it so he was waist high, he seemed more lucid.

Turning his head toward her as they conveyed him toward the front door, he raised a hand briefly. "Wait." His voice was still weak. "I want to thank my angel." He spoke with a thick Polish accent, which had not been apparent when his communication had been limited to grunts and moans.

Bethany stepped closer. "I'm glad you're looking better."

"You have saved my life." His eyes roamed over her face. "Are you really an angel?"

"Ha. No. I'm just a girl. Just someone ... who listens to Jesus ... sometimes."

Chapter 22

Layers

After she left Mr. Pienkowski's house, Jesus appeared to Bethany again. She found him waiting next to an elm tree, as if they had an appointment. A late-night rendezvous. It was well past ten.

"Thank you, dear. Thank you for saving Mr. Pienkowski."

She shook her head and snorted. "I didn't do much. You just gave me directions and the paramedics did the rest."

"You had your part, and you did it obediently and with compassion."

"Hmm. Okay. I guess I have to admit that. If you insist." She chuckled from deep in her throat. The evening was still temperate, though it seemed a bit cooler. Mr. Pienkowski's house had been slightly warm, as if he didn't have a working air-conditioner. "Will he be okay?"

"Yes, his prognosis is good. They got to him soon enough to diminish the risk."

"Diminish the risk? What about healing? You could have healed him entirely."

"I could have, back in the day." He smiled when this attracted a skeptical look from her. "These days I do my healing work through my people. People like you."

"But ... you just had me calling 9-1-1, not healing him."

"Would you have preferred that I told you to heal him?"

"Preferred?" She took a deep breath. "No, that would probably have freaked me out completely. Like, freaked me out the rest of the way."

"Yes. I know. I only ask you to do what you're ready to do."

"And you figured I could handle calling 9-1-1."

"I knew you could."

Though they were at a natural place to turn toward campus, Jesus showed no inclination to cross the intersection in that direction. Bethany didn't try to persuade him. They ambled together down the tree-lined street, mostly in shadows, passing occasional streetlights at the corners. She could smell lilacs, even though she couldn't see them. The call of crickets ruled the night. It was too early in the year for cicadas.

"Did he really think I might be an angel?"

"It was his way of explaining how a stranger would come into his house uninvited and save his life."

Bethany bobbled her head. She tried replaying in her mind what she had told Mr. Pienkowski about how she happened to be there. She had hesitated to admit it, but she did explain that Jesus had directed her to help. She sniffed another laugh, self-conscious in retrospect. The dispatcher must have heard that part as well.

"I suppose some of them will think I'm crazy."

Jesus nodded. He had a hand gently resting on her upper back. Then he let go. "You did what you were asked to do, and you told the truth."

"Eventually I did. I was trying to think of ways to hide the truth."

"But you repented quickly from that."

She examined his face. "You always seem like you're ready to give me excuses."

"Not excuses. But I am your advocate and I offer you forgiveness instead of excuses." They took a few steps in silence. "Forgiveness is something that has to be received."

That awakened a troll who had been snoozing in a cavern inside her head. "Do I ... need to receive forgiveness for not ... forgiving my mother?"

"I know it sounds ironic when you say it that way, but it's true." He turned toward her but didn't stop walking. "Are you ready?"

"Ready to receive?"

He simply nodded.

"So, you're offering me forgiveness for being too hard on my mom. And I just need to accept it?" She jogged her head to get her ponytail loose from her collar.

"That's a good summary."

She took a deep breath, as if that might help. Then she snickered. "Okay. I accept." That seemed inadequate. "I accept the fact that I have been unforgiving to my mother, and I accept the fact that I need to be forgiven for that." She looked at him. "In the name of Jesus." Then she laughed out loud.

He laughed too. "Yes. You are forgiven." He sobered. "Now, one more layer."

"Of what? Forgiveness?"

"Yes." He pursed his lips. "Will you forgive *yourself* for your resentment against your mom?"

"Wow, this is getting complicated."

"I have noticed that. People do tend to be complicated, and relationships are a complication times a complication. In fact, the more important the relationship, the more complicated it can be."

"And my relationship with my mom is, of course, important."

"Yes. As is your relationship with me."

"Yeah. But ..." There seemed to be a knot here that she needed to untangle, like when she pulled a necklace from her jewelry box. She couldn't just pull the chains apart without looking closely. "Forgiving myself is about my relationship with *you*?"

He smiled in a way that could only be described as proud. "Yes, dear. Because when you choose *not* to forgive yourself, you are taking over my role in your life. I am the only judge, just as I am the only savior. You cannot save yourself. Neither should you judge yourself."

"Wow." A chill of recognition ran up the back of her neck. "I can see it, I think—this urge to be better, wanting to be right all the time." She took another of those purging breaths. "It's like I wanna be the one in control, so I wanna be the one to decide when I deserve to be forgiven."

"And you do that because being in control is part of your human DNA. The trick is to discover which things you do control and which ones you don't."

Her chest bounced with more laughter. "I think this is too much for the end of a very exhausting day."

"Okay. I understand that you feel that way, but I think you will retain some very important truths from what we've been talking about."

She smiled at him. "Well, I'll trust your judgment on that."

Laughing appreciatively, he turned at the next corner and accompanied her back to campus. This time he didn't disappear before they passed a few scattered students.

Bethany had to trust his judgment on that as well. He knew who would see her with him, and he knew something about what it would mean to them. He also knew what it might mean to her later, having been seen with this older guy out late at night. Just then, she felt too tired and too overwhelmed to worry about any of that.

He did disappear when they entered the stairwell but he kept talking to her. "I bless your sleep tonight, my dear. I bless your dreams, and I promise to be there with you as you rest and as your subconscious mind does its work."

"Thank you. Thank you for everything."

"You're welcome. I love you, Bethany."

And that was the last thing she heard him say to her that night.

But that didn't mean she felt alone as she washed up and got ready for bed. She could still sense him with her as she listened to Sandy talking on the phone in the other room. And Bethany could sense him as she slid between her sheets, pushing her blanket down to the bottom of the bed.

Was this sense of his presence just a matter of recalling her talk with him or was she really aware of him there in her room?

Those questions accompanied her into her dreams, dreams which included Jesus and her mother and Ash, Sandy, Lucas, and Savannah. The details of those dreams didn't stick with her, but her sense of being accompanied remained until she woke the next morning.

Chapter 23

Saturday

That Saturday swelled with Bethany's need to get work done, driven by having a day ahead when she would get none of it done. During the transitions between tasks, she paused to consider what she had learned from Jesus and what difference it would make. Did those recollections of walking with Jesus constitute awareness of his presence? They did at least remind her of his promise of staying present.

Around lunchtime she noticed how tight her shoulders were. She was rotating them and rubbing her neck when Sandy walked past her dorm room.

"You getting sore from doing laundry?" Sandy stepped in where she could see the folded shorts on top of the pile still warm from the dryer. She was shorter and a bit heavier than Bethany, with her hair colored blonde.

Bethany gave one more shoulder shrug. "I really think it's me worrying about stuff."

Sandy maneuvered behind her and began to massage her neck and shoulders with small and strong hands. "Oh, yeah. You are tight in here. Maybe it's from the diner."

"Hmm. Maybe."

Sandy patted Bethany's shoulder and turned back to the door. "You going to lunch?"

"Yeah. Sure. You?"

"Yes, I am. I'll get my stuff together." She looked down at her shorts and t-shirt as if trying to decide if they were appropriate for the cafeteria.

"Eating downstairs, right?"

"Yeah. That's fine with me."

Bethany knew Sandy had a deluxe food package, which allowed her to eat in some specialty restaurants at the student center without paying more. But that meal plan still required Sandy to eat most of her meals in a dorm dining hall, where Bethany took all her meals.

They arrived downstairs a little past noon. The hubbub in the dining hall was a muted version of the rush hour roar during the fall and spring. There were still students living on campus and taking part in the meal plans, and there were conferences and guests using the dining halls. But sections of the buffet were shut down even during the lunch peak.

Those darkened serving stations gave Bethany a feeling of sneaking in when things were closed, though the dining hall was technically never closed. The promotional material for the service promised food availability at all hours. Bethany had seldom tested that availability between meals. Emily and Jacqueline had each tempted her downstairs after midnight once.

Following Sandy to an open salad station, a grand salad buffet that included various carbs and proteins for a complete meal, Bethany glanced around at the occupied tables. She thought she saw someone she recognized at a big round table, but she couldn't be sure from that distance. His back was to her, and the person with him was collecting his tray as if to leave.

Hurrying a little so she could investigate the sighting, Bethany assembled a familiar combination of ingredients, adding a few more black olives than usual and some sunflower seeds that she hadn't seen available yet this year.

With Sandy trailing behind her on shorter legs, Bethany headed toward that guy who was seated alone. He was looking at his phone, but there still seemed to be food on his plate. She was not too late to join him.

"Lucas?"

He turned and smiled at her. "Hey, Bethany. I thought I saw you still on campus. You staying around for the summer?"

Bethany nodded but turned her attention to her social responsibilities. She shrugged one shoulder toward Sandy. "This is Sandy, one of my suitemates."

Sandy said hi somewhat blandly and set her tray on the table. She was less likely than Emily or Jacqueline to light up at the sight of an attractive male. Sandy was shy, compared to those other girls. "Anyone want milk?" She gestured toward the row of drink machines, tugging self-consciously at her red hoodie.

"Yes, please. Two percent." Bethany settled her tray and pulled out a chair. She focused on Lucas. "You're around all summer? Working?"

He wore a generic royal blue polo shirt with two buttons left free. "Yeah. I'm working on my master's project and getting paid for helping a professor with some data analysis for her experiments."

"Oh, okay. Do most graduate students stick around and work through the summer?" She took a seat almost directly across from Lucas, and closer to where Sandy had left her tray.

"I don't know about *most*. In my department there are usually ongoing experiments that need data collection and analysis. And it's nice to have some more lab and computer time available, with the undergraduates away for the summer. So, it's an attractive option."

"Right. I get it."

"So, what are you doing here this summer?"

Bethany described her work situation and her arrangements with housing and the dining halls, but she didn't describe her relationship with her mother.

When Sandy arrived back at the table, she explained she was still at school because she had an extension for a couple classes she had been taking when she responded to her father's sudden illness. She didn't dwell there long, instead digging into what Lucas was working on. Sandy explored his data collecting work more closely than Bethany had. Sandy had taken more statistics and data analysis courses than Bethany would ever consider, so she could ask some intelligent questions about Lucas's summer job.

He was finished eating, but he stayed seated. "Where's this diner you work at?" He laid his kind eyes on Bethany. His face was clean-shaven today. That was unusual in Bethany's experience of Lucas.

She collected his inviting attention with eye contact that lasted a bit longer than casual conversation might require. She was looking for interest, measuring his level of curiosity about her personal life. His eyes were definitely brown.

Bethany described the location, the staff and management of the diner, and she outlined her regular work hours. "Sunday is a day I try to take off so I can get to church. I miss the young adults' group about half the time because of work, but I carved Sunday mornings out. I also do laundry and homework that day." She felt like she was sharing too much.

"You gonna be there tomorrow? Church?"

"Ah, no, actually. I'm going to visit my grandma down in Illinois. She's been sick and I wanna go check on her."

"Oh. Is she doing better now?"

"Yes. She had water around her heart. They drained it and she seems to be doing lots better now."

"Well, that's good to hear."

"Yeah. My grandma is my favorite person. It really worried me when she was in the hospital."

"How old is she?" Lucas leaned back in his chair, still making no move to push away from the table.

"She's in her eighties." Bethany knew the exact number but couldn't access that data in the moment.

Sandy set her fork down and squinted at Bethany. "Sorry, I forgot to ask you about her. I'm glad she's better."

"Thanks. Yeah, I considered going down to see her during finals, but my aunt and my grandma both talked me out of it." She reached for her milk glass. "Now I'm kinda dreading seeing her sick tomorrow. But that feels selfish." Where did that confession come from? Why was she saying this to Lucas?

He nodded slowly and seemed to be considering something. "It is hard to see people we love getting old. It's hard to think of letting go, especially if she's your favorite grandma." His brow tightened. "Have you lost someone else recently? Or seen some other elderly relative ... in distress?"

"What? No ... not really. Though yesterday was ... strange." How had she gone there? What was Lucas asking?

"I don't know what it's about, but I have this feeling that you had a significant experience recently with an ailing older person." He shrugged casually, as if acknowledging the odd assortment of fragments that had informed his question.

Bethany resisted the temptation to examine the space around Lucas, to see if Jesus was whispering into his ear. That's what it felt like. Sandy was just crunching lettuce and scowling, perhaps too confused by this part of the conversation to even know what she thought about it.

Now Bethany had to decide how much to say. She tipped her head and looked at Lucas. "Are you, like, getting some kind of download ... from, like, Jesus?"

Sandy stopped chewing and turned toward Lucas, perhaps expecting him to laugh or to get up and run for the exit.

But he was nodding. "Yeah. I don't know if it's something you wanna talk about, but I feel like there was something ... significant that happened to you recently."

Facing the realization that Lucas had said approximately the same thing three times now, Bethany knew it was up to her to advance the conversation. She paused to consider again what to tell him. She didn't want to make herself out to be some kind of hero or some kind of kook.

Go ahead. Fear not. Just say what happened. Her invisible advisor helped her decide.

"Well, something significant did happen and it was the weirdest thing." She laughed uncomfortably, not sure she was ready to tell this story in front of Sandy. "But ... on the way home from work last night I ... I thought I heard Jesus tell me to stop at this house." She laughed again. "Telling you about it just reminds me how crazy it was."

"*What* happened?" Sandy held a fork in one hand but was doing nothing that looked like eating. Her deep blue eyes were aimed at Bethany like lasers.

"Uh, well, I felt like I was supposed to go up to this house because there was an old man in there having a heart attack. And he couldn't call 9-1-1 for himself. He needed help right away." She shook her head. "I knew it was insane to follow that thought ... but it was so random that it couldn't have just been my imagination."

Lucas and Sandy both listened closely as Bethany told the story of entering Mr. Pienkowski's house and finding him lying on the floor. They both had their eyes latched on to her, but Sandy's face was frozen in horror. Lucas's face was warm with fascination. Bethany mostly kept her eyes on Lucas as she spoke.

When she finished, Lucas pulled out his phone. "I wonder if there's something on the local news about it."

"What? Why would there be?" As outside the box as the experience had been, Bethany couldn't imagine it was newsworthy.

Sandy was dumbstruck, shaking her head and looking concerned. Was she trying to think of who she should call to help Bethany with her delusions? Was she wondering if it was safe to stay in the same suite as this crazy girl?

"Here. Here it is. Listen to this." Lucas read a story about a good Samaritan who found a neighbor lying on his living room rug having a massive heart attack yesterday evening. "Paramedics have not disclosed the name of the person who called them, but Mr. Paul Pienkowski has been telling everyone in the hospital about the angel sent to save his life."

"Where is that? Where did you find that?" Bethany's voice shrilled. She was feeling a bit lightheaded.

"A local neighborhood news site. I've seen some fun human-interest stories about deer wandering into people's garages and things like that. I thought they might be interested in a story like yours."

"I don't believe it. I never thought anyone would report it or anything." She wondered if the dispatcher had told someone the explanation Bethany gave Mr. Pienkowski for coming to his house.

"So, it's real. It really happened." Sandy was not asking. It was more like she was registering the status change of Bethany's story.

"That is so cool. And Jesus told you to do it. He, like, directed you to that guy's house?" Lucas's voice rose and his grin grew. "That is so cool."

Bethany just nodded, still stunned.

Chapter 24

Grandma

On Sunday morning, Bethany woke to find a text from Lucas. He had asked on Saturday what time she would be leaving for Illinois, but Bethany hadn't pinned down the exact schedule at that point. **"Can I give you a ride to the train station this morning?"**

It was 6:30 a.m. That was early to be texting on a Sunday morning but not too early to be arranging a ride to the train station.

She held her phone above her face and typed with her thumbs. **"Wow. Sure. That would be great. I live in the dorm where we had lunch yesterday."** She wasn't sure if he knew that. Then she added, **"Train leaves St. Paul Street at 8:05."**

"Pick you up at 7:30?"

"Yes. Thanks!!!" She pondered her three exclamation points for a second but rebuked herself for overthinking. The offered ride was a triple-exclamation blessing, especially coming from Lucas.

She lay still in bed for a whole minute, wondering whether she was reading too much into his offer. But that only led her to the exasperated conclusion that she had *no idea* whether she was reading too much into it. She would just have to wait and see.

One cost of accepting a ride from Lucas was the extra time she needed to tend to her hair and makeup. She would have done something to prep for traveling and for seeing Grandma, but she admitted to herself that she was delaying breakfast over getting her makeup just right for Lucas. As if she knew what *just right* looked like.

Straight from the dining hall, carrying her backpack and wearing a big smile, she met him in front of the dorm. The wonder of a ride from the kind and interesting graduate student was getting swirled together with the way he had listened so appreciatively to the story of Jesus leading her to help an old Polish man. That Lucas was now privy to that story was another shiny connector between them.

When she arrived at his compact car, she realized she hadn't told him what she had told about her seeing and talking to Jesus. Telling Lucas about those miraculous interactions felt like full disclosure regarding what she did for Mr. Pienkowski. She didn't take time to study whether that feeling made sense.

"So, are you excited about going to see your grandma?" He turned toward her, his long chin rubbing against the collar of his quarter zip pullover.

"I am, though I'm worried about how she is. You know how a major illness affects old people sometimes."

He nodded then talked thoughtfully about his grandfather's recovery from cancer surgery—a surgery that included the amputation of his leg. "He hasn't been the same since that, but we've all gotten used to the new him. And he's still living a good life, I think."

"Oh. That's encouraging to hear." She allowed a lull in the conversation as he negotiated a turn at an intersection with a few cars moving in various directions.

She cleared her throat. "I wanted to tell you more of the story about Jesus directing me to help that old man. I told part of the, like, background of that to the people on the church van, so I wanted to include you on that part too."

He raised his eyebrows at her, as if impressed that there was more to the already extraordinary story. And those dark brown eyebrows stayed arched toward his hairline as she talked and as he continued to drive. They were parked by the Intermodal Station downtown when she reached the end of her tale. Bethany stopped at the point where the visible Jesus stayed behind while she entered Mr. Pienkowski's front door.

"That is ... amazing!" He shook his head. "And something like this happened to your grandma?"

She nodded. "I also met a couple when I was at music camp one summer who had a similar experience. Both of them did."

He was still shaking his head. "I am ... well, to tell the truth ... I'm really jealous." His voice cracked boyishly. "I would love to meet him like that." He took a huge breath while still smiling at Bethany. Then he glanced at the digital clock on his dashboard. "Ah. You need to go."

"Yeah. Thanks for the ride, Lucas. And thanks for listening to my story." She pulled the door handle. "And for believing me."

"Of course. Jesus can do anything. And I gotta say I have a lot of confidence that your story is true. It just feels real to me."

She didn't know how to respond to that, but she paused after closing the car door behind her and gave him a little wave. "Thanks again."

Bethany managed to get on the right train, doublechecking with a conductor once she was on board. She easily found an empty seat with room to stretch her legs. The weather was questionable, a fifty percent chance of rain both in Milwaukee and Chicago. She assumed that kept the train ridership low—that and it being only eight o'clock on a Sunday morning.

Treadmilling over the details of her conversations with Lucas—all the accumulated conversations she had with Lucas over the course of their acquaintance—overlaid the trip south to Union Station in Chicago. She kept picturing his eyes as she told him about seeing Jesus. Those soft brown eyes had golden stars at the center.

During a half hour wait at the station in Chicago, she got on a Metra train bound west toward Naperville. She pried her spinning thoughts away from Lucas as she neared her destination. She hoped to have about seven hours with Grandma and with Katie. She was hoping Katie would be with her dad, Derek, when he picked Bethany up at the station in Naperville.

Off the train and standing on the parking lot side of the station, Bethany texted confirmation of her arrival to both Derek and Katie.

The reply came back from Derek immediately. **"Katie should be there soon."**

There was no reply from Katie, who must have been driving.

Of course. Her cousin was seventeen. She was of driving age. Apparently, Katie had scaled all the walls required of teens wanting to operate a vehicle in Illinois. Bethany possessed a Wisconsin license. She had no idea whether it was harder to qualify for one south of the border.

Smiling and waving, Katie pulled to the bottom of the stairs in a dark red electric car. Her dad's car, no doubt. Her blonde ponytail and big blue eyes seemed timeless.

She jumped out once the vehicle was parked and greeted Bethany with a vigorous hug next to the passenger door. "Oh, so excited to see you. And I get to spend the whole day with you and Grandma. Then I'll bring you back here."

"Awesome!" Some scheduling uncertainties, of which Bethany was not fully appraised, had left Katie's availability questionable. As much as Bethany looked forward to being with her grandma, having Katie along all day would add to the pleasure.

Inside the car, she confirmed that Katie knew the time of the return train, but she skipped ahead as soon as that was clear. She didn't want to darken the day with dwelling on the shortness of the visit. As they reviewed summer plans and updated each other on news they had shared over the phone, Bethany comforted herself that she would come back down for a longer visit later in the summer. She could take a couple days off work when she had a chance to plan further ahead.

"So, any boys you're interested in?" Katie was an attentive driver, but she bounced in her seat as she asked that question.

"Boys?" Bethany laughed. "It's *men* these days, actually. Or it's supposed to be."

"Yeah, but ..."

"Well, I'm not dating anyone, if that's what you mean. But there is a guy I'm interested in. A graduate student. So definitely not a boy."

"Oh. An older man?" She bounced again.

"Well, I'm sure we're not beyond the *just friends* stage. We're still getting to know each other and mostly what we talk about is Jesus."

"Oh, really? Sounds like a guy Grandma would like."

Bethany chuckled. "Yeah. But she can't have him. I saw him first."

Katie let out a growly laugh. "You gotta save jokes like that for Grandma."

Bethany smiled out the window for a couple seconds. "You think she's okay for joking around?"

"She's okay. I think she feels a little stronger every time I talk to her."

"When did you see her last?"

"In the hospital. Like, three times. She was in there for, like, five days."

"Yeah. I talked to her once after she was back at home. I guess they're figuring out if she needs more care from the retirement facility."

"Sure. She's hoping to keep it like it is, living in the apartment. No kinda care involved in that." A pause followed.

"So, tell me what's the latest with soccer."

"Nothing new. Season is over, with school being out. I'm teaching at a kids' soccer camp next month. It was a good year. Making it to the state semifinals was good. We need to work on scoring next year—I scored the only goal for us in the semis."

"One more year."

"Yeah. Well, I'm pretty sure I'll play in college. I just need to decide whether I wanna go with a big scholarship program or go somewhere that might not even have soccer scholarships for girls. I'll still play. Mom and Dad are gonna help me with school. I mean, I can get some academic scholarships too."

"Great. That sounds great. Yeah, it's good to leave your options open. I'm glad you're willing to take a step down in ... like, competitiveness to get the school you really want."

"Yeah. Offers will come in the fall. We don't have anything formal yet, so I don't even know what my choices will be."

"Got it. Well, I'll keep praying for it to work out the way Jesus wants."

"Yep. Thanks. If Grandma's prayers aren't enough, I'm sure yours will help." She grinned. Maybe it was a joke.

Katie drove like a lifelong resident of that large suburb. Her constant traveling to soccer practices and matches probably taught her something about how to get around Naperville. How often did she drive herself to Grandma's retirement home? Bethany didn't ask.

They parked in a small lot near the front of the complex of buildings. Bethany knew there was a larger long-term lot for visitors around the side, but she assumed Katie knew what she was doing. Bethany was determined not to treat her younger cousin like a little kid, even if her enthusiasm for lots of things was still childlike.

The retirement home always seemed to smell like vanilla cookies and cedar chips. The carpet was probably new, or maybe Bethany just hadn't noticed it before. Katie's spry steps highlighted the cush of the plush carpet.

Bethany was feeling much less spry after her dual train journey, and she was not looking forward to the return trip. She did hope to get some class reading done on the way home, as opposed to staring out the window and obsessing about Lucas or Grandma.

When they exited the stairs to Grandma's second floor hallway, Katie reached into the pocket of her gray joggers and pulled out a key. Perhaps noticing Bethany's curiosity, she explained. "We have a key so Grandma doesn't have to hustle over to the door every time we come to visit."

Bethany laughed. "I know you and her are a lot alike, but I think you're the only one who *hustles* around here."

Katie rolled her eyes and bobbled her head, always full of motion, whether directional or merely kinetic.

Unlocking the door, Katie opened it and knocked. "Hey, Grandma. It's your favorite teenagers." She pushed through and Bethany followed.

"Well, hello, hello." Grandma's voice escalated as she seemed to be coming to greet them.

Bethany faltered at the sight of her grandma gripping the handles of a walker.

Grandma probably saw her concerned expression. "Don't worry, kid. Just a temporary setback. I'll be right as rain in no time." She was dressed the same as Bethany expected, wearing comfortable stretchy slacks and a floral print blouse—heavy on the pinks and purples.

"Good to see you, Grandma. The video chats just aren't the same."

"But I am proud of myself for pulling those off." Grandma reached one arm, inviting a hug.

Bethany slipped past the walker and carefully wrapped her arms around Grandma, regretting her backpack, which kept Grandma from getting an arm around her.

"You brought stuff with you? You're not staying overnight, are you?" Grandma looked a little confused.

"No. Just a couple books. Or a notebook and an eReader, really. And a small gift for you."

"A gift for me? And it's not even my birthday. Is this in honor of my escape from death?"

"Uh. No, but your escape from the hospital is worth celebrating." Bethany was still off balance, and Grandma mentioning death so glibly didn't help settle her.

"How's that walker working? Is it too awkward like you said?" Katie escorted Grandma back toward the living room, where a path to her favorite chair had been cleared.

"I'm getting used to it. Your dad moving things around helped some. I just need to get more practice. Then, about the time I have it mastered, I won't need it anymore."

"That makes sense." Bethany was absorbing the situation in a way she hadn't done from long distance. "As you get stronger, the walker will get easier and then you won't need it."

Grandma had aligned herself in front of the highbacked chair. "I might use a cane though. I can use that to fight off the suitors." She punched one hand, as if imagining a cane in her grip.

"That sounds like a good idea." Katie took hold of the walker. Bethany assumed her cousin's idle affirmation was aimed at the cane, not fighting off suitors.

Grandma lowered herself into the chair with hands firmly planted on both arms. She puffed a big breath, once she landed. "All right. No *Adventure Grandma* this weekend, I can tell ya."

"You feeling pain or anything?" Bethany waited for Katie to wheel the walker around the side of the chair where Grandma could reach it but keep the space open in front of her.

"Just a little sore." She pointed at a spot on her side. "The worst is the way I get tired faster, I think. Still getting my wind back." She perked up. "Oh, I probably forgot to mention to you two. Someone is coming here to pray for me. She's with the same order of nuns as Sister Alison, my old spiritual director. Or I should say former, not old. She's just a kid compared to me."

"What?" Katie scrunched her brow.

"I hope you don't mind. I told her she could come over and pray for me. She believes in healing and thinks she can help me. I forgot this was the day you girls were visiting when I first said, 'yes' to her."

"Oh, that's no problem. We can tag team with her." Bethany sounded like one of the people at her church. But she didn't regret that, not when it came to healing.

"Good. I thought you girls wouldn't mind lending a hand." She raised her head to see Bethany through her glasses, which had slid half an inch down her nose.

"Well, we can give it a try." Katie sounded less enthusiastic than Bethany.

Chapter 25

Sisters

Bethany, Katie, and Grandma teamed up to get lunch together. Seeing how quickly Grandma tired, Bethany didn't let her roll her walker around the little kitchen for long. Half of the items were storebought anyway, delivered to her apartment by a grocery service, no doubt.

After they stowed the last of the storage containers after lunch and slid the dishes into the dishwasher, the doorbell rang.

"That must be her. Sister ... Sister Juanita." Grandma took Bethany's arm and let herself be ushered back to her favorite chair.

Katie headed to the door. "Cool, a sister."

"Another sister, I'd say." Grandma made that exhausted sound again as she landed in her chair. "I talked to her on the phone a couple times and Alison recommended her. Juanita is down here posted in Lisle, or whatever they call it."

"Lisle is right next door to Naperville?"

"Right." Grandma waved a hand toward the window.

Bethany thought that wave was northward, not that she would know the difference. Geographically, she was still a displaced Oregonian.

A cheerful conversation by the apartment door drew their attention and a second later Katie appeared, leading a woman who was a bit shorter than she was. Sister Juanita had a face shaped like a lemon, with a small, pointed chin. Her skin was, however, much closer to the color of a caramel than a lemon. She wore a white cotton blouse and a dark skirt. She wasn't wearing anything that looked like a habit. Not even a head covering.

"Hello, Gladys. Good to see you. And with your girls gathered 'round. Such a blessing."

"Hello, Sister, come on in. My door girl is on duty today, saving me the trip to let you in."

"That's nice. That works out just right. And I'm counting on you girls to help me out. I could have brought one of the other sisters along, but I came alone knowing help was waiting here already."

This sister was nothing like Bethany's picture of Sister Alison, about whom she had heard a lot. But Bethany had never met Alison either, so she was adjusting an already secondhand impression.

Their introductions and greetings were followed by a rumble of thunder.

"Oh. Is it raining out there?" Grandma made a weak effort at turning her head to look at the window.

"It just started. Just sprinkles. I hadn't heard any thunder till now." Juanita's voice coasted lightly, as if the weather didn't interest her. Her tone was the opposite of sharp, but her focus on Grandma seemed quite pointed. "Shall we get to it? I'm sure you all have plans for the day."

"Yeah, sure. Let's do this thing." Grandma looked at Katie and half winked. Obviously, she was imitating her youngest granddaughter with that phrase.

Bethany nodded and started to stand, but her knees nearly buckled when she saw a fifth person in the room. He was there, standing behind Grandma's chair. Visible. She gasped, despite herself, then she looked at Katie and Juanita for their reaction.

Nothing. As if no one was there. As if a Middle Eastern man with a broad smile was not standing behind Grandma's chair. He was wearing his ancient Jesus costume.

He looked directly at Bethany and spoke. "The others can't see or hear me right now. This is how it was for me and your grandma back in the day, so you get to see what that was like for her."

Bethany was stuck in Jesus's tractor beam. She couldn't move. The impulses between her brain and her limbs were getting interrupted, mostly by questions.

"What are you looking at?" Grandma squinted slightly, a hint of good-natured suspicion. If that's even a thing.

"Uh." Bethany started to raise her hand to point at Jesus then some part of her brain—a childish part, no doubt—told her not to point. "Jesus." She nodded her head toward him, leaving her hand hanging half raised.

"Jesus?" Katie yelped.

"Thank you, Lord. Thank you for appearing to this young sister. Lead us now in healing your servant, Gladys." Juanita's voice skipped and quivered, as if tamping an urge to shout *halleluiah.*

Jesus replied to Juanita with a smile. "All right. I will lead you, but you will all need to cooperate. I want you to coordinate with each other." Then he nodded to Bethany.

She took that nod as her prompt to pass on what he had just said. "Uh ... he ... I mean Jesus ... just said he would do what you asked, but we have to work together."

Grandma was staring at Bethany as if she could see the reflection of the man standing behind her in the eyes of her granddaughter. "You can hear him too? He's giving you instructions for us?"

Bethany nodded.

"Really? You really see and hear him?" Katie squeaked, then she groaned. "Why don't I ever get to see him?"

Sister Juanita seemed to be swimming right through all the countervailing currents of craziness. She kept her head up, above the water, and waited for instructions.

"I want Juanita to put her hands on Grandma's head. You girls each touch a hand." Then Jesus nodded, prompting Bethany to pass it on.

She explained those arrangements even as she struggled to imagine why it had to be just so. What difference would it make if Juanita touched Grandma on the shoulder instead? What if Katie touched Grandma's head? When Bethany focused on Jesus again, he had a tolerant smirk on his face. She wouldn't have been surprised if he had rolled his eyes at that moment. But he didn't. Instead, he nodded toward their three places.

And then it got even weirder. Jesus slid around the chair and stood where Sister Juanita would have to stand to touch Grandma's head. For half a second it was Jesus there, then he was invisible, and Juanita had sort of merged with him.

"She can go ahead. She knows how to pray." He said it from where it seemed like he was sharing space with Juanita. He waited. "Tell her."

"Oh. Okay. Oh, he ... uh ... he is right where you're standing, Sister. Uh, he says you know how to pray."

Juanita shivered slightly and then quirked a surprised grin, like someone receiving an unexpected compliment.

"Okay, then. Thank you, Jesus, for guiding us. Thank you for your presence. And thank you for your shed blood on the cross that has made the way clear for the salvation of our souls and of our minds and our bodies. I come in your name to bless this sister. To Gladys's heart, and also her brain, I say be healed of the trauma and of any setback caused by the water and previous infection. Full recovery. Let that come to her, in the name of Jesus."

She turned toward Bethany as if she had finished her part. *Next.*

Bethany followed Juanita's model but focused her blessing on Grandma's hands and legs, their steadiness and strength. When she was done, she looked at Katie.

Katie shrugged. "That all sounds good to me. So, I say, go for it, Jesus." She nodded decisively.

An unorthodox prayer, but it seemed just right to Bethany.

With a satisfied smile, Jesus slipped back to the space behind the chair. His expression was similar to that proud look Bethany had seen on his face two days ago. Maybe this one was proud times three. Or four. At this he raised his eyebrows at her.

Time for another translation, evidently, this time relaying the sights, not the sounds. She told the others about the proud smile on his face and that he seemed to be satisfied.

Grandma turned her head again, this time more vigorously. She leaned forward and twisted her whole torso. "I wish I could see him. I miss ..." She stopped and stared at the place where Bethany could see Jesus. Grandma chuckled. "Well, thanks for that."

Then Jesus went invisible to Bethany and apparently invisible to Grandma as well.

Katie was staring open-mouthed, her eyes wide and glistening.

Juanita, still beaming, breathed heavily. Her hands were clasped together beneath her chin. She stood in reverent silence.

Closing her mouth, finally, Katie shook her head. "What just happened?"

"Well, I feel a whole lot better, for one thing." Grandma's voice contained a bit of a giggle, calling to mind a toddler being tickled. She seemed to be reserving outright laughter, as if waiting for something even merrier to come along.

Juanita took a deep breath, transitioning back to the business at hand. "You feel stronger, then?"

Grandma nodded. "I do. I feel good. I think I could stand up on my own pretty easy right now."

Bethany considered the significance of her grandma's self-evaluation, wondering if that restoration might only be temporary, or even imaginary. Grandma had witnessed healings over the years. She was probably more inclined than Bethany to associate Jesus's appearing with people getting well.

Placing her hands on the arms of the chair, Grandma scootched forward. Juanita reached toward her but pulled her hands back in obvious self-correction, and Grandma nodded her agreement with that restraint.

"Let's give this a try." She leaned her head over her knees and pressed with her palms on the golden, plush arms of the chair. Her hands shook only a little with the effort.

Was she stronger? Why the strain? Bethany was piling up these questions but keeping them contained entirely in her head.

Katie leaned toward Grandma with one outstretched hand, but she didn't touch her either, only mutely offering to serve as spotter in case she needed it.

But Grandma didn't need a spotter to execute that move. She stood, with just a little hesitation on the way up. She looked steady when she was upright. Of course, Bethany knew she had been able to stand before the prayer time. This was no miracle. A spark in Grandma's eyes and the intensity of her grin, however, promised something more. Maybe even something miraculous.

"Okay. I did that. Not too difficult either." She passed her mirthful gaze over the three women watching her. All three still held their hands toward her, reserved but ready.

"Clear the way, I wanna walk some." Grandma made a swimming motion with both arms and giggled—a giggle that seemed impossible from the frail, old woman that had greeted Bethany in this apartment just over an hour ago.

Juanita chuckled and stepped back, gesturing with her right hand like a doorman welcoming a resident home for the night. Katie took a succession of backward baby steps, staying close while still making a path. Her pale brows were tightened to her eyes and her lips pursed.

Wondering where Jesus was in all this, Bethany noticed a sort of hum at her left ear. That led to a question about why he had to be invisible now and why he was making that noise next to her ear. Not that she minded, really. It was the warm sort of comforting noise she would have welcomed throughout her life, if her mother had been different. And her father too. Or, perhaps, if Jesus had made his presence known earlier.

Grandma forged ahead. One small step for her, one modest leap for Bethany's faith. The eighty-something-year-old grandma did not run laps. She didn't even really stride. But her steps looked steady, similar to the way she got around the last time Bethany saw her in reasonably good health.

"Does that feel good?" Juanita struck a caregiver's note, checking in as she would with elderly folks recovering from this or that.

Grandma turned back toward them, standing now at the near end of the little hallway to her front door. Her eyebrows jogged playfully. "Anybody wanna race?"

And they all laughed.

Chapter 26

Katie

All four women had tea, which Grandma insisted on serving without any assistance. She was showing off, as far as Bethany was concerned. But showing off something Jesus had done for her was probably allowed.

Juanita kept trying to excuse herself, insisting on letting the girls visit their grandma without a strange person in the apartment.

"I don't consider you a stranger anymore, Sister." Grandma set a plate of windmill cookies on the coffee table that had been returned to its rightful place in the center of the living room rug.

"Thank you, Gladys. I agree with you, but I will be getting on."

Grandma took her hand and walked with Juanita toward the hallway.

The sister turned and bowed slightly to the two young women who were rising from the couch in unison. "Thank you, girls. Thank you for showing me Jesus in a new way."

Bethany held her breath for a second. "Well, I'm not taking any credit for that, but I'm very grateful for you coming to pray for Grandma. You and Jesus." She wasn't sure about the exact words she was saying. Her heart was full of gratitude, but her mouth didn't seem to know exactly what to do with that trove of thankfulness.

Juanita just smiled and followed Grandma to the front door.

With the other two women out of sight, Bethany looked squarely at Katie—maybe for the first time since Grandma's remarkable improvement.

"What are you thinking?"

Katie blinked at her cousin a few times. "I'm thinking about other times I was with Grandma and things like this happened. It's been a while. I guess I keep wondering why that is. Like, what changed from then to now? Or in the in-between time?"

Grandma was returning to the living room. She was not striding boldly, but she had returned to the pace Bethany had seen on earlier visits—maybe as far back as her first visit to Grandma's house.

Before those days, Bethany had only known her other grandmother. And Grandma Marconi was a prickly character who kept Bethany at arm's length. She was the most likely person to criticize the cut of Bethany's hair or the length of her skirt. Grandma Marconi favored shorter skirts back then. "You have to show your wares, young lady." She was probably in the beginning stages of Alzheimer's at that point, though it had not yet been diagnosed.

Contrast that with the smiling, hugging little lady that greeted Bethany in her living room in Wisconsin. Grandma Hight, despite the name, was half a head shorter than Grandma Marconi, and shorter than Bethany as well.

Back then, Bethany spent a full day with Grandma Hight without hearing a single criticism of anything or anyone, not even a jab at Bethany's mother, who had kept them apart all those years. Grandma Marconi was constantly poking at her own daughter.

Grandma Hight seemed just the same now as on that first visit, though the venue had changed.

"Looking good, Grandma," Katie spoke playfully.

Bethany grinned and pushed back her small doubts about the dramatic change in Grandma's movement. Could it be permanent?

Chuckling, Grandma waved a hand at Katie. "Doesn't take much to impress you people, I see."

Katie giggled and shook her head, which caused her blonde ponytail to dust the back of her collar.

"I'm actually feeling a little tired. Like I could use a short nap just now." Grandma stood at the edge of the rug, looking an implied question at the cousins.

"Are you okay?" Bethany let her shoulders droop a bit.

"I am fine, just a bit tired. I have been known to take a little nap after lunch." She gently scolded, raising her head to see Bethany through her glasses.

"Maybe getting healed is ... an exertion." Katie tilted her head to one side. She probably didn't know more about healing than Bethany, but she did know a lot about exertion.

Bethany had seen a few people recover from physical ailments when folks at her church gathered around to pray. Most prayers there were about emotional or spiritual healing, but there were a few noteworthy physical healings within their moderate-sized congregation. Being tired after one of those experiences seemed entirely plausible, whether Bethany had heard about that post-operative symptom or not.

"We could go for a walk." Bethany looked toward the window. The thunder hadn't lasted long, and the rain tapping on the window had ceased. Only now was Bethany noticing any of that. Other things had been crowding her attention during this visit.

"That's an excellent idea. Take the big umbrella I have in the closet there in case it rains again. Rain and no lightning." Grandma wagged a finger at them to punctuate that electrical storm warning.

Bethany lifted her phone off the coffee table. The weather app claimed it wouldn't rain during the next hour. "Okay. Katie has a key, right? So we can let ourselves back in if you're still asleep."

"Yes. That's true." Grandma glanced at Katie, but even the pace of that glance betrayed some weariness.

Aware that Grandma generally took an afternoon nap, Bethany had nevertheless gotten used to her skipping that daily rest when her granddaughter visited. But today was different. Certainly, before the prayer time Grandma would have begged off in favor of a little rest.

So Katie and Bethany each kissed Grandma on the cheek and wished her a good nap before heading to the front closet and out the door. Bethany carried the long navy blue umbrella as Katie pulled the front door gently shut, even though Grandma was probably not in her bedroom yet.

A large sigh from Katie raised a question for Bethany.

"Are you still worried about Grandma?"

"Oh. Not more than usual. I just ... well, I guess I always worry about her getting older. And I kinda ... worry about her having to count on people coming over to pray for her to be healed like this." She released another sigh as Bethany gestured toward the stairs, bypassing the elevator.

"Like, feeling that the healing stuff just proves she's ... like, fragile?"

Katie paused her answer as she pushed through the door. "Yeah. I guess that *is* it. I mean, it's okay with me that Jesus heals Grandma once in a while. I've gotten a couple things healed before too, a few years back. So that's fine with me. I believe in that." They approached the bottom of the stairs and Katie surged ahead to push the lobby door open. "I guess needing Jesus to bail her out—health wise—just makes the point that she's getting old. She won't be around forever."

"Does that make you think differently about going away to college?"

Her head snapping toward Bethany as a preliminary answer, Katie barked a laugh. "I haven't said that to anyone. How did you know?"

"I had the same thought when I was offered a piano scholarship on the east coast. I didn't wanna be so far from Grandma."

Katie laughed again. "You're like me. Not worried about being far away from our parents but not wanting to leave Grandma."

Bethany laughed too. "Okay, guilty as charged. But Grandma is a lot older than my dad ... or my mom. So I have that excuse."

"Mm-hmm." Katie held the outside door for Bethany.

The post rain air was one of the most convincing signs of summer Bethany had inhaled yet that year. Sunny days in the eighties in the spring seemed flighty, abandoning the area at the first threat of some weather front. But warm air that stayed after a rainstorm was a sure sign that summer was coming, or even here already.

"So, you said you were looking at some smaller schools. Are those around here?"

"Yeah. There's a couple private schools and some Christian colleges that have a pretty good women's soccer program. Not the kind of scholarships they have at big universities, but some financial help and a chance to play competitive soccer."

"Football, you mean."

"We stick with *soccer,* so people don't boo us for being football snobs."

"We?"

"Us soccer chicks." A nasal laugh followed.

"You could probably be the star of the team if you went to one of those smaller schools, right?" Bethany didn't know how much that counted as either an advantage or a disadvantage. Most of what she knew of the sporting world came from listening to Katie talk about her school team, her club team, and her summer soccer camps. A year-round occupation.

"That's something that has me checking my ... motives. Like, am I just wanting to be the big star?" She shrugged. "It's something the coaches talk about—getting to go to college to play with other girls that are used to being the best on their high school team. But I guess there could be others like me that just go to the smaller school for other reasons, not interested in the big scholarships or in trying to play professional soccer someday."

"I've never heard you say anything about playing professionally before."

"Uh. Well, it's far off. And ... well, I guess I feel like talking about it could, like, jinx me, or something."

"Hmm. Better not let Grandma hear you talking about jinxes." A moderately ominous tone came with that moderately facetious warning. Bethany tossed her head to send a strand of hair away from her face.

"Ha. Did she catch you saying something like that?"

"She must have, though I don't remember exactly what I said to get that warning."

"Like, that we have Jesus, so we don't have to worry about jinxes and stuff?"

"Something like that."

"Do you ever wonder if you just believe ... well, all of it, just because of Grandma?"

Bethany admired the row of townhouses they were walking past. Maybe they had new white paint on the trim. They looked stunning in the emerging sunlight. She laughed a little self-consciously. "Yeah, I have thought that." She recalled one of her early conversations with Jesus, then she snickered. "Grandma would say you and me are two peas in a pod."

Skipping briefly and chuckling, Katie said, "Yeah. She would." Her chuckles wound down. "I don't mind. I think she's right." She rested a winning smile on her cousin.

Bethany didn't ever want to be far from Grandma. She would also stay in touch with Katie, no matter where either of them went in the future.

Chapter 27

Rests

The grass painfully green, the trees fully leafed out, and the sun dazzling on the droplets left by the storm, Bethany's walk with Katie sparkled. The air was sweet with roses and honey-suckle.

The girls returned to Grandma's apartment after forty-five minutes of touring the neighborhood. The silence of her place was as thick as the pile carpet. Bethany opened the coat closet and settled the unused umbrella next to the doorpost, where it joined one of Grandma's canes. Katie carefully closed the front door with only the gentlest click.

Being in Grandma's apartment while she slept was new. Bethany had, of course, been in the living room while Grandma went to some other part of the apartment. But this afternoon felt like Katie and Bethany were explorers entering a holy place—a place they should not venture on their own. Katie might have been feeling it, stepping into the living room as stealthily as a watched rabbit.

After a faint shuffling and the clearing of a familiar throat, Grandma's bedroom door made a low creak, a note on the bass clef. Something about that tonal observation made Bethany want to play the piano. Strange how that urge snuck up on her.

"How was your walk, dears?" Grandma was straightening her short-sleeved blouse and squinting at them even though she was wearing her glasses.

"It was great. Your neighborhood is beautiful after the rain." Katie plopped onto the couch.

"And the company was grand." Bethany used a phrase she had heard from Grandma.

"Yes. I do believe that. Both of those things." Grandma stopped next to Bethany. "I expect I can get out for a walk soon."

"But you won't go out by yourself. Not around the neighborhood." Bethany's tone was leading, not demanding, but meant to persuade.

Grandma looked Bethany in the eyes. "You're right, of course. I'll get someone to come with me. Maybe one of the eligible younger men around here."

"Or me?" Katie sounded like the twelve-year-old Bethany had first met with Grandma in Chicago.

"Or you." Grandma gave Katie a wistful gaze. "I suppose I could tell my beaus to wait until my granddaughter goes off to soccer practice before they take me on an excursion around the neighborhood."

"There's always that. Soccer practice." It was a throw away comment from Bethany, just gliding along with the friendly banter.

Grandma was still eyeing her. "What about you? Are you practicing piano these days?"

It had been a while since Grandma had asked anything like that. Bethany had never resented questions about piano when they came from Grandma. She had been grateful for Grandma's gentle restraint when she did inquire. This current query startled her a bit, however, given the thought just a minute ago about wanting to play. Interesting coincidence.

As Bethany nodded distractedly, something occurred to her. "There's a piano downstairs, isn't there?"

Smiling, as if she had done this play before and knew not only her own lines but those of her costar as well, Grandma gave one deep nod. "Shall we go see if it's available?"

"Sure. Let's do that." Bethany turned toward Katie, wondering if she should apologize to her cousin for this unplanned musical interlude. Assuming the piano was available.

Walking to the elevator with Grandma and Katie was something Bethany had done a time or two before. Still, it felt unfamiliar. Was that because of the complications regarding Grandma's health? Bethany had drastically reduced her expectations after Grandma's trip to the hospital. Now she had to adjust again after the healing.

As soon as the elevator door opened to the lobby, Bethany's heart sank. She could hear someone playing a Gershwin tune on a piano. She couldn't recall the name of that tune immediately, but that point was academic. The gift of music she had hoped to give her grandma would have to be shelved for some indeterminate time.

But Grandma pushed on, with a beckoning wave for the girls to follow. "I think that's Mr. Peyer. He won't mind giving up his seat to a prodigy."

That was Grandma's word for Bethany's talent, as if she knew no other way to say it. It was like Bethany was a member of a guild, the prodigies' guild. Bethany carried this whimsical observation silently, trusting her grandma for what lay ahead.

"Hello, Allan. How are you?" Grandma raised her voice above a restful passage in the tune the old gentleman was playing.

He sat placidly at the baby grand piano, sharing his smile with all three of the new arrivals. He addressed Grandma easily, while still playing. "Gladys. I am well. Has my playing disturbed your nap?"

Bethany caught a glance from Katie. Apparently, Mr. Peyer knew Grandma well enough to know about her afternoon naps.

"Of course, not. No. We came down to see if we could use the piano for a bit. My granddaughter would like to play me a song."

"Oh, that would be wonderful. I've heard you are quite the piano maestro. Maestra, I guess it should be." Mr. Peyer continued to play, but Bethany noted a slight increase in his tempo.

She knew the tune well enough to see the end approaching. She admired Mr. Peyer's touch—the gentle caress of his fingers on the keys and the ease with which he played while speaking to the new arrivals.

When he finished, he bowed to the small patch of applause. Another woman had stepped into the lounge, behind Bethany and the others. She clapped the loudest and longest.

"Are you giving up your seat so easily, Allan?" The woman teased with flirtatious familiarity.

Mr. Peyer was a handsome old man of gentle charm. He was tall and hunched, with a sweep of gray hair around a spotted baldness at the back of his head. Bethany knew the math of old age. She could guess at the disproportion in a facility like this, the number of men versus women and how many of them would be single.

"I am yielding the bench to a greater talent. I was merely the warmup act this afternoon."

Bethany grinned at his outgoing generosity and noted that she only blushed a little. She was not shy about her talent, and she didn't intend to hide from it, even if she had chosen not to spend any more of her life on stage, tallying the encores.

She took the seat offered by Mr. Peyer. The cushioned bench was as warm as the greeting she felt from the old man.

With no sheet music, she had to select something she knew well and something she had practiced recently, if only on her electronic keyboard. She thought of Chopin's Sonata Number 3. She liked it for its brash start, followed by gentle passages that never seemed to rise again to that opening announcement. The adamant start would rouse her, get her going.

She took a long slow breath, settled her hands on the keys and let the music begin. It flowed into her soul first before it coursed through her arms and hands and fingers.

The piano was just slightly out of tune on three keys she had noted during Mr. Peyer's playing. She used that observation to adjust her contact on those offending keys to minimize their impact on the feeling of the song.

It took only seconds before she felt as if she were alone in the room. Alone with the music. The piece was not very long. She had taken that into account, with three elderly people standing on the parquet floor watching and listening. The few minutes of playing skated past her and away—dynamic with crescendos but twirling on ballet slippers for most of the composition.

The feeling of time rushing past turned the tune more melancholy. Could her listeners sense her deepening mood during the contemplative sections? None of them had known her when she lived almost exclusively through music. They wouldn't recognize the sense of loss she was encountering now—this journey into music, the land of her childhood. That homeland had been populated by performances and tainted with pressure for perfection.

With no real pressure today, she grinned at the applause from Grandma, Katie, Mr. Peyer, and his lady friend. And she smiled at herself to some extent. Then she noticed another figure standing just past Grandma, a familiar face visible only for a moment, appearing long enough to send affirmation with his eyes. She was beginning to believe that he was proud of her no matter what she did or how she did it.

Then he was gone.

But not gone.

Just invisible.

Chapter 28

Celebration

While sitting in Grandma's living room late that afternoon, Bethany thought she could see an idea land on her grandma, who was generally not inclined to conceal her discoveries from her own face.

"I think we should go out to dinner. I got a nice little tax refund check from the federal government last month, and I feel like celebrating tonight."

Bethany's train was supposed to leave the Naperville station at 6:33. She checked her phone for places to eat near the train. Katie and Grandma tossed restaurant ideas back and forth.

"You know, I haven't had a good steak for quite a while. The stuff they serve at the dining hall here is okay but it's not the best. Is there a nice steak place? Not too fancy. You know." Grandma was watching the two girls searching on their phones.

Through her dad, Bethany knew that Grandma had an IRA from grandpa, as well as her social security checks. She got along simply and with little help from either of her kids, as far as Bethany knew. She had learned from Katie how to deflect Grandma's attempts to spend money on her grandchildren. Apparently, Katie's siblings had dumped on her once for accepting too many gifts from Grandma. Bethany hardly knew her older cousins, but she thought well of them, as fellow devotees and protectors of Grandma Hight.

Bethany assumed accepting a nice dinner from Grandma was okay just this once, especially because Grandma had reason to celebrate and needed some companions with whom to do that. Companions and a good steak.

The three ladies drove to a moderately-priced restaurant not far from the train station. The worst-case scenario would have Bethany trotting half a mile with her supper unfinished, if service was particularly slow. But they walked into the restaurant before five, which was the only reason they were able to get a table on a Sunday in downtown Naperville on short notice.

"It's what you have to expect when you eat with old folks," Grandma said, as they walked along the dark red carpet and followed a slender young hostess with long black hair.

"We're always glad to have early diners." The girl was evidently assuming she was included in Grandma's explanation, or apology.

When they took their seats, Bethany thanked the smiling hostess with a feeling of amity for a fellow restaurant worker.

"Sky's the limit tonight, girls, though no drinking. I don't wanna get anybody in trouble." Grandma's voice grumbled through that mock warning.

"Good thing I'm not a vegetarian." Katie ignored the drinking comment and targeted the menu. Maybe she was checking to confirm Grandma could afford this place.

"They do have vegan and veggie options." Bethany was curious if this was one of those places that charged extra for the privilege of not eating meat or if it offered a discount based on the lack of an animal sacrifice. Working in a restaurant had sharpened her skepticism about food and business. And the business of food.

But this was a celebration, and Bethany had no trouble keeping that in mind. Dinner with Grandma and Katie was a special treat.

Katie was grinning at Grandma, her menu resting on the table.

"Why are you smiling like that, my dear?" Grandma peered over her glasses at the dimpled blonde across from her.

"I'm just so happy you're feeling better, Grandma. I can't get over it."

"Oh, well, me too. And I don't think you have to get over a thing like that. Gratefulness is the best attitude all the time." She bobbled her head and returned her eyes to the menu. Then she looked at Bethany as if just recalling something. "Do you see him now?"

Bethany recoiled at the surprise inquiry and glanced around, grateful her grandma hadn't said explicitly who she was talking about. Shaking her head, she reported the current state of Jesus's visibility. "I do try to remind myself that he's here even when I don't see him, but I don't see him right now."

"Well, my senses aren't super sharp, I suppose." Grandma peered left and right, still holding her menu. "But I do feel his presence now."

"You think he came to dinner with us?" Katie bounced her eyebrows. She must have been joking. Surely, she had heard Grandma's assurances that Jesus always accompanied her to dinner. *Her* being Grandma. And *her* being Katie.

"It does make me wonder ..." Grandma cut herself short when their waiter approached the table.

"Hello, ladies. Let me guess—Grandma is paying for dinner." He raised his eyebrows and looked for confirmation of his insight or his lucky guess.

"I am doing that. These are my granddaughters, and we are celebrating."

"Oh, is it a special occasion?"

"It's always a special occasion whenever I get together with my grandkids. Having these two lovelies with me is reason enough." Grandma leaned back a little, the height of the waiter challenging her bent neck.

"That sounds just right to me. Can I get you started with some drinks? Though I will have to see some ID from you three."

He leaned his head toward Grandma, his blue eyes wide with mock suspicion.

"No drinking. It's a Sunday. There was a time when places didn't even serve alcohol on a Sunday. But us girls are too young to drink, anyway."

"Understood. We do have some alcohol-free cocktails, or I could bring you iced tea or lemonade. We have freshly squeezed lemonade this evening."

"Squeezed it yourself, I'm guessing." Bethany teased him, letting the menu rest on the table.

"Don't ask to smell my hands." He took a whiff without getting his hand very near his nose. If he did squeeze the lemons, he would have worn a plastic glove, but she knew that didn't keep your hand from smelling like freshly polished furniture the rest of the evening.

"I'll take your word about that part." Bethany returned her eyes to the menu.

"Let's get an appetizer. I see they have quesadillas. I had that with Bill, your dad." She looked at Bethany. "Enough cheese to make a Wisconsinite happy."

"Spicy cheese?" Bethany looked at the waiter, thinking Grandma shouldn't be ordering jalapeno-laced cheese.

"No. Very mild, but we include three salsas with it. You choose." He pointed to a list on the menu in Bethany's hands.

After a brief back and forth on flavors and ingredients, they ordered the quesadillas and salsas, as well as salads. Katie was still pondering her main course, so they postponed ordering entrees.

While they waited for the server to return, Bethany asked something about Grandma's healing that had been percolating in her brain all afternoon. "Do you think you got ... better because of the combination of things that came together today? Was it, like, the right ingredients or something?" She kept her voice down. There were a few other early diners at tables in the wood-paneled room. No one was seated right next to them, but Bethany was conscious of ears around her.

Grandma sort of shrugged her face, her cheeks tightening and her brows bending. "I gave up trying to figure out that kinda thing a while back. The folks I've met that had similar things happen, with Jesus visible and such, are just glad it happened. They have no idea why it happened and had no way to be sure the things they saw with him around wouldn't have occurred if he wasn't visible." She shrugged her shoulders now. "I'm not much on speculating." She glanced at Katie, who was setting down her menu. "I think I get myself in trouble when I try to add it all up and say I know the whys and the wherefores."

Katie nodded. "I'm ready to order."

The waiter was on the way toward them with a tray bearing one lemonade and two iced teas. Perfect timing. At least for ordering. Bethany regretted losing the strands of the answer Grandma had offered. But *I don't really know* was basically the answer she had given so far.

Their drinks were followed soon after by a heaping plate of tortillas stuffed with cheese and sliced into wedges. The waiter promised salads soon and Grandma glanced at her watch as he walked away.

"I'm thinking it still might get a little tight on our time at the end, and I feel like I have something to tell the waiter—a message Jesus wants him to hear." She raised her eyebrows at each of the girls.

Katie froze with a slice of quesadilla between her lips. Then, chewing with her mouth full, she nodded.

"When did you get this ... idea?" Bethany wasn't sure what Grandma called it or if her label would be the same as what the people at church would call it.

"It's been sort of stirring in me since we first talked to him, and I wanna do it before we have to hustle off to catch the train, if it comes to that."

"That's okay with me. Good idea to take the pressure off in case time gets short at the end."

Katie sipped her lemonade before responding. "It makes me nervous to think about it. I mean, telling someone that Jesus is talking to them seems risky." She picked up another quesadilla wedge. Apparently, she wasn't nervous enough to spoil her appetite.

"We'll be just fine. Even if I think it's from Jesus, I don't worry about whether other folks believe it. I can't control that. It's the sorta thing Sister Alison talked about in our video calls."

"Virtual spiritual director. That's very modern of you, Grandma." Katie grinned her playful admiration.

That comment deepened Bethany's curiosity over how much Katie talked to Grandma about her spiritual journey. The poke was mildly funny, but Bethany was getting the impression that her cousin was keeping herself at the edge of faith. Not diving in like Grandma or like Bethany intended to do.

The waiter came by and dropped off their salads, moving the appetizer into the center of the table to accommodate.

Grandma introduced her message. "You said your name is Kurt, right?"

He nodded, unloading the last of the salad plates.

"Well, Kurt ..." Grandma paused to clear her throat. "When is the last time you called your sister?"

"My sister?" He scowled, reddish brown eyebrows conspiring together over vigilant eyes. "How did you know I *have* a sister?" His face brightened, as if he had discovered a cheat to this game.

Bethany was thinking it was a percentage guess, whether he had a sister, though not a very high percentage. His animated response implied that there was something significant about Grandma discovering the existence of his sibling.

"I don't know if you have a sister, or I didn't know before you said that. I just had this inkling. Sort of a leading from God, I think. I think he's saying that you'll find an opening with her if you make the call, instead of waiting for her to call you. And she has some good news she wants to tell you."

"What ...?" His voice climbed more than an octave on that one word.

"Grandma's had messages for people before like that and usually they're right on." If Katie was doubtful about fully investing in God, she wasn't doubtful about Grandma's gifts.

"Really? That's interesting." Kurt was already a step away from the table. "I'll have your dinners in just a few minutes."

Grandma sighed. Was that frustration or just a release of tension? "Well, all I can do is give it a try." She stared after Kurt and fell silent for a moment.

Bethany suspected her grandma was praying for Kurt. She said a silent prayer as well.

It took more than a few minutes for their entrees to arrive. And Kurt didn't bring them. Bethany had seen this at other restaurants, including her diner. Food was ready, and the server was not, so someone covered for them. This restaurant might even have a designated plate presenter, though the woman who brought their main course made little ceremony of it.

For a second, it looked as if Grandma would ask that other server about Kurt, but she appeared to stow her question. And the look on her face was more satisfaction than surrender, which, of course, made Bethany curious.

They were cutting their meat and comparing the quality of their selections when Bethany next sighted Kurt. Grandma was dividing her steak to reserve half to take home, but she seemed to notice Bethany's attention and lifted her head.

Kurt arrived beside their table a few seconds later. His tousle of red-brown hair looked like he had been running his hands through it. "How are your meals?" As bright and enthusiastic as he had sounded when they first arrived, this question clunked hollowly, like a formulaic recitation. He seemed to be breathing harder than normal.

"This is fine. Just like I ordered. Thank you." Grandma looked up at him as Bethany and Katie also said their meals were good.

"Did you call her?" Grandma set her fork down.

Bethany snickered, amazed again at Grandma's boldness. But was it boldness if she simply believed something Jesus was telling her?

Kurt inhaled a huge breath and held onto it an extra second. "I don't know what to think. I mean, I guess I should thank you. But I gotta admit, I am, like, weirded out."

"You did call her." Grandma's face softened.

He was nodding. "I did. And she was happy to hear from me." His eyes wandered around the room. "And she said she'd been wondering if she should call me with her news but wasn't sure what I'd think." He paused and looked hard at Grandma. "Did you know ... did you, like, get the message that she was pregnant?"

"Oh." Grandma's hand rose toward her mouth. "No. I didn't hear *that*, but I had a feeling. I kinda guessed it was something like that." She chuckled. "So how do you feel about being an uncle?"

"How do you know I'm not already an uncle?" Again, he offered playful resistance.

"*Are* you?"

He hissed a laugh. "No." He continued to laugh so that his chest shook. "No, this will be my first niece or nephew."

"You don't know which it is?"

"Not yet." He raised his eyebrows. "What do you say?" Perhaps he was still teasing.

"Oh, I'm not even gonna take a chance on that. I really don't know, but I suspect it doesn't matter to you. You're gonna be happy to be an uncle to that little person, whoever they are."

Kurt covered his forehead with one pale hand and stood still like that for two heartbeats. He shook his head and then smiled at Grandma. "You're amazing."

Katie snorted at that. Of course, Grandma was amazing. She was amazing even when she didn't know everything. She was amazing when Jesus didn't show up and heal her, or when he didn't give her a message to pass on to a waiter.

"I don't think that's it, but I am thoroughly convinced that God is amazing." Grandma deflected the praise with a winning grin.

Chapter 29

Strangers

As melancholy as was the goodbye at the train station after dinner, Bethany imagined how much harder it would have been if Grandma was still struggling to walk and constantly worn out by that struggle. Nothing inhibited the repeated hugs and laughter at the bottom of the station stairs.

The two trains back to downtown Milwaukee provided opportunity for Bethany to get ahead on her reading for World Literature Survey, her class that started after Memorial Day. It was a sampling of all the modern literature of the world in four weeks. Lots of reading. But keeping her mind latched onto the assigned short stories was like a sword fight in an old swashbuckling movie. The hero prevails for half a minute, then the villainous forces of distraction get an advantage, then the hero ... etc. She was just glad the hero of productive concentration didn't succumb during that dangerous final twist where it looked like he was a goner.

Bethany preferred being the hero in that kind of story and was not at all interested in being a damsel in distress. Her mother had taught her that and Grandma Hight reinforced it. Her Grandma Marconi had made the most of that damsel role, as far as Bethany could tell.

These distracting thoughts about Grandma Marconi versus Grandma Hight were part of that mental struggle toward the end of the trip. She took a deep breath as the train pulled into the station in downtown Milwaukee. It was late. It had been a long and eventful day. She wasn't going to beat herself up over the strain to stay focused. During the bus ride toward campus, the final short leg of the trip, Bethany didn't even try to read, which worked out for the best because her dad called.

"How are you, Bethany?"

"I'm good, Dad. Had a great visit with Grandma and Katie."

"Oh, good. Did you see Patty?"

"No. Was I supposed to?"

"She was hoping to see you. I guess she was too busy or something."

"Yeah. Katie picked me up and drove us around. So that's new."

"Right, you girls are aging fast."

"Ha. Look who's talking."

"Uh-huh. I'm glad you got to see your grandma. How does she seem to you?"

"Exactly the same." That response jumped the turnstile. Only after she heard herself say it did Bethany realize she needed to fill in some details about what happened.

Her dad replied before she could add that backstory. "Well, when you say she's the same, you mean her attitude is still good?"

"No. More than that. It was amazing, really. Grandma was healed, I think. I mean, I saw this really big improvement when me and Katie and this Sister Juanita prayed for her."

"Sister Juanita?"

Bethany laughed. She wasn't doing a great job of telling the story, so she went back to the beginning of Grandma inviting Sister Juanita over, or maybe accepting her offer to come pray. She finished her synopsis when the bus slowed, approaching the stop next to campus.

Staggering against the wobbles of the bus, Bethany gripped the overhead rail. Her backpack grazed the seat of a woman who was sitting with a small child.

"Sorry."

"Oh, no problem. Bless you, sister." The woman raised intense, dark eyes and offered a knowing smile with the corners of her mouth.

"Oh. Bless you too." And, with that, Bethany was out the door. As she landed on the pavement, she calculated how much that woman might have heard of what she had been telling her dad.

"Who was that?" Dad had waited patiently for her commuting transition.

"A woman on the bus. I guess she was listening to my story."

"Ha. I wonder what she thought about it."

"She called me *sister*."

"Maybe she thinks you're a nun too."

"After meeting Sister Juanita, I consider that a compliment."

"Well, not everyone sees Jesus or sees people getting healed. So, I guess you don't have to be a nun, but you've got something special, dear."

"Yeah? I guess I do, and I got most of it from Grandma. Along with Jesus, of course." When she said his name, she tossed a wishing well hope that he might appear, but she saw no sign of him.

"Okay. Good to hear your story. I'll have to call your grandma now to see how she's doing. Or call tomorrow, I guess."

"Yeah. She was way better, but she needed a nap in the middle of the afternoon. So, I suspect she'll be going to bed soon."

"Sure. That makes sense." He paused. "Well, goodnight, Bethany."

"Goodnight, Dad." As she ended the call, she wondered about her dad's mild response to yet another miracle story. He reminded her of Katie—friendly to the idea of Jesus and healing, but only in a neighborly way. Not ready to move right in.

Bethany used her keycard to enter the dorm lobby. It was past ten. Her feet dragged with weariness. She was learning about the impact of positive stress. Even being with her two favorite people could be tiring.

On the stairs she listened again for her invisible friend. Though hearing no sound from him, she smiled when she recalled his appearance in Grandma's apartment.

The next day was Memorial Day. Bethany slept until eight and took her time getting awake and ready. The diner was open. It was an all-hands-on-deck holiday. Tables would be full from breakfast until closing. She was glad she didn't have to work breakfast. She ate a big meal in the dining hall, with lots of protein, to prepare for another high-stress day.

Bethany had forgotten about playing piano for Grandma and Katie and the other residents until she was walking to work. She was a little early when she approached a piano store. It was open. A bright yellow sign said, "Memorial Day Sale."

Her journey to or from work had taken her past that store several times when she chose one of her alternative routes. Maybe spending the previous day with Grandma and seeing a miracle from Jesus was the sort of thing that sent her in an unconventional direction. The open door of the piano store seemed to vacuum her up.

When she stepped into the shady store, a middle-aged man was talking to a couple next to a baby grand. The brand name of the pianos was unfamiliar. Maybe she had heard of them, but they were not the Steinways or Yamahas she played in concert halls or in most practice rooms. As she cast her gaze around the shop, it occurred to her that it might be easy to sign up for a piano practice room at the university during the summer.

She felt the salesman glance at her. She was dressed for work—black slacks and a white cotton blouse. She wasn't exuding anything like the wealth required to be a paying customer. Though she could buy sheet music here, if she were so inclined.

Today she was following a longing that gained intensity as she stood next to a glossy new piano. Bethany glanced again at the salesman and the couple he was talking to. They were laughing about something, ignoring her. She was of no concern.

Sitting down at the grand piano closest to the door, Bethany took a deep breath. Without thinking about it, she started to play a Bach piano concerto she knew very well. It was a piece she had used in competition when she was thirteen. At first, she felt like she was forcing it. Where was the longing to make music that had attracted her into the store? She found some of it in the composition itself. Bach's brilliance awakened her heart and enlivened her skills. The keys welcomed her. The room filled with the shiny black instrument's resonance. A few measures in, she no longer thought about anything else.

Something—some sound or change in the light—awakened her again to the world outside that concerto. The world which was not connected to her hands. And she confronted the fact that she needed to be on her way to work. She was headed for a busy day at the diner.

As her fingers sprinted too quickly to the end of the piece, in a way that would have annoyed her teachers and infuriated her mother, she thought about the possibility that she might arrive late for her shift. And she shrugged off some gathering sense of loss that she couldn't name.

Then there was applause.

Ah, the applause.

She raised her head and turned her neck. Three people stood in the doorway, as if they had been passing by and had stopped to listen. There were two older women in the store that she hadn't noticed before, and the salesman was now approaching her.

He was still clapping and smiling an open and honest smile. "Wonderful. Just wonderful. I'm guessing you're a student at the school of music."

She nodded, not attending closely to his exact conjecture and its inaccuracy. "I rushed the ending. I have to get to work."

His smile faded. He was a pale man with bright green eyes, dark hair, and a high hairline. When Bethany stood, she realized he was slightly shorter than she was. "Stop by and play anytime."

His voice had gentled, as if he now recognized the shy creature he had attracted into his store.

"Thanks. It's wonderful." She gestured toward the piano, feeling she owed him something—at least a compliment regarding the grand instrument. It did sound good, though she wasn't ready to sign an endorsement.

Excusing herself, she squeezed past the little crowd by the door. Two more people seemed to have been listening from the sidewalk. She could feel herself blushing as she stepped around them and sped toward the diner.

Why did she stop? Why did she play?

"Because the music is in you." Striding up next to her was the man with the ponytail.

That man.

After a startled jump, she snickered at seeing him. She was caught off guard by the joy of it.

He laughed merrily, a full-chested laugh, and his eyes greeted her joy. His smile was just like that of the music store salesman.

"He's the owner. Mr. Goldberg."

"You know him?" She chuckled at her silly question, picking up her pace that had faltered when she first saw him.

He laughed more intimately this time.

She shook her head at herself. "Oh. I'm ... sort of spinning." Bethany attempted a stabilizing breath. Her swift pace required more air. The head spin required something else.

Jesus put a hand on her shoulder, and calm spread from that point of contact throughout her body.

"Ah." She allowed her shoulders to relax. Now on the main road where the diner was located, she could see her destination. The sight of the humble diner lifted and dropped her heart in turn.

"It'll be a good day. Lots of tips. Opportunity to reconnect with your coworkers and opportunities to serve strangers."

"Serve strangers?" It was, of course, an apt description of her job, but she had never formulated it that way. "You like that I'm serving strangers?"

"Yes. It's part of my culture. Serving the stranger is at the very heart of God's people. That's why my people valued it in the generations before I was born on earth. That is also what I did in my life here. That is who I still am, and what I pass on to you."

Waiting to cross the street at the next light, Bethany thought about how inspired she was by people who readily served strangers, including some who even devoted themselves to that kind of service.

"When you serve a stranger, you cannot expect anything in return. You don't know what to expect, but you serve because it's right and because it's a true expression of love. That's part of your true self." He stepped up the curb in unison with her. "You have served several people this weekend, including with your playing."

She turned her head toward him before heading up the alley. She didn't mind walking past the dumpsters in the company of this wise man. Being on her feet all day didn't sound so bad now, either, as long as she could keep in mind that she was doing God's work of serving strangers.

Chapter 30

Intervention

The whole staff was working the lunch and dinner rush, including Janet, Ralph's wife. Maybe she was the co-owner. Bethany didn't know the details of the diner's finances. Janet coordinated the wait staff and augmented their service on the busiest days.

"And Ralph just sits in the back room counting the money." Annabelle pushed a strand of golden hair off her forehead, her hand finding where to slide it behind her ear.

As usual, Bethany just walked away, not encouraging disrespect toward even someone that might deserve a little dissing. She spent no amount of time figuring out the faults of her bosses. She was learning to pray for them instead, even if she didn't know exactly what they needed. Not knowing probably made it easier to turn them over to Jesus.

Only ten minutes allowed for lunch break and another fifteen for supper, Bethany's day barreled past. Between posting orders and delivering plates, she thought about the piano store. She wondered why she had stopped in to play today and why she hadn't even thought of doing that before. Maybe it was a holiday thing.

The holiday crowd included all kinds of people. Some she expected were just looking for a decent meal in the middle of their festive day. For some, she could imagine this was a special pleasure. Eating in this diner didn't feel like a luxurious celebration to Bethany, until she met people for whom it seemed to be just that.

Janet had just seated a family of three in the last window booth across from the counter. The booths beyond that were windowless and were closer to the bathrooms and the kitchen.

"This is good. This is one of the best spots." The man was sinewy and dark, with the kind of skin that comes from overexposure to the sun. There was a pale line across his forehead just below his hairline and his hands were not what Bethany would call clean.

"I want french fries." The little boy announced it like he was in a medieval inn, shouting out his order to the proprietor.

"Shut up." The man raised his hand, though there was no way he could hit the boy all the way across the table, not without standing up. "Can't you control him?" He directed this challenge to the woman seated next to the boy.

She was compact and pale, her hair dark and long. Bethany guessed she had made an effort to put her hair into that braid for the holiday. The woman leaned down and said something into the boy's ear.

"Hello. I'm Bethany." She surged her friendly voice past questions about what she had just witnessed from the weather-beaten man. "Can I get you something ..."

"I'm Darrell." The little boy had tilted his head upward and was staring at Bethany as if waiting for something.

"Well, hello, Darrell. I'm glad to meet you."

The man made a disgusted noise in his throat and shook his head.

"Can I get anyone something other than water to drink?" She had to pry her eyes away from the boy, sensing that she needed to cover him, protect him somehow. It was a nascent thought—nothing she could imagine acting upon.

"I'll take a Coke. Regular." The man ordered without looking up from the menu.

"Me too. But diet." The woman offered a very slim smile and their eyes met.

Again, Bethany felt an obligation. This time, it was something for woman. She felt it was some kind of ... mission for her, but that was no more than a seed of an idea.

"And for the boy?" She kept her eyes on the woman.

"He can have juice. Do you have, like, apple juice?"

"Aw, let 'im have a soda. It's a holiday." Even that grand gesture came with a belittling glare from the wiry man.

"You want a Sprite, Darry?"

"Uh. Okay. And I want french fries."

Bethany smiled. "I'd be glad to bring an order of fries out as an appetizer. Since it's a holiday." She had never offered that before and she wondered why she was doing it now. Maybe she was searching for the start of her mission.

"Huh? No. He can wait. We don't give him everything he wants." The man cut through Bethany with his eyes—evidently unimpressed with what he found as he measured her.

"Oh. Of course. My mistake."

"It's okay. Of course, he can wait." The woman was looking at the boy, who was sucking his thumb, though he must have been five or six years old.

The man growled across the table, his head low, like a panther preparing to pounce. "Git your thumb outta your mouth or I'll smack it outta there."

The woman looked up at Bethany. This time there was a question in her big brown eyes. What was the question? Was it about whether Bethany was registering the violence with which the man ruled this little family? Or was it more? A cry for help?

One night when Jose was in charge, Bethany had gone into the kitchen to talk to him. She needed to know what to do about a customer threatening to hit the woman he was with.

"Ummm. Girl, you gotta just mind your own business. We can't deal with nothin' like that." Jose was older, more experienced. And, since he was managing the diner that night, Bethany had yielded to him, not doing anything beyond praying for that woman.

She was praying silently again.

"Okay. I'll get your drinks. Waters for everyone. Cokes. Sprite for ... the boy?"

The woman nodded and offered that thin smile again.

Bethany intensified her prayers as she headed behind the counter. Another table's order had come up, so she muttered to Jesus as she delivered the chicken fried steak and chef salad to that other couple. She glanced at the little family and saw the surly man watching her. She tried a genuine smile in his direction. Attempting to fake a genuine smile slowed her maneuvering around the end of the counter.

Amid the rattle of the ice and the shush of the soda machine, backed by the general hubbub of the restaurant, Bethany heard a voice at her ear.

You can help. But we will have to take a long view of what will be useful tonight.

She pulled back from the soda dispenser and snapped her head around. Who would talk into her ear like that? And what was he talking about?

Misgivings about the insightfulness of the advice was the only reason she doubted that she was hearing from the only invisible whisperer she knew.

"Long view?" She muttered that then stopped moving her lips when Savannah squinted at her.

Just follow my lead. His internal answer.

"Mm-hmm." It was easy to agree with that, even if she had no idea what he meant. Like one of the suspenseful stories she had read for her summer class, she expected the author to make things clear before the end.

Jesus was the author. He had a long view of things, apparently.

She crashed into Annabelle with the drink tray, but they avoided broken glass or even much of a spill by leveraging their accumulated experience. Annabelle especially had a circus performer's juggling skills.

"Whoopsie. That was a close one." Annabelle spoke absently, as if she wasn't even sure who she had bumped into.

Bethany chastised herself for losing focus and delivered the drinks to that table of three.

"Are you ready to order now?" She consciously avoided the common formulation, "Are *we* ready to order." Annabelle said it that way but that sounded phony to Bethany.

The three diners ordered food, Darry reiterating his desire for french fries. The adults insisted that a hamburger accompany those fries. The man called the boy a foul name when Darry begrudgingly agreed to the sandwich. Bethany looked at the woman but she was avoiding eye contact, looking instead at her hands where they rested on the melamine tabletop.

Bethany repeated their orders back. "Is that right?"

"Yeah. Yeah. You got it." And the man made a shooing motion with one hand. They were back in that medieval inn, the maiden being dispatched to fetch his vittles.

Shivering as she walked away from that table, Bethany was thinking that someone needed an intervention. Either someone should do something about that man, or someone would have to talk her off a rooftop somewhere. Fortunately, the diner was only one story.

I have what it takes, even with him in the picture. Jesus spoke into her ear again. It was the sort of intimate voice that blocked out everything else, not only for its warm proximity to her ear but because of its solid confidence.

Bethany just had to stay present—do her job and Jesus would handle the rest. She hoped.

Bouncing between two other tables, correcting a mistake from the kitchen, and taking a bathroom break delayed the food order for that table of three. A slight delay.

"About time. Sheesh. Did you have to order out for it?"

Bethany actually laughed. "Now there's an idea." She grinned at the man, which seemed to soften him a little. "Sorry for the wait. I promise the french fries are worth it." All three had fries with their meal, whether with chicken fried steak, a kids' burger, or the French dip sandwich.

The man crunched one. "Mm-hmm. Damn good. Hope you're happy there, squirt." He looked at the boy.

Darry had his mouth full and his little hand back in the stack of fries.

"Don't you want ketchup?" The woman reached for the bottle.

The boy nodded vigorously and kept chewing.

"Okay. Anything else?"

"No, thank you. This looks really good." The woman surveyed the plates and raised her head but again avoided eye contact.

A few minutes later, Bethany stopped to check with that table and got affirmative head nods and grunts from the trio. She aimed a covert inquiry at her invisible advisor. *So, when do I do whatever it is you have for me?*

When you leave the check, they will be talking about something. That will be your opportunity.

To do what?

You'll see.

She scowled at that and bore down once again on filling orders and collecting credit cards or cash. Seeing the bundle of money stuffed in the register, Bethany sniffed a laugh at Annabelle's joke about Ralph counting in the back room. Bethany felt free to laugh at that jibe as long as she didn't let Annabelle witness it.

Annabelle left at seven-thirty. It had been more than a twelve-hour day for her. Bethany waved goodbye to her while carrying the check to the table of three. Not until she overheard their conversation did she recall that this was her time to intervene.

"We could send the little sh** to church or somethin' so we could sleep in. Or you could go with him while I sleep it off." The man chortled at his own words, then he noisily sucked the last of his second Coke through the straw.

"Hello. How was everything?" This part was standard.

"Oh, fine," said the woman.

"I overheard you talking about church." Bethany suppressed the urge to also say she overheard the man calling the boy that rude name. But she was on a mission. "I go to church, if you're looking for a place."

The man leaned against the window ledge and glared at Bethany.

She started to apologize, but the woman interrupted her.

"Really? What church is that?"

Bethany gave the name of her church and the street it was on.

"That ain't too far from us." The man was still contemplating Bethany but with a more subdued glare.

"Oh, yeah. I know where that is. I've seen it from the bus." For the first time, the woman looked at Bethany directly with no plea in her eyes.

Bethany pulled a page off her order pad and wrote the church website address on it. "If you're interested, you would definitely be welcomed."

"Oh, ain't that sweet." The man's sarcasm was sickeningly sweet.

But all he got from Bethany was a tight grin like the one the woman had started the evening with.

The woman wore a more relaxed smile now. "Well, I sure will look it up. They got kids programs and all?"

"Oh yes. Lots of things for kids. Some really good people in charge of the program."

The man snorted a laugh. "Would you believe I went to Sunday school when I was a kid?" He noisily sucked air, looking at the woman with a sort of proud irony in his eyes.

"Everyone's welcome." Bethany was still forcing it but her smile survived.

She breathed a satisfied sigh when she got to the break room for her supper. She nodded to Ralph who was heading up front to fill in for her. And she offered quiet gratitude to Jesus for giving her something to do for three strangers, even if it was a small thing and the outcome was uncertain.

Thanks for sticking with it, girl.

That reply made her smile with satisfaction because *he* was satisfied.

Chapter 31

Offering

Memorial Day at the diner had been draining. Bethany was glad for her usual Tuesday off. She knew things would be slower at the diner that day but not nearly as restful as a day of reading and attending class—a single class she only had to pass, just to check off a line on her transcript.

Awake for breakfast almost an hour earlier than the day before, Bethany climbed out of bed and heard Sandy knocking around in the bathroom. They had never been close, but Bethany hoped to connect more intentionally with her suitemate during these four weeks. Bethany tapped on the bathroom door. Sandy called out in a dull tone. It sounded like an invitation.

When Bethany opened the door, she found Sandy staring at her phone. Perhaps she was between things. Maybe headed to the shower.

"You going to breakfast?" Bethany was hungry. She had seen a lot more food yesterday than she had eaten, of course, and had forgotten the takeout bag she had packed for herself toward the end of the shift.

Sandy mumbled something. Her mouth seemed not to be working.

"What's up? Are you okay?"

Shaking her head, Sandy raised a hand to her cheek. "Something wrong with this tooth, or the gum or something." She talked as if she had a large piece of soft candy in her mouth but her expression was bitter.

"When did this happen?" Bethany felt like she had missed something. She hadn't spoken with Sandy since before her visit with Grandma Hight.

"It's been there for a while but not this bad." That was the translation of her mumble-mouthed reply, which seemed to include the word *thith*.

Without worrying what Sandy would think about it, Bethany offered to pray for her.

"Oh. Thanks, I appreciate it." Then Sandy went back to looking at her phone.

"What if I prayed for it right now?"

"Like, prayed for it ... now?"

As uninspiring as that reply seemed on the surface, Bethany was sympathetic. She had never done this sort of thing with Sandy before, and she hadn't explained what she meant by the offer. But pressing through Sandy's confused state seemed the easiest next step.

Bethany moved a bit closer and put a hand near Sandy's cheek, where a small swelling was apparent. "Lord, let your healing come right here to Sandy's mouth. Thank you."

That was how Colson would do it. Or Sister Juanita.

Sandy rocked her head side to side. A gesture that seemed to suggest the experience wasn't too bad. She also didn't burst into joyous celebration.

"Thankth." Sandy chuckled at her own speech impediment.

Laughing was better than moaning, Bethany thought, as Sandy left and she got the use of the bathroom.

When Bethany came out of the bathroom, Sandy was back, with her towel. "I could have some breakfast. Something soft."

"There are lots of soft things for breakfast." Bethany grinned at her suitemate, noting her speech had improved. A willingness to eat was probably a good sign as well.

After they had each showered and dressed, they met by the door of the suite, both with mostly wet hair.

"So, what was that? Was it, like, a Jesus thing?"

Bethany stared dumbfounded for a couple seconds. So much of her life recently could be described as "a Jesus thing" that she didn't instantly guess which one Sandy was referring to. But she finally understood, even without breakfast or coffee yet.

"Yeah, I guess you could say that. I feel more ready to do it lately because of all that's been happening with me and Jesus. But my church does stuff like that. I was just sorta shy about it before."

"I can understand that. I've never been a very good Christian ... in lots of ways."

Maybe it was just because it was still early, but Bethany again felt like she and Sandy were not connecting. Nevertheless, she followed Sandy out to the hallway instead of standing there staring at her.

Yogurt and pancakes seemed soft enough for Sandy. She ate with only occasional pauses to suck air past the offending tooth. And, when her mouth wasn't full, Bethany could understand Sandy's words much better.

"Is your tooth feeling better?"

"Is it? Yeah, I guess it is. Maybe that's from eating."

Only allowing her nose to wrinkle for one beat, Bethany decided not to contest that explanation for the change. She couldn't prove that her prayer had produced results, but that didn't stop her from believing it might have.

As she chewed her granola, Bethany wondered at her own shyness about God things when she was at school. That probably had to do with fear about what her friends would think—and perhaps something to do with the prevailing suspicion about traditional religion at the university. Doing Jesus stuff at the diner seemed easier somehow. At least it had been so far. Doing the same kind of serving at school would take more courage.

She exchanged a grin with Sandy as they each chewed their food. A text on her phone interrupted Bethany's thoughts.

"I would like to talk in person. Willing to fly out this week."

From her mother.

"Talk about what?"

A long pause. **"Want to catch up and see how you're doing."**

The disconnect between being willing to fly out to talk about something and merely wanting to catch up was suspicious. At least confusing. Bethany breathed a prayer for wisdom. **"Sure. When will you be here?"**

"Could arrive day after tomorrow."

Her mother's habits and tastes had always been more expensive than her father's but paying for a last-minute plane ticket seemed extreme. On the other hand, Bethany had to admit she hadn't priced out plane tickets lately. Maybe her mother was getting some kind of deal online.

Next, she had to consider her work schedule. The day after tomorrow was Thursday. Could she get off work that day, on short notice? Even for part of the day?

Sandy raised her eyebrows as she began to gather her dishes and napkins onto her tray, finishing her meal.

Nodding to Sandy, Bethany tested an idea with her mother. **"How early? I work late on Thursday and Friday."** She said goodbye and waved weakly at Sandy, who grinned in return on her way to depositing her tray.

"Could fly in late Thurs. and see you Friday morning ??"

Again, Bethany prayed. Something was up with this visit, obviously, but she was more inclined to accept the offer than she might have been a few weeks ago. This time she heard an answer or maybe just recognized an inserted thought.

This will be good for both of you. She glanced around, a new habit when items like that landed in her mental inbox.

"That sounds good."

"Breakfast Friday then? You pick the place."

"Pick me up on campus?"

"Yes."

Later that day, Bethany saw Sandy in the suite again. "How's the tooth?"

"Much better. I have a dentist appointment and I'm sure I can last until then."

"That's great."

"Hey, thanks for praying for me." Sandy smiled sheepishly then ducked into her room.

A return smile was all Bethany could manage as she wrestled with the question of what Sandy believed and what she herself believed about the power of that prayer. Further inhibiting her response was the dangling question about her mother's reason for visiting. The pending visit seemed to hover behind even wholly unrelated things, much the same way her mother had always seemed to hover behind Bethany for most of her life.

Having read all she could take in before and after attending the first class of that summer course, Bethany set aside her reader for a walk through the forested park near campus. She packed a bottle of mosquito repellant but hoped the little suckers weren't active yet. And she wore a hat and long sleeves, just in case.

The temperature was in the upper sixties in the middle of the afternoon. The shady woods seemed cooler than that. The scents of pine and rotting leaves accompanied the tiny blossoms of viny shrubs and bushes near the path. The dirt and gravel walkway crunched beneath her running shoes, and her own breathing was the second strongest sound nearby. At a distance, the sound of bird calls obscured a hum of traffic from the surrounding city.

Other footsteps on the crunchy path made her slow down and look behind her. Expecting a faster hiker was overtaking her, she moved to the right. She checked again to find a man approaching, hiking sandals on his feet, wearing long pants and a long-sleeved zip up.

A familiar-looking man.

"Good place for us to meet." The man with the ponytail grinned warmly at her.

Bethany allowed a snicker to leak between her teeth. She took his hand when he reached it toward her.

As soon as she felt the warmth of his hand in hers, her heart stirred.

Then he became invisible. This time, she was sure she could still feel his hand, even though he was no longer crunching the path next to her, no longer adding the sound of his breathing to hers in the silence of the woods.

Fending off fears and frustrations, as if she could keep them in a glass room where their noise would be muted, she focused on that warmth. Warmth in her hand and warmth in her heart. The goodness of that living presence drew her away from the questions raised by his appearing and disappearing.

She walked in the woods for half an hour, savoring the experience, and she wondered why she didn't walk there more often. She resolved to come back during these warmer months. There were, of course, good reasons to stay out of the woods in the winter, though even then she might venture out if she could hope for a warming presence to meet her there.

Chapter 32

Visiting

The customer traffic in the diner was moderately heavy on Thursday night. The tables were only completely full for a few minutes at about seven o'clock. Then the crowds tapered and Savannah left. Calm settled as the evening went dark under a slow-moving rainstorm. Distant thunder warned of the start and then more rumbles signaled the storm's end, just before Bethany left for the night.

"Goodnight, girl. Have a good time with your mama tomorrow." Annabelle stood at her bus stop, a sympathetic tilt to her head and a lipstick smile.

As unlikely as Bethany was to ever call her mother *mama,* she headed for campus thinking she was also unlikely to have a good time with her. At this thought, she turned to check next to her. Did someone clear their throat? She twisted her neck to determine if there might be someone in a second story window watching her pass. No sign. She might have misinterpreted some other sound.

Whatever the case, that throat clearing—or its equivalent—caused her to think about what Jesus wanted for her visit with her mother. The notion that it would be good for both of them remained as his last words on the subject. At least those were *likely* his words. She wouldn't want to take the proposition to debate class, but his brief appearance in the woods felt like a confirmation that she had indeed heard that assurance from him at breakfast on Tuesday.

Her mother confirmed her safe arrival around eight that evening. Bethany acknowledged that text but let two more messages land unanswered as she worked through closing time. On her way home, she remembered the unread messages and pulled her phone out of her pocket.

"Delayed by storm."

So long since I've been in Milwaukee"

"Remember the time it snowed here when we were on tour?"

That last message made Bethany laugh. She didn't count herself a Wisconsin native, but she was surrounded by them, including her dad. Asking a Wisconsinite if they remembered the time it snowed would draw a deer-in-headlights stare at best. But Bethany did, in fact, recall the snowstorm to which her mother was referring.

She replied to her mother two hours late. **"Almost didn't get to play that night."** The snowy evening in Milwaukee didn't seem so long ago. Maybe that was because Bethany had seen a few more days like it since.

She was passing Mr. Goldberg's piano store now. Without premeditation, she had taken the route past his place. That ran against her usual habit, especially on evenings when she walked Annabelle to the bus stop. She looked in the windows as she passed, but it was dark inside and she mostly saw the reflection of herself walking on a lonely street. Though she made the walk home from work several times a week, something about the young woman in that window looked out of place.

Maybe it was just her lack of a coat. Bethany had started working at the diner the previous October. Until the past two weeks, she would have been wearing a jacket or coat every time she saw herself in a nighttime reflection.

She might also be missing the companion she had seen in a store reflection the previous week. Two people visible in the glass, not just one.

Why did he show up sometimes and not others?

In the woods he had said it was a good place to meet with him. She thought of that now as a sort of spiritual advice, not just a geographic note. Advice to get quiet and go for a walk, a walk on which she is conscious of Jesus being with her. She could do that in the woods. And she could do it on the way home from work. She settled that truth into her soul with a long sigh.

Bethany lay awake in bed that night trying to fit various answers to the riddle her mother had sent her—the riddle which started with something she wanted to talk about and then turned to just checking in. Why now? Why check in now?

Obviously, something had happened. Something had changed. Maybe her mother had a boyfriend now. Maybe she was getting married.

Or maybe she was feeling bad for not supporting Bethany's schooling. Maybe she was coming to offer financial help.

Maybe. Maybe. Maybe.

Tossing and turning at the start of her sleep meant rousing herself in the morning was an ungainly struggle. Her alarm on her phone insisted it was time. She had left the phone across her room, to force herself to get out of bed to silence it. She briefly considered *not* silencing it but decided to have mercy on Sandy in the next room.

Standing now next to her dresser, Bethany thought of breakfast with her mom and she looked again at that riddle. She had not set her alarm as early as she might. Tired from an evening in the diner, she opted for as much sleep as possible. Now she was grateful for the slender segment of time until breakfast. She could pack it full of getting cleaned up and dressed instead of leaving herself time for frustrated conjectures.

Dressing took longer than usual. Sandy poked her head in the door when Bethany was trying on her third blouse. Her suitemate noted the growing pile of clothes on the bed and laughed.

"Kinda early for a date. You got breakfast with someone special?" Maybe she was thinking of Lucas.

Bethany realized then that she hadn't spoken with Sandy about her mother's visit. "My mother is here. She's taking me to breakfast."

Sandy stepped a foot into the room now and leaned on the doorpost. "Wait. Your mother came here from Oregon to have breakfast with you."

"Right. You sound as suspicious as I feel." Bethany pulled that dark blue blouse off and tugged a dark pink one out of the pile on the bed. She had already tried that one. She was surrendering. Her time was up.

A buzz on her phone confirmed that conclusion. "That's probably her. She's picking me up downstairs. You wanna meet her?"

If Bethany had stabbed her with a pencil, Sandy probably wouldn't have grimaced more harshly. "Uh, is it okay if I opt out?" She flipped her fingers through her shoulder-length hair that was still wet. Only a few loose strands were dried enough to show her manufactured blonde.

"Sure, it's fine. I understand." Bethany laughed gently. She didn't want to meet her mother either but she had her obligations.

On the way down the stairs, she argued with herself about the exact nature of her obligations to her mother. Financially, it felt like her mother had disowned her. She did that when Bethany walked away from her concert career and chose to teach music instead. Her mother's rejection of that life choice—her rejection of Bethany's sense of calling—was worse than her refusal to provide funds for college. A deeper cut. A stab at Bethany's sense of herself.

"You're young. How could you possibly know what you want to do with your whole life?" That was what her mother said, or something like it, the last time they discussed her education.

Bethany could understand that skepticism. She had watched her friends try on career paths the way she had tried on blouses that morning.

All those thoughts slammed to a halt when she stepped into the lobby and saw her mother approaching. She was thinner, maybe. Still relatively pale but maybe a little tanner. The Pacific Northwest wasn't known for its sun, of course, but her mother could get a tan if she wanted. Her complexion was on the light end of olive. Her mother's parents and one of her brothers were darker, even without sunbathing.

Was she thin because she was dating or was it something less positive? Stress? The lines in her face seemed to have been darkened by the artist who sketched her. It was a face an artist would like to sketch. In Bethany's mind, her mother was more beautiful than she was, at least by the conventional standards of beauty.

"Dear! How are you? You look good." Her mother held out her hands, but not for a hug. She took both of Bethany's hands instead, a familiar maneuver, and one that harkened to her mother's childhood on Long Island. At least she didn't do the air kisses next to each cheek.

"Hi, Mom. You look the same." It was mostly true. Her daughter had no trouble recognizing her across the lobby, even though she hadn't seen her since spring break freshman year.

"Oh, I think I look tired when I force myself to look in the mirror." That might have been a joke. Being forced to look in a mirror was not a suitable description of the mother Bethany knew.

Still puzzling over the meaning of this visit, Bethany's distracted response was subdued and wordless. Briefly, she wished Jesus could join them for breakfast. He would certainly be a good mediator. Despite her mother skipping past all the obvious conflicts still standing between them, Bethany knew they needed some kind of mediation.

"Did you choose a spot for breakfast? A nice place, I hope."

On a Friday morning, Bethany was hoping they could get into a popular breakfast place a couple miles from campus. She knew her mother would want an expensive breakfast, no matter the purpose of this visit.

She gave her mother the name of the restaurant and described where it was. Her mother pulled out her phone and found it. "Oh, nice. Good choice. Well, let's go then."

Her mother had rented a new electric car, though not the deluxe model Katie had picked her up in.

"Glad I didn't get a ticket." She had left the red sedan in a marked *no parking* zone.

"Campus police aren't super strict, especially in the summer. And especially if they think it's a parent's car." Bethany had observed this and had heard stories from her friends.

In the car, Bethany tried to end her suspense. "So, you said you wanted to talk to me about something."

Her mom checked the directions on the LED display on the dash. The route was not complicated after the first few turns. Perhaps she was noting that she couldn't credibly claim to need to concentrate on the driving. There wasn't much traffic this far from downtown.

"Well, of course, I missed you. I wanted to see you." This answer was a stall. Was she waiting for Bethany to stuff herself with Belgian waffles before hitting her with the real reason for the visit? That would fit into her usual arsenal of tactics for controlling their relationship. Here was part of the wall that separated them.

"Dad said I should go see you if I could. I was thinking Christmas."

"Hmm. Well, we'll see about Christmas. When did you talk to your dad?"

"This was some time ago. A couple weeks. We've talked since."

"How is his mother doing?"

"She's well. I spent Sunday with her and Katie. We had a great time."

"Oh. I thought she had a heart problem, and her health was failing." She sounded more invested in that old news than Bethany's positive update.

"No, just water around her heart. She recovered. She's feeling much better. She was back to normal by the time I left her Sunday." She could leave out vital facts as well as her mother could and skip over controversial topics too. She expected her mother would be more willing to listen after she got her latté. Certainly not Belgian waffles.

"Oh, I'm surprised. I guess I thought it was more serious." She slowed the car to a stop at a light. "Doctors don't know everything. They present the worst-case scenarios just to protect themselves."

Tempted to come to the defense of the unnamed doctors in this indictment, Bethany resisted. She really didn't want to hear what her mother thought about the idea that Jesus had healed Grandma. That fact was too precious for Bethany to set it out where it would likely get roughed up by her faithless mother.

Surrendering to her mother's timetable for the big reveal, Bethany rode the last few minutes in relative silence. She offered only small answers to small questions about classes, friends, and work. Her mother seemed only a little interested in the answers to these polite queries, which might have been the point. At this stage in their meeting, she just wanted filler.

The restaurant was near the river, along the edge of the Third Ward, a fancy European breakfast place at which Bethany had not eaten before. It looked inviting online but was out of her price range. It wasn't out of her mother's, though. She was dressed in new clothes, a new gold watch on her wrist and a diamond pinky ring. Her real estate business must have been going well, unless her big revelation was about a rich boyfriend she was planning to marry.

There had been one man her mother contemplated marrying. She had contemplated that aloud, using her twelve-year-old daughter as a sounding board. But Bethany didn't ever hear the part about why it didn't happen. She wasn't briefed on the final negotiations, but it would have been difficult to fit a stepdad into their travel and competition schedule—hers and her mother's.

Locking the car by touching the handle or something that Bethany couldn't see, her mother started toward the restaurant at an athletic pace, despite her three-inch heels. They had parked a block away from the front door. It was a clear, sunny and crisp morning. The storm last night had cleaned the air, leaving a bright summer day.

To Bethany, the clarity of the air was inappropriate. She was used to her mother obfuscating, hiding her intrigues until a precisely planned moment. If she wasn't forthcoming about her true purpose, the optimistic sunlight didn't fit. Or, at least, it was wasted on Bethany.

The restaurant was nearly full, but no one was waiting to be seated when they entered. A lithe young woman with a boney chest under her black leotard top greeted them with the briefest smile. She might have been a dance student working her way through school at this restaurant. Such was Bethany's concocted story on the girl's behalf. A jolly, middle-aged man with a mustache that practically covered his mouth led them to a table. He introduced himself as their waiter and gave her mother a flirty grin.

He was not her type. His white shirt strained to keep his round belly concealed. Mom was much more likely to be attracted to a trim and athletic doctor or lawyer. The gray ponytail on the waiter was the punctuation mark on Bethany's pessimism regarding his prospects.

"Order whatever you want. This looks marvelous." Her mother had set her purse in an empty chair next to her and lifted the menu. Her approval felt formal. She was rarely enthusiastic about anything.

After they placed their breakfast orders, Mom opened a touchy topic between them. A topic that might have provided a clue to the purpose of this trip. "Have you been playing?"

Between them, *playing* only meant one thing. Perhaps that was part of the problem. If Bethany asked Katie if she had been playing, Katie would surely pause to wonder exactly why she asked it that way, but she would guess the question referred to playing soccer. With Bethany's mother, there was no need to guess.

"I played a couple times in the last week. Some Chopin, some Bach."

"Oh, really. Where?"

"At Grandma's retirement home and at a piano store on my way to work."

"Huh." That was the sound of her mother containing the full impact of a shock. She was speechless, probably astonished about those humble venues hosting Bethany's precious talent.

Her latté arrived to interrupt what Mom might have said next. Perhaps she was relieved by the interruption. It gave her a chance to recover from batting her eyelids so furiously.

After a few sips, she tried again. "Don't you miss it? Playing? The concerts?"

Bethany set her orange juice down and shook her head very gently. She allowed herself an internal hunt for anything that felt like *missing* performances. "No. I'm especially glad to not be on stages anymore."

Her mom took a deep breath. The sort of air intake that might be a gasp from a more sensitive soul. Maybe it was the preparation for an argument. Whatever it anticipated, she held onto it. Perhaps she really *was* waiting for Bethany to eat first, though there would be no Belgian waffles on their table.

When the food arrived, Bethany surveyed the smoked salmon English muffin, piled with savory ingredients, the salmon bright and inviting. Her mother's fruit bowl was tempting, but Bethany could have fruit, yogurt, and granola in the dining hall, even if not so artfully presented.

As good as the breakfast was, Bethany was still focused on the waiting. The big revelation. The questions about playing piano gave her a hint that this probably wasn't about her mother finding a new man.

"So, I got a call the other day." It sounded innocent enough, but Bethany supposed this was the prelude.

"Really? From whom?" She was quoting a line. The vocabulary and tone were dictated by the story—her mother's story. Bethany was thinking of the short stories she was reading for class. She probably hadn't seen this particular narrative among them.

"Do you remember that kind judge out in San Francisco, the one who came to us afterward and personally congratulated you? Even though it was only second place. He had such generous things to say."

"Hmm. Maybe I remember." Bethany sliced off another bite, careful not to squeak the fork on the ceramic plate.

"Well, he called—out of the blue—to offer you an opportunity."

"He called you to offer me an opportunity?" She only noted how brash her question was after it escaped into the clatter of the brunch crowd, but she hadn't hit the personal pronouns as hard as she might have. *He called* **you** *to offer* **me** *an opportunity.*

Her mother smiled slyly. The sort of smile that says, *I get the joke, but I'm not laughing at it.*

Bethany wasn't joking. At that moment, she was thinking of what Jesus had said about this visit being good for them both. Good for her and for her mother. So far that prediction had not proven true, she was certain of that. What Bethany wasn't certain about was whether she had to do something to change the account balance.

"It's a very grand opportunity, really, dear. With a prestigious youth symphony from Southern California. The fact that you are still under twenty is a bonus, but you wouldn't be sent packing on your next birthday." She was selling but not in a desperate way. As if she was showing a property to a client but knew there were other homes she could sell them if this one wasn't to their liking.

"He's hiring a pianist for a youth orchestra? A tour?"

"A national tour and several dates in Los Angeles."

"But you told him I was in school." She suddenly noticed a missing bit of data. "Did you send him a recording? An audition?"

"No, I didn't. He called me. He might have seen something online, because he was talking about your development since he judged you in that competition. Perhaps he's been following your career."

"Perhaps he *was* following my career before." She allowed a more forcefully corrective tone this time. "Did you tell him I'm not available?"

Her mother set down her fork and lifted her water glass. "I didn't want to close the door on it. They're offering ten thousand a month with travel expenses paid. Hotels, et cetera. Even in L.A., they would put you up at their expense."

"If I were interested, they would, but you know that I'm not interested." Again, the impact of what was happening was hidden behind a screen. Some part of it still wasn't fully visible. "You came all the way here to talk me into taking this position because of the money?" That last point wasn't certain. Her mother might have just been trying to entice her back to their old life.

As if reading her mind, her mother clarified something. "This would not be you and I traveling together. You would be on your own. I would stay in Beaverton, I still have houses to sell. But you could get back on stage without your stage mother." The tone of her voice was subtly complex. Full of competing emotions—enticement mixed with apology and accusation entwined with acknowledgment.

Bethany took a deep breath. If this was going to be good for both her and her mother, she would have to reply with grace. Surely Jesus would want that.

"I ... I appreciate ... the time and effort this has cost you, Mom. And I appreciate your concern for me. I know you think this sort of thing would be better for me, but I still disagree. I respectfully continue to disagree."

Her ability to say all that taught Bethany something about herself, and in the glow of that revelation, she didn't want to continue this conversation with her mother. She wanted instead to explore the lessons she had been learning, including what she had already absorbed from Jesus.

Her mother's sad stare told Bethany something about *her* as well.

Mom was making her last plea.

This was her final attempt, and she was facing the possibility that she had failed.

Chapter 33

Accompanying

Even though Bethany had maintained her resistance against her mother's attempted overthrow of her life, the victory left a residue of exhaustion with no hints of triumph. Having to work a long shift at the diner on Friday, with that background noise, was even more tiring. The echoes of the drama that was her tragic relationship with her mother would not fall silent.

But Bethany was comfortable in her job, and she welcomed the living distraction her customers could offer. Usually, they offered and sometimes they demanded.

"Do you have sweet pickles? I would just love to have some sweet gherkins on the side. And could you cut those into little slices?" The old woman pinched her thumb and forefinger to less than half an inch.

"Slices of sweet pickles. Gherkins. I'll see what I can do." She answered with no annoyance in her voice, she was pretty sure. If the customer had been a college student, Bethany would have known it was a joke or some odd hazing challenge.

The blue-haired woman did smile appreciatively, as if she recognized that she was asking for something special. Bethany backburnered her past observations about customers with special requests who had tipped poorly, or not at all. She would ignore that history and do what she could to serve this woman.

Interrupting her work throughout the afternoon and evening were texts from her mother. Mom's flight was leaving Saturday afternoon. Tomorrow. She wanted to see Bethany one more time before heading home.

Of course, it's not too much for a mother to ask to see her daughter twice when she has flown all the way from Portland to Milwaukee. But that *of course* was part of her mother's mode of manipulations, and Bethany's instinct was to resist and resist some more.

Then, around six-thirty p.m., Bethany received a text from Grandma.

"How are you doing dear?"

Even that simple greeting seemed to reset Bethany's heart, including her heart toward her mother. She answered Grandma during her supper break nearly an hour later. **"Doing ok."**

"I'm praying for your time with your mother. Praying it will be good for both of you."

Bethany stood breathless before sitting down to eat. Grandma's prayer was exactly what Jesus had promised. Wasn't it a promise? When God tells you something will be good for you, that has to count as a promise, doesn't it?

But now something else became clear, even as she was quickly cutting through her grilled chicken. In the past, what was supposed to be good for her was always curated by her mother, who often had to strive to convince Bethany that her plans were good. Imposing her will on Bethany was what it generally felt like. Bethany had finally responded by completely cutting herself off from her mother, the only way she could hope to find the life *she* really wanted.

However, to make any part of her relationship with her mother good for both of them, they would have to negotiate and compromise. No longer could they play the roles of dictator and exile. They would have to be more diplomatic.

Hadn't Jesus taken the role of mediator in their negotiations by revealing his promise to Bethany directly and then through Grandma? He was offering a way forward—concession and settlement. It would be hard, of course. It would be a complete culture shift, but now Bethany had a comprehensible goal at which to aim.

Carrying these intense thoughts back from her break, she had to stop and take a few deep breaths to get her head into her work. She had to let her mother go, at least for the evening.

Bethany was carrying a paid check toward the register when she noticed a ten-year-old girl sitting in a booth with her family—a man and a boy on the other side of the table, a woman next to the girl. It was one of Savannah's tables. Bethany assumed the order had been placed and the family was waiting.

The red-haired girl had her fingers on the edge of the white surface. She was practicing piano. This was something Bethany had done most of her childhood. And when Bethany paused to watch, she knew the song the girl was playing. "Fur Elise" by Beethoven—a song every young student of piano in America will encounter at some point.

Without even introducing herself, Bethany pocketed her order pad, stopped by the table, and bent her knees so she was closer to the surface. She set her fingers on the edge, waiting for the girl to start the next measure, then she played in unison with her, humming the tune as they played.

Only a hiccup of a hesitation interrupted the girl's playing. Then she surged with new intensity. Her hands moved more like they would on actual piano keys, mirroring Bethany's precise fingering.

Instead of just playing a few measures, as she had expected, Bethany kept playing and humming. The girl had joined the humming, the mother joined next, then a voice behind Bethany had piped in.

The girls kept playing—the girl who was probably practicing for a ten-year-old's recital, and the girl practicing for a new life with her talent, with her mother ... and with her calling.

When they reached the end, after playing a bit faster than Beethoven surely intended, a half dozen hummers hit the final note. Laughter surrounded the table and Savannah hooted.

After surveying the folks applauding, Bethany zeroed back to the little girl who was displaying all her teeth in a huge grin.

"That was great. You must be a teacher." The little redhead blinked her questioning eyes at Bethany.

In most people's eyes, Bethany surely looked like a student. She never had any trouble convincing people she was a teen, even if only technically a teen for a few more weeks. But apparently the younger girl saw something more in her. At least she saw someone older.

"I am *studying* to teach music. Good call."

"And you're working as a *waitress*?" The surprise in the mother's voice came across as confidential and sympathetic.

"Paying for school." Bethany shrugged.

"You couldn't get scholarships?"

"I did, just not enough to cover everything. My dad's helping some."

The tanned man across the table fished in his wallet, which made Bethany nervous. But instead of a scholarship donation, he pulled out a business card. "You give us a call if you're ever taking on new students."

"Yeah!" The girl bounced in her seat, reminding Bethany of her cousin.

"Wow, that's nice." Bethany couldn't keep amazement out of her voice. "I'll hang on to this." She held up the card. The man was apparently an attorney. "I'm Bethany." She said that to the girl.

"Cassie." She held up her hand for a shake.

"You have good rhythm and fingering. I pulled you along faster than the real tempo of that song, you know."

"I know. But it was exciting, so I was glad to speed up."

"It *was* exciting." Bethany lent her squintiest grin to the whole table. "Well, have a good evening."

As if that wish rebounded to her, Bethany had a very good evening after that. The most demanding customer had been the lady with the sweet pickles. And Jose had found what she wanted, muttering something in Spanish as he sliced them to order.

After closing, Bethany said goodnight to Ralph and Savannah as she headed out the front door. It was finally dark by ten o'clock, especially in the shadows of buildings. Golden and blueish lights on the streets, and along the business fronts, sent multicolored shadows all around her as she walked the quiet concrete on the way to campus.

A car rolled slowly past, and a guy shouted something out his window. Bethany was glad not to understand the words, but she took the first opportunity to get off the main road. Her heart rate returned to normal after half a block, when she thought she felt someone next to her.

That sensation would have frightened her two weeks ago. This night it was reassurance and another promise.

Chapter 34

Breakthrough

Her mother had only fired back two text objections before agreeing to meet Bethany at the dining hall in her dorm for Saturday breakfast. It was a negotiated meeting on Bethany's territory, a meeting in which she hoped to make peace without surrendering. Most of her knowledge of history had to do with composers and symphonies, but she recognized the influence of her history survey class in that characterization of this impending summit.

Her mother surveyed the dining hall with bland disapproval when they entered together. "Is there a private dining room we could use? They used to have one or two of those at my college."

Victoria Marconi had certainly been a popular beauty in her college days. Bethany could picture her mother as one of those aloof undergraduates who could flirt with her eyes and captivate with a smile ... when she wanted to. But she had heard only a few stories of her mother's college days.

"No. Not that I know of. It's okay, though. It won't be crowded. We can sit over there by the windows, once we get our food."

"Buffet style." Another bland comment, with neither approval nor disgust. Mom rummaged in her purse for her wallet, while Bethany swiped her card and waited on the other side of the automatic cashier.

"It takes any card?"

"Well, I don't know about Diner's Club but standard credit and debit cards." Bethany was trying to tease her too-posh mom, but she saw no indication that her mother recognized the joke.

Mom was wearing white slacks and a teal blouse with a white sweater around her shoulders, the sleeves tied loosely across her chest. Preppy had not died for her, and it definitely had a Long Island accent. Her obvious discomfort probably came from her privileged upbringing as well. She was uncomfortable in a university dining hall, which was not the same as the cafeteria at the private school she had attended in New England.

Inhaling renewed resolve to make the best of this time with her mother, Bethany understood those seizures of discomfort. Mom was out of her territory, outside her safe zone. Bethany would do what she could to make her mother comfortable. She thought she knew the best place to start.

"You'll have to show me how to use the espresso machines. I've never tried it." Bethany gestured toward the hot drinks kiosk. Three students were there, in various stages of tea, chocolate, or coffee creation. She had mostly watched the espresso machine in operation from a distance before this. If she wanted coffee, Bethany would draw a mug of the regular from the large urn, but Jacqueline was a great fan of the espresso in this dining hall. That fact gave Bethany some hope.

"Oh. Well." Her mom's exclamation was modest but upbeat. A significant change in tone from bland disapproval. They paused to procure trays on the way to the prospect of a latté or two.

"Looks like two of us can do it at the same time." Bethany took two large mugs from next to the duel spout espresso machine. "Show me how?"

Her mom set her tray down and accepted the mug. "I do espresso sometimes, but I can show you how to do a latté." She glanced at the printed instructions. "This looks familiar enough."

Her hands only hesitating once or twice, Mom demonstrated the creation of a flavored, creamy coffee drink that Bethany had seen her consume many times. Bethany had rarely joined her.

The creative process, however, made the foamy drink more attractive. Her mother's advice proved helpful during each step, and the result was nothing like the disaster Bethany had imagined her freshman year when she first considered using the espresso machine unsupervised.

Mom was a natural teacher. Bethany recognized that in the steady instruction she received throughout the little project. She had never noticed this before, or maybe had never allowed herself to respect that skill before. Past instruction had generally felt like her mother forcing conformity on her.

Allowing her mother to teach her something peripheral, something noninvasive, seemed like a good place to start this round of negotiations. Small steps.

Her voice more animated, her eyes venturing toward the various breakfast bars, Mom had shifted gears. Foraging for food, as required by the buffet arrangement, was natural for some people. Bethany's mother was used to sitting and waiting to be waited on. She seemed now to be inflating her courage to attempt the uncomfortable, if not the impossible.

Bethany led her mother to the foods she liked. As she had noted yesterday morning, the fruit, yogurt, and granola Mom favored were all here in the dining hall. Though no mangoes or avocados awaited them—not this morning, anyway. The summer fare was a bit pared back, by Bethany's estimation.

At a table next to the far windows, with no one sitting nearby, Bethany placed her laden tray on the clean wood veneer tabletop. She had probably overloaded her tray just because she could. Not only were the food options for the two of them abundant, but her skills at carrying a tray of food were well beyond the average college student's. Some of what she carried today was for her mother.

Her mother had protested. "I don't think I can carry all this or eat it all."

"If you need to take the muffin or something with you, they won't search your purse on the way out."

"Right. The muffin and not the pineapple or the yogurt." A small joke with a smile to match.

For one fleeting moment, Bethany dared hope that she was seeing the reward for her effort—a peaceful advance in their negotiations. But it was a fleeting hope.

Surveying her food as if to decide where to begin, her mother said, "So, have you reconsidered the audition for the youth orchestra?"

"You didn't mention that they wanted me to audition. It sounded like they were already offering me the position." Bethany had never had a position with an orchestra. She had accompanied three different orchestras for at least two engagements each. The former judge who was recruiting for this position might have seen a video of one of those performances. Those were busy times for a teenager. She had resented that busyness, but Bethany bypassed addressing all that right then.

"Well, he was glowing in his praise, so I think the audition is just a formality."

"But does he know that I haven't been playing? I've barely practiced." She considered again that she should try signing out a practice room. She could do that on her phone right now, if she were serious about it.

"Barely practiced? Really?" Her mother's incredulity seemed to be coated in something. Maybe low-fat yogurt.

"I've ... I've been avoiding it, I think—I mean, avoiding practicing on a real piano. I still do exercises on the electric keyboard in my room." This last note was not intended to provoke her mother, who would surely not approve of that method. It was actually a confession. A confession to herself. Bethany had accumulated her own coating over her fear of her mother's opinions. Though not a yogurt coating, certainly.

"Avoiding the piano? Avoiding practice?" Her mother stopped chewing and scowled at her. "Why would you do that?"

The toddler that was not far beneath the surface whenever Bethany was with her mother had a ready answer to that question. *Why? Because of you. You have poisoned music for me.*

But she kept that toddler on timeout. Instead, she just shook her head. She paused to face her dissatisfaction over her own decisions. She had given up the concert and competition circuits, but she was not giving up music. She would not play for applause, but she would not stop playing.

Bethany thought of the girl at the diner last night as she sipped her latté, which was lukewarm now. She didn't mind the tepid, creamy sweetness. It still went well with her low-carb quiche.

Her mind was wandering away from the conversation. She hadn't answered her mother. "I have to get back to practicing. I know that. I've ... I guess I've thrown the baby out with the bathwater." That phrase was her mother's, not something her friends would say. But negotiation surely required translation—speaking her mother's language while not allowing her to dictate terms.

Eyebrows bobbing and head nodding in a way that might count as twitching, her mother cut a piece of pineapple in half and inserted it between her perfectly white teeth.

"I didn't do any of this to hurt you, Mom. Not really." Bethany gazed past her mother at some students hugging as if they hadn't seen each other for a while. "I think that was part of it at first. Or I should say, I thought that was part of it when I first told you I was quitting. But really, it wasn't to make you feel bad. I just had to break away, and I knew you wouldn't like it and I had to tell myself it was okay. I had to let you feel bad if you ... if you chose that."

"Chose that? Since when do we get to choose how we feel? Or who we care about?"

"I never doubted that you cared about me. The question was always about how ... about what was the best way for you to care about me." She paused to assess whether her explanation was connecting with her mother. "And, I guess, now I'm admitting I have no way to judge your ... your best guess on how to do that. I just felt like I needed something else." She shrugged. "I feel like I was right. I've seen it in lots of little ways lately. I was made to be a teacher. For kids. A piano teacher, a music teacher."

Her mother slowly placed her knife and fork next to her plate. Then she raised her eyes to meet Bethany's. She seemed to search for something there. Or, perhaps, that search was internal. She began nodding. "Yes. I see it. I can see it." She sniffed a laugh. "I probably should have been a teacher myself." She shook her head. "I just never developed the patience for it, I think."

Bethany breathed a laugh that was also a sigh. "I know you *are* a teacher. I was just thinking that and I know I'm like you. But I'm also like dad, and a little like Grandma Hight."

"But nothing like your grandma Marconi." Her mother chuckled knowingly.

"Ha. Yeah, probably not so much like Grandma Marconi."

"We left her generation behind, you and me. We're ready to make our mark on the world." She took a deep breath. "And, of course, teaching is a way to make a very important mark on one life at a time."

The *one life at a time* characterization must have assumed Bethany would be a piano teacher, working with individual students. She could probably start that career with Cassie from the diner if she wanted to. She smiled at that notion, but she was still planning to teach in a school at some point. The summer camp experience, with a dozen kids at a time, was an eyeopener. But she wouldn't bring all that into what was a preliminary conversation with her mother.

She and her mother had both said more this morning than they had ever said to each other on this topic, at least in a way that the other could hear.

Bethany had been nodding for several seconds, which stood in as an answer to her mother's concession speech, her allowance. And before she could say anything more, her mother surprised her.

"I should help you out with the finances, shouldn't I?"

Wording it as a question, as a request for advice or approval, lengthened Bethany's ruminating silence. She had stopped nodding, but she gave one more nod after she recovered. "I'll leave that up to you. Maybe you could talk to Dad." She kept her voice small. There were complications regarding financial aid that wouldn't fit into this breakfast breakthrough discussion.

"Oh, yes. Sure. I suppose there are things to work out." Her mother let her eyes rest on Bethany in a way that implied admiration, which was something Bethany hadn't seen in her mother's eyes as long as she could remember. There were the admiring gazes locked on trophies or ribbons or certificates, and even admiration for a few checks received, but seldom an affirming gaze that felt this personal and lasted this long. Even if it only lasted a few seconds.

Maybe she did it to prolong that look from her mom, but Bethany reached across the table. Her mother took her hand. Bethany had held hands with Jesus more than she had held hands with her mother, at least since she was twelve.

This time her mother didn't let go.

Chapter 35

Practicing

During the church announcements on Sunday morning, Bethany finally checked on the availability of a piano practice room at school. Though the idea was not new, the resolve to make it happen was fresh and clean. Some of that new resolve came from her mother, ironically. Their last conversation over the phone, before her mother boarded the plane to Portland, had been different.

"Get back to practicing, dear. You know you should." Her mother's phone voice sounded peculiar, lacking the usual forecast of anger or disapproval. Also missing was the wounded shock of Bethany not having done what her mother wanted already.

In the context of church, it was easier to imagine forgiving her mother, even if Bethany hadn't done a thorough job of that yet. But she could also forgive herself for that whole *baby with the bathwater* reaction.

Playing music, especially piano, was her passion. Maybe even enough to merit the baby analogy. She was thinking about this when Mildred drove her home from church.

"What are you thinking so hard about? Did Jesus come see you again?" She signaled the turn into the drive that ran in front of the dorm towers.

"Ha. Well, no, I wasn't thinking about that." She paused to wonder how many encounters with Jesus she'd had since last updating Mildred. "I was just thinking about practicing piano. It's easy to get a practice room during summer term, it turns out."

"Oh, that makes sense. So how often do you practice?"

"Not often enough. I need to get back to it."

"That's good. Sounds like a good idea." Mildred's innocence was real on this point. She had no investment in Bethany's piano practice, her performance, nor even her preparedness for teaching. She was just generally supportive.

Maybe her mother's relationship to Bethany's music could become more innocent in the years ahead. Would her mother really help pay for her degree in music education?

"I had a very good visit with my mother. Much better than I expected."

"Yes. You said that. How was it better?"

Bethany fluttered her lashes at the reminder. Of course, she had already told Mildred about her mother visiting. She dug for something more substantial to say about it. "Uh, well, I think we understood each other better this time, and I think she's ready to let me follow my dream with my music and teaching and all."

"Oh, nice. Praise God for that."

"Yes. Jesus helped me get into the right mindset. That's for sure."

Mildred grinned, perhaps waiting for more of the story.

But Bethany wasn't in a mood for storytelling. A piano in the music building was calling to her. Actually, a text message reminding her of her reservation had just pinged her phone, but the piano may as well have been the source of that communication.

She did have time to eat lunch before going to practice. She hoped the excitement of this first time in a practice room would be enough to overcome the usual afternoon nappishness. She ate light, just in case adrenaline wasn't enough to keep her alert.

Someone was running through scales at an impressive speed when Bethany entered the long corridor lined with music practice rooms. The lighting in the hallway appeared to be set at half brightness, contrasting with the sunlight outside. She had reserved a room with a baby grand piano. Not all the rooms had a piano but she found a variety of options. The baby grand would be perfect for her. It was a Yamaha. It would be familiar, similar to the one her teacher had in her home when Bethany was seven or eight years old.

The scales ended when she reached the reserved room, as if the rapid runs up and down the keyboard had been the soundtrack for her return to regular practice. She would have preferred a Handel piano suite for her soundtrack. Bethany sniffed a laugh at herself.

The room was cool. It was in the seventies outside, with ambitions toward the eighties. The air conditioning in the music building might have already anticipated that likely rise in temperature. The room was kept dry to protect the instrument. The chill was part of that preservative environment. Bethany recalled complaining to her mother more than once about being refrigerated with the piano when she practiced at a local high school. She wouldn't complain today.

Seated on the hard wooden bench, no cushy seat for this practice session, she took a deep breath, stretched her hands, and loosened her shoulders for a whole minute. Then she touched the keys. Instantly she began running scales like that unseen pianist had been doing moments before. She noted two keys that were slightly off, but only slightly, of the fifty or so she tested with her scales.

She was ready. Her instrument was ready, and she started one of those Handel suites she had been thinking of. She couldn't recollect all of it but would play through the parts she recalled more than once if necessary. She hadn't thought of bringing sheet music. There was plenty in her dorm room. She could buy more at Mr. Goldberg's piano store, something she might do out of gratitude. And perhaps she would play one of his pianos while she was there.

She played through approximately three quarters of the Handel suite and played it again. She returned then to the Bach she had played in the piano store. When she finished that, she smiled at herself and played “Fur Elise.” She played it at the proper tempo and thought of little Cassie the whole time. The girl had become an inspiration.

Thinking about inspiration seemed to awaken something in the room. Then she stopped playing because someone was behind her.

Wearing his Jesus costume, the man she had been thinking of as *the guy with the ponytail* tapped her on the shoulder. “Slide over.”

After a frozen second, she did. She slid to the left and stared up at him, trying to understand what he was doing.

Deftly arranging his robes as he slipped into the seat next to her, he eyed the keys in front of them. “Can you teach me?” He looked at her with childlike simplicity.

“Wha ... at?” Her voice caught in her throat.

He sat up straight and carefully rolled up his sleeves with the kind of precision that recalled her mother’s hands. Even her own hands. He might be a good pianist with those hands. Bethany began to laugh at that idea, and her belly rocked with the thought of teaching Jesus piano. She had to lean her head on his shoulder to settle herself down. He laughed with her, but his was a *patiently waiting* sort of laughter.

Apparently, he was serious about the piano lesson.

Taking a deep draught of air to purge those giggles, she looked at him. “You want me to teach you from scratch? From the beginning? What do you know?”

He tilted his head toward hers. “I know this.” He played chopsticks. Carefully. Woodenly. With a hitch or two, and only the two-fingered version.

She started to laugh again but questions were bursting in her head. “Wait. Aren’t you ... the Son of God? Don’t you know everything?”

He turned and grinned at her. "Yes. Of course. I even know how to be a beginning piano student." He raised his eyebrows. "So, teach me."

There was a mental trap door just beyond where Bethany was sitting. She leaned away from it. She decided she just had to think of it as agreeing to play along. That was the best way she could approach this odd challenge. She slid a bit further to the left so her student could sit in the center of the piano.

First, she introduced him to the white keys, and she showed him the letters assigned to each of those keys. She showed him how to always find the A key. She showed him the difference between a half step and a whole step. Then she demonstrated a major scale. She was still playing a part, even playing a game. She had learned the rules of this game from others who had played it with her.

Her first piano teacher, when she was five years old, was instantly with her now, in her head at least. Bethany was reviewing what she had learned from Mrs. Maxwell and from others, old ways and means from early in her life. Those ways came back easily, spilling out as if she had been storing them at the front of an overfull closet shelf. She could, of course, recall teaching kids at camp last summer, but those kids had already started piano lessons. So, she hadn't begun with them on such a rudimentary level.

The reverberations of her own early piano lessons seemed to grow and to fill the practice room, as they had at Mrs. Maxwell's house back then. Those vibrations woke wonder and presented possibilities. The big piano, with its pure white and black keys, held magic in it. Music could be coaxed out of it. If you knew the trick, you could create enchanting sounds. Five-year-old Bethany wanted to learn that trick. She *had* to learn that trick.

Bethany was introducing other scales to her new student, other keys, leading Jesus through one octave and the next. As she did that, she wasn't thinking about what she was saying. She was thinking instead about how fun it was to go over this with

Jesus. With him she revisited the primal level of discovery that had fascinated her from the start ... and clearly still did.

Jesus, the man who literally knew everything, knew how to be a perfect student. He struck the keys as she directed, and he observed and repeated what she did. He turned to watch her with seriousness, but also with that same kind of admiration her mother had allowed herself at breakfast yesterday. Admiration Bethany had seen in Cassie's eyes as well.

When she remembered that Jesus was only playing the part of a first-time piano student, she skipped to one of the exercises she had done with students last summer. And he didn't object. He didn't whine about her going too fast. Of course, he didn't.

With that, the game expanded. She would jump to a lesson a year past the last one, and he would jump with her without a breath of hesitation—just an occasional clarifying question then compliance. Not once did he step outside their game. He could be a first-year piano student and a second-year and third-year and on and on.

How far could he go? Well ...

Bethany got off the bench. There were small piles of discarded sheet music on the painted shelves to her right. On her wristwatch she noted that her hour would be over soon, but she hoped no one had booked the room directly after her. She wouldn't have done that, with so many rooms available on a summer Sunday afternoon.

She found a Debussy composition she recognized. "Reverie."

She returned to the piano and spread the pages in front of her student in the Jesus costume.

"Oh, good. I like that one." He was now an advanced student and he rose to the challenge.

But he played somewhat mechanically, attending to hitting the notes, trying to anticipate, to read ahead, as if he had never played it before.

Had he? Had Jesus ever sat at a piano and played Debussy's "Reverie" before? Perhaps Bethany would ask a religion major that question someday.

For now, she was coaching. Coaxing. Urging him to pull feeling out of the music he was playing. Leading, listening, guiding, encouraging him. Then the song was over.

Her mouth was straining with an irrepressible smile. And she said, "Again."

After a long breath, Jesus played with more feeling, like a skilled pianist who had seen this piece before. Bethany spoke over sections where he needed to adjust his touch, to hold a rest longer, to evoke more of what the music was offering. To find that trick hidden inside the big, shiny black instrument.

And he did it. He did it very well. By the end of the second time through, he was playing like an accomplished pianist.

He was playing like Bethany.

"You're a good teacher." He grinned at her as the last note faded.

"I have a very good student." She shook her head before landing it on his shoulder again. This time she released the laughter. And she didn't resist the tears.

Chapter 36

Companions

Later that day, and the next day, and the day after that, Bethany's mind kept returning to the experience of teaching Jesus to play piano. She hadn't seen him since. But those recollections kept him close, it seemed.

On Wednesday she was wandering toward the dorm before lunch and before her shift at the diner. Lucas was walking toward the physics building when he spotted her.

"What are you up to? You look like a kid on summer vacation." There was no edge to his voice, no judgment, not even a tease. It felt like a spontaneous observation. An observation by Lucas, the scientist, who was practically a professional observer.

"I look carefree?"

"That's it, I guess. Though not the sort of clueless carefree of a Disney movie or something."

Bethany blurted a small laugh. Then she got more serious. "Hey, I have a story to tell you."

"Really?" He looked at the academic building half a block ahead of him. "Can you walk with me and tell me on the way? I have an appointment in a few minutes."

That time constraint was a relief, really. Bethany had no way of knowing how he would respond, or where her story would lead. Having to pack it into a few minutes offered useful guardrails around her worries.

She walked with Lucas as she told him about Jesus showing up in the practice room, including only a brief background about not practicing enough and about working on reconciling with her mother.

Mom had been texting every day since she returned to Beaverton. Bethany pictured her mother composing a text and deleting it, or heavily editing it, and doing that before finally sending every message. She was clearly making an effort.

"So glad to hear you are making it happen." That was Mom's reply to the news that Bethany had reserved a piano room two days a week for the next six weeks.

When Bethany and Lucas stood in front of the glass doors to the physics building, listening to the wind rushing through the artisanal grass in the small garden there, he stared at her, speechless.

"I know. It's a whole new layer of crazy." She said that to give him space to decide not to believe her. But the intensity of his gaze implied that he didn't need that space.

Lucas stretched his thin lips. "I was just absorbing what this might teach me about Jesus. Like, a whole new insight on what he's really like, what he's about."

"Really, you could get all that from my wild story?"

He smiled some more, glancing at his watch. "I gotta go. Can we talk more about this?"

"I'd love to." She wanted to delete the word *love* as soon as she said it, resisting the twitch it inspired inside her.

"Good. I'll text you when this meeting is over and see when we can get together." He patted her on the shoulder. "Thanks for telling me your story, Bethany."

"Thanks for listening." She wanted to edit that line too. It sounded like something she had said to him before.

She inhaled deeply as she watched him swing through the glass door before she turned to walk back toward the dorm. She recalled then that she was supposed to be meeting Sandy for lunch. She pulled out her phone and sent an apology, assuring her suitemate that she was on the way.

The follow up conversation with Lucas, about teaching piano to Jesus, was just the first of many meetings in coffee shops and restaurants, and on the paths of the forest park next to campus. They got in the habit of riding to church together on Sunday mornings, though Mildred still provided Bethany transport to small group on Tuesdays.

During the few weeks that Sandy attended class that summer, Bethany did get to know her better, including sharing laughs over the story about the dentist's confusion over what happened to Sandy's tooth. Someone else had repaired it, apparently. Sandy told him Jesus was her other dentist. It was a joke. Sort of.

Grandma's recovery also inspired amazement, though no jokes that Bethany heard about. The doctor was speechless at the first appointment after Grandma had left the hospital. Her recuperation was so thorough that he questioned whether the diagnosis in the hospital had been accurate but reviewing the notes on removing the fluid from around her heart silenced him.

And Grandma started going for walks around the neighborhood again. Not alone, of course. Katie assured Bethany that Grandma was being safe. Katie even served as chaperone for Grandma and Mr. Peyer once.

"It's strictly a *just friends* thing, dear." Grandma's phone chuckle left Bethany wondering which part of this assurance was funny. Was it Grandma imitating Bethany's *just friends* summary of her relationship with Lucas? Or was it the notion that the old folks needed to report their relationship status to the youngsters?

Bethany was happy she had friends to tell about her relationship status. Sandy, Katie, Jacqueline, and Emily all listened to her phone ponderings about Lucas. And Lucas listened to her tell about her relationship with Jesus.

Her mom and dad worked out a financial arrangement which made working at the diner unnecessary. She stayed on through the rest of the summer, glad for a chance to save some money. And Ralph talked her into planning to come in when one of the other waitresses was on vacation, or to help out on a busy holiday—Labor Day was just a week away when the manager removed Bethany's name from the regular weekly schedule.

With that settled, she contacted Cassie's father about giving piano lessons. Apparently, Cassie had graduated from her former teacher at the end of the school year, after one last recital. She was ready for a more advanced instructor this year.

Bethany went to Mr. Goldberg's store to purchase sheet music she needed for her own practice, as well as to teach Cassie. He talked her into playing his newest grand piano each time she stopped in. She began to stop in more often, eventually not needing any urging to play.

On her last day of working at the diner, Bethany received congratulations, via text, from Emily and Jacqueline. Jacqueline may have orchestrated that.

"Whoo hoo! Free at last!" That was Jacqueline's celebratory message.

As over-the-top as that exclamation was, Bethany wasn't feeling like shouting. She was already missing her coworkers.

"You can enjoy being a student, for a change." Savannah offered that magnanimous consolation after Bethany hugged her during dinner break, before Savannah left for the day.

"I hope I see you when I fill in for Annabelle or someone." Bethany had seen signs that Ralph was interviewing waitresses, but he hadn't yet hired her replacement.

"Oh, yeah. And if not that, you better come by and have a piece of Boston cream pie on occasion." Savannah stopped patting Bethany's shoulder and briefly touched her cheek.

Hopefully no one else would do that. Bethany was having a hard time holding it together. No longer coming to work at the diner would be like emigrating to another country. These were her people. The diner was like another home.

"At least you can come by for a real meal once in a while." Jose stood next to Annabelle after closing, taking his turn at the farewells.

They were letting her off easy, not making her stay long after the *Closed* sign was hung in the window. It seemed that none of the others were looking forward to a long goodbye either.

After hugging Bethany, Annabelle said, "I'll let your regular customers know where to find you, including that guy Jesús."

Bethany practically choked on the laughter that rose amidst her tears. "I ... I expect ... I'll probably see him around."

A flash in Annabelle's eyes said she knew something beyond what she was saying.

The heart-felt farewells implied the others didn't expect her to really fill in at the diner in the future but Bethany was determined to do it, even if she didn't feel the financial need. The opportunity to serve strangers would be impossible to surrender entirely.

That late August night was balmy. More than two months into the solar summer, it was dark when Bethany walked away from the diner. The humid air enveloped her like she had just stepped out of the shower. She luxuriated in having that moment to herself, to simply feel her own skin.

Then she felt something else. A presence. Someone close.

She turned when she heard the first footstep. She turned quickly, though she was feeling no fear.

"Hello, dear." The man with the ponytail wore no jacket this warm evening, just like an actual human being.

She smiled at him, too full of gladness at seeing him to find words.

He didn't hesitate to take her hand and didn't comment on her stunned silence. They walked casually, hand in hand, all the way to campus, eventually finding plenty to say to each other. Then he turned to the right, still holding her hand and they walked on. A gentle breeze rose and clouds covered half the night sky. Bethany and Jesus strode through the neighborhood, avoiding campus and avoiding having to say goodnight.

One more time.

At least one more time.

You may also be interested in:

Seeing Jesus Series:
https://www.amazon.com/dp/B074CGZ26F
Get to know Jesus through this thriving series with ordinary people's extraordinary encounter with Jesus.

Sophie Ramos Series:
https://www.amazon.com/dp/B08NGWQWF5
She sees angels and demons. Can she break free from her fear and embrace her gifts?

The Prayer Raider Series:
https://www.amazon.com/dp/B09YCFPQFG
A celestial visitor takes Josiah on miraculous rides, revealing the power of prayer.

The Reign Series:
https://www.amazon.com/dp/B0753CSQ13
Set in a post-tribulation world, a carpenter struggles to rebuild a shattered community in this mind expanding series.

I Am Not Alone In Here
https://www.amazon.com/dp/B0C6FLJPY6
A witty children's book author finds himself questioning his sanity when a shape-shifting creature appears on his stairway. In this captivating blend of psychological suspense, supernatural revelation, and humor, discover the truth that sometimes the scariest things are the ones we conjure ourselves.

Get Up, Eleanor
https://www.amazon.com/dp/B08B1LN3VK
When her mother the artist dies alone, she has to sort her old farmhouse where she discovers a disturbing secret about her parents.

Alice's Friendship Bench
https://www.amazon.com/dp/B09F1CVXVK

Instead of only tending her garden Alice meets with people searching for hope, sitting on a park bench.

Sign up for our Newsletter to keep current on what Jeffrey is working on, to be the first to know about free promotions and more.

https://www.jeffreymcclainjones.com/subscribe-1

Visit Jeffrey's website for all his books

jeffreymcclainjones.com

Printed in Great Britain
by Amazon